Miss Lister's Guest House

A Lesbian Romance by
A. L. Aikman

Library of Congress Control Number: 2023901570

Published by Aikman Publishing
8724 Cascadia Avenue
Everett, Washington
First paperback edition: April, 2023

Editor: Jane Crisi Tufts, Rye Beach, New Hampshire
Cover Illustration and Book Design: Geraldine Aikman, Aikman Design, Kennebunk, Maine
Character Illustrations: Jane Dillon Wingfield, @olysketcher, Olympia, Washington

ISBN: 979-8-9874643-0-4 (paperback)
ISBN: 979-8-9874643-1-1 (e-book)

Dedicated to the memory of Anne Lister, 1791-1840, of Halifax, Yorkshire, and to all the Lister Sisters and Misters — especially those in and around Halifax — who have created a supportive and creative worldwide community to carry on her legacy of courage, daring, and love.

～

Table of Contents

Characters
Illustrations by Jane Dillon Wingfield

Celia

Claire

Daisy & Evie

Dawn

Devon

Glo

Honour

Imara

Jess

Kim

Larkin

Lindsay

Miremba

Nicola

Perry

Stephanie

Walker

•••《●》•••

Prelude: Polk County, Oregon

Francine stifles a yawn and looks at the big clock above the cold beverage refrigerators. It's almost midnight, so two more hours till her shift is over. The rain is sheeting down, keeping most people away on this Tuesday night. That's fine with Francine; she likes peace and quiet.

The door beeps and Francine casts a suspicious eye on the newcomer, a tall, bedraggled teenager wearing an army surplus jacket and a green knit ski beanie, both soaking wet.

"Good evening," Francine says. "Backpack at the register, please."

The teen — it's a girl, Francine sees now — says "Sure," and drops the navy-blue backpack at the counter.

"Anything I can help you find?" asks Francine.

"Just looking for some protein," says the girl, attempting a jaunty grin as she pulls off her sodden cap and flips her short brown hair back. She starts to browse the food aisle.

Francine looks idly down at the backpack. It's a good quality one, battered but intact. There are several patches sewn onto its cover. Francine can just about discern the biggest one, "Polk County 1999 H.S. Softball Champions," and then the girl is standing at the counter again. She's holding up a package of crackers, salami, and cheese.

The girl clears her throat. "Can you tell me the price on this, please?"

Francine squints. "Three ninety-nine."

The girl's face falls. "Oh." She turns away, back towards the shelves.

For some reason, Francine feels moved to follow up. "What's the matter, hon?"

The girl looks ashamed. "I only have three-fifty. It's okay, I'll find something."

"Come here," Francine says, brusquely. "You can have it for three-fifty. Just don't ever tell my boss."

The girl brightens, drops the package on the counter, and digs in her jeans pocket for the money.

Francine rings her up and hands the package back. The girl is practically slavering, looking at the food. "There's a couple of tables over by the soda pop," Francine says. "Feel free."

The girl smiles broadly, says "thanks" in a quiet, husky voice, and Francine sees that despite a broken nose, she is quite pretty, in a boyish sort of way. The girl goes to the tables, throws herself into one of the faded orange molded-plastic chairs, and rips into her food.

Francine looks around. No other customers, no cars outside except her own — did the girl walk here? She locks the register and saunters back to where the girl is sitting. "Mind if I join you?"

The girl, her mouth full, looks startled, then waves her hand to indicate that Francine should take the other seat.

"Go ahead, eat," says Francine, running her hand through her grey curls and remembering a time in her own youth when she was this ravenous herself. Francine looks out at the rain that is hissing down.

The girl finishes her paltry meal and grins shyly at Francine. "I guess I needed that."

"I guess so," replies Francine. She leans forward a little and says, "Can I ask you something?"

The girl looks scared, but nods.

"Are you in some kind of trouble?"

The girl shakes her head, making what appears to be a conscious decision to be brave. Then she suddenly tears up. She wipes her eyes roughly with the back of her hand and says, "My parents threw me out. I don't know what to do. That was the last of my money."

Cursing herself for getting involved, Francine takes a deep breath and asks, "You got anyone you can call?"

The girl shakes her head. Then she says, "I have an aunt in California I could call, but my phone is out of juice."

Francine says, "Oh for heaven's sake. Let's see your phone." The girl shows her a Nokia flip. Francine asks, "You got a charger for this?" The girl nods. They go to her backpack and fish it out.

Within five minutes, the girl's phone is charged enough to make a call. Francine goes over to the canned-goods section and busies herself tidying the shelves, far away enough so as not to be a creepy eavesdropper. But she overhears the call anyway.

"Aunt Amy? Yeah, it's Devon. How are you? Were you asleep? Oh, I'm so sorry. It's just…no, I'm not really okay. Mom and Dad threw me out last night. I don't have any money or any place to stay… A convenience store. The lady's been super nice, let me recharge my phone." There is silence for a minute.

Francine can't help herself, peers over the counter. The girl is wiping away a fresh flow of tears, but her face is lit up by relief now. "Okay, yes, thank you, thank you so much, Aunt Amy! Okay, well, I'll call you in the morning and let you know. Yeah, thanks again, bye."

The girl clicks the phone shut and lets out a sigh of deep relief. Francine inches around the shelves, says "Good news?"

The girl dissolves in sobs, but nods vigorously. Francine goes and fetches a small box of tissues. "On the house," she says, pushing the box to the girl.

When the girl has mopped her face dry and is breathing normally again, she says, "My aunt in California is wiring me some money by Western Union. She told me to get a motel room and then catch a Greyhound tomorrow. Is there a motel here? And I guess most important, how on earth do I find a Western Union office? In the middle of the night?"

Francine grins at her. "We've got a Western Union office right here in the store. Come on, let's get going on that. The motel next door is gross but there isn't another one for miles, so it's your best bet. And there's a Greyhound station in Rickreall, just ten miles or so. You can get a taxi there tomorrow."

Devon beams at her. "Really?"

Francine smiles back. "Yes, really."

For the rest of her life, Devon will remember the convenience-store lady and wish she had asked her name.

••• ‹‹ ● ›› •••

PART ONE: Summer
Castro Valley, California

Rough Sketches

It's a late afternoon in June and the sun is still far from setting. The front door of the little house is open to the street. Devon, in shorts and T-shirt, is in the middle of her living room, kneeling on a tarp spread over the carpet. Despite the breeze, she's sweating lightly as she carefully hand-sands the repairs to Glo's antique rocking chair.

The TV is on. She is half-watching the movie about Anne Lister. She whistles along with the soundtrack music. Every now and then she stops sanding and looks up — whenever Anne Lister, played by that hunky Celia Denton, is onscreen. Devon can't get enough of her.

She hears a car pull into her driveway. A door slams, and a moment later, familiar footsteps trot onto her porch. A sturdy woman peers in through the open front door. "Hey, Dev."

Devon grins at the sight of her best friend. "Hey, Glo."

Glo takes a step back, looks up. "The new roof looks great."

Devon winces — *it cost a fucking fortune.* "Thanks. Come in. Look! I'm working on your chair."

Glo comes in, a mock scowl on her face. "Why are you so far behind schedule?" She pulls off her Oakland A's cap, revealing a rumpled mess of blonde hair, and glances at the TV. "Oh, dude, are you watching the Anne Lister movie *again?* You're too old to be a fangirl."

"Shut up," Devon replies. "You want a beer?"

"Yeah, you?"

Devon nods. Glo goes into the kitchen and gets two beer

5

bottles out of the fridge. She re-enters the living room, unscrewing the cap of one bottle, and takes a long drink as she sits on Devon's comfy old brown couch. "This is the part where they kiss for the first time, right? How many times have you watched it? Five? Ten?"

"Not that it's anyone's business, four times in the theater and…a few times on DVD. And you?"

Glo ponders. "I think five times." She waves the unopened bottle at Devon.

"Five times, but *I'm* the fangirl." Devon abandons the chair, dusts her hands on a rag, and goes to join Glo on the couch. They sip their beers and watch silently as Anne Lister sweet-talks Ann Walker into giving her a kiss. When the scene ends, Devon turns off the TV and they both sigh deeply.

Glo takes a swallow of beer and looks pensive. "Important question for you, Dev. I want you to think very carefully."

"Shoot."

"Would you rather be Ann Walker or Anne Lister in that scene?"

Devon laughs. "I don't care if she *is* butch, Celia Denton is the hottest thing I've ever seen. So I'd be Ann Walker. Puffy sleeves and all. What about you?"

"Same, same. Embarrassing but true."

"I'm glad you liked the movie."

"Thanks for forcing me to go see it with you. You were right, it's the best film about lesbians I've ever seen. And incredible to know it all really happened."

Devon clinks her bottle against Glo's and takes a drink. "That's good, because we've been friends for a long time and I'd hate to have to ditch you."

Glo looks at her incredulously. "You'd end our friendship over a woman who lived two hundred years ago?"

"In a heartbeat."

"Cold."

"Did you know they filmed it at her actual house? And it's a museum now — people can go and visit it. Shibden Hall." Devon looks wistful.

Glo says, "You want to go?" Devon shrugs. "What's stopping you? You still have that U.K. passport, don't you?"

"Yeah," Devon replies. "The one thing I'm grateful to my stupid mother for."

"You went over there once, right? When you were, what…?"

"Thirteen. Man, I hated it. My parents spent the whole time at this church revival in some horrible London suburb. I didn't get to see a thing."

Glo says, "Well, at least you got the passport out of the deal." She gets up, walks over to take a look at her chair.

Devon hastens to her side, points at the area she's been sanding. "It's got a ways to go, but I'm working on it every chance I get."

Glo punches her gently on the arm. "Sure, sure. Hey, I don't give a crap about the chair. I really came over because, a, I haven't seen you since early May…"

Glo trails off. Devon elbows her. "Is there a 'b'?"

"…and, b, I was worried you'd be sad after you and Julie broke up."

Devon laughs briefly. She gets up, goes into the kitchen, fills a bowl with tortilla chips, brings them to the dining table. "Need another beer?"

Glo shakes her head, goes to sit at the table with Devon. "You're avoiding my Julie comment."

Devon sighs deeply and plays with the label on her beer bottle, peeling it off with her close-bitten nails. "You know, she's a really nice woman. Super nice. I know you liked her, too."

Glo shrugs. "It doesn't matter how *I* felt about her. What about you, though? Why did you end it?"

Devon tilts her head down, looks up at Glo from behind her eyelashes. "She was starting to throw the M word around."

"Monogamy? Marsupial?"

"Marriage."

"No!"

"Yeah."

"She gave you that gorgeous silver bracelet."

"Yeah. I liked it. I liked a lot about it. About her. But then — " Devon hesitates. "She hated everything about Anne Lister. She made fun of the costumes and the hairstyles. She teased me relentlessly about it. I didn't understand why. Maybe she was jealous, I don't

7

know. But of a movie? I got tired of trying to figure it out." Devon lifts her eyes to Glo's. "Is that a stupid reason to break up with someone?"

Glo looks away. "It doesn't sound like you tried to make it work."

"I tried for a while," Devon says, defensive.

"I have to wonder," Glo says slowly. "Did you do a pre-emptive breakup?"

"What are you talking about?"

"I've known you for a long time."

Now it's Devon's turn to look away. "So you think I wanted to beat her to it? Like, 'you can't fire me, I quit'?"

"Maybe." Glo pauses. "I always felt you liked her family more than you actually liked her."

"I did like them a lot," Devon admits. "Oh well, easy come —"

"Ah, Dev, you're such a heartbreaker."

"I know. I don't want to be."

"How did you return the bracelet to her?"

"Drove to her house, gave it to her mom, probably mumbled something, left."

Glo gives an ironic thumbs-up. "My hero." She pauses. "Well, since we're talking about serious shit — what *do* you want, Dev?"

"In my life?"

"Yeah. What do you want right now?"

Devon looks into Glo's forthright blue eyes and sighs. "I don't know, Glo. I just feel so fucking…restless. You've known me longer than anybody. You were my catcher for, what, a hundred games…"

"At least."

"At least. And you took care of me when Aunt Amy died…and when I broke my ankle sliding into second in that tournament in San Mateo…"

"Hey, you drove in the winning run. The team appreciated your sacrifice. How is it now, by the way?"

"I can walk fine, just can't really run far without pain. No more softball for me I think. Maybe ever."

"Such a bummer," Glo says sincerely. "Let's see it." Devon rolls down her sock and they pause and look at the scarred ankle. "Ooh, sexy," says Glo.

8

Devon rolls up her sock, sighs again and asks, "So what do *you* think I want?"

Glo looks thoughtfully at her friend. "I think you want something like what softball used to give you. I remember how much you loved all that. A community — even if they were dumb jocks…"

Devon sighs deeply and nods.

"Women pursuing you all over the East Bay — remember that girl I heard in the stands? 'Oooh, that tall, dark pitcher is so hot. I'd love to see what's under that uniform, giggle giggle.'" Devon rolls her eyes. Glo continues. "And, but seriously, Dev — I mean, here you are all on your own since Aunt Amy passed away. Am I wrong to worry about you?"

"You're probably not wrong," whispers Devon, picking at the beer label again. Glo reaches out and grabs her hand. Devon pulls back, then submits as Glo examines Devon's nails, which are bitten to the quick, the skin around them ragged, raw. Glo pats the hand and releases it.

"Lovely," she says. Devon hides her hands under the table.

Gently, Glo asks, "Been doing any painting?"

"I wish. I have zero time. I'm pretty behind on my bills, so every time Steve calls me in for a job I have to take it. We did three kitchen rehabs last week, working fourteen, sixteen hours a day. The minute I get off work I just grab something from the taco truck and bite it when I get in my door …"

"You're not cooking, either? Aw, Dev."

"… and go straight to bed."

"You can't live without doing your art, or cooking," Glo says.

Devon laughs bitterly. "Yes I can. What I can't live without is a non-leaking roof over my head."

"At least Aunt Amy left you the house all paid for."

"Yeah, but I still have the repairs, and the loan for art school. The truck payments. And, you know, other little luxuries, like groceries."

"I do worry about you, being all alone. And now, oh shoot, Baxter. It doesn't feel normal to come over here and not have him slobbering all over me."

"Jesus, I know, I'm so pathetic. It's like a country-western song!

The dog died, too!" They laugh, then Devon looks out the window and notices that the shadows are lengthening. "Hey, you need to be home anytime soon? Wifey making dinner for you?"

"No — Tanisha's out till late. I wouldn't mind eating something."

"How about a banh mi?"

"Perfect."

Glo gathers up their beer bottles and takes them into the kitchen where the recycling bins are. She comes back after a minute with a crumpled sheet of paper in her hand.

"What is this?"

"Oh, some stupid sketch I did."

"It's Celia Denton."

"Yeah, okay, I sketched her when I was watching the movie."

"It's really good, Dev. Why'd you throw it away?"

Devon shrugs. "Why'd I draw it in the first place? Ready to go?"

"Can I keep the sketch?"

"Oh my God, sure, if you really want it."

The two women walk through the well-worn neighborhood with its brown lawns and modest cars. The breeze wafts mouth-watering cooking smells and the citrus scent of eucalyptus trees. Conversations in English and Spanish float from the houses. Three dark-haired boys on skateboards race each other down the street.

After their dinner at the quiet little Vietnamese restaurant, they walk back slowly to Devon's house in the gathering dusk. Glo clears her throat and asks, "Anything else going on? Anything you haven't told me?"

"Jesus, you're nosy, woman!"

"Well?"

Devon kicks a eucalyptus nut along the sidewalk. "I miss Aunt Amy like crazy. Especially in June. It was three years last week."

"Jeez, three years? Already? I was concerned about you for a while — you were drinking way too much."

"I know. I've cut way back. The whole thing really made me think about how unpredictable life is — she was diagnosed in January, died in June. And you know what, Glo, I don't want to waste a day. For a while I was working really hard on just being contented and calm, you know. But then I learned about Anne

Lister and all the great stuff she did — the mountain climbing! The travel!"

Glo chimes in, "The women!"

"The women! So I've been reading about her, too. She lived her life so completely. It's all kind of riled me up."

"Thank God for vibrators, huh?"

"Thank God for vibrators. But two or three times a day? It's super annoying."

They arrive at Devon's house as the street lights come on. Glo's phone chimes. She checks it.

"The ball and chain?" Devon asks.

"Yeah, time for me to go."

Devon walks Glo to her car and they hug. As Glo gets in, Devon says, "I'm glad you came over. It was good to hang out."

"Same here," says Glo. She starts her engine, then looks up at Devon again. "Dev. You need an adventure."

"What kind of adventure?"

"Something different. Maybe you should go visit Anne Lister's place in England."

"Right, like I really have the money —"

Glo holds up her hand, laughing. "Okay, forget it. Love ya, Dev. Night."

"Night. Love ya. Come back soon, okay?"

Glo drives away and Devon stands outside for a while, looking at the stars, before sighing and going back inside the quiet little house with the incredibly expensive new roof.

Devon is grateful to her core that it is Saturday. She has a lot of chores to do around the house and yard, but does them gladly, with an attitude of devotion, almost of reverence.

Aunt Amy had welcomed young Devon in eighteen years ago with quiet, unconditional love. The little house in Castro Valley became a haven to Devon, a safe space to become herself.

Aunt Amy never probed, but Devon eventually told her all about it — her evangelical parents had thrown her out when they caught her kissing her high school girlfriend, Kathy. Aunt Amy just sighed. She and her sister had migrated to the States from England when they were teens. They shared the traces of an English accent but otherwise were radically different — Devon's mother having become a rigid religious zealot; Amy having become a successful, though modest and frugal, pharmacist.

Devon was never completely sure what Aunt Amy's own sexuality was — she was fiercely private, even with her beloved niece. She was brusque and hard-edged, but there was never a doubt that she supported Devon whole-heartedly. Aunt Amy, who ran her life on science and facts, believed in naming things. When Devon pressed her for her opinion about Devon's sexuality, Aunt Amy said, "You've got plenty of time to figure things out. It sounds to me as if you might be a lesbian. If you are, claim it. The word has a proud history. But whatever you are, listen to your heart and you won't have regrets."

Aunt Amy supported Devon through her last two years of high school, then helped her with art school and later, when Devon realized she also needed a trade, a cabinet-making program. She attended most of Devon's softball games, even going all the way to the Sacramento tournament when Devon's pitching carried the team into the state finals. Amy welcomed Devon's rowdy teammates to the house; persuaded her own friends to hire Devon to help with their kitchen remodels; gave her freedom, responsibilities, and respect.

When Aunt Amy fell sick with cancer, a heartbroken Devon had nursed her through her final, terrifyingly rapid illness. A month before she died, Aunt Amy told Devon that she was leaving everything to her, and instructed her thoroughly on how to care for the immaculate house and its little yard. To Devon, the house is not a humble single-family dwelling in the East Bay foothills; it is a sort of holy place. She tries hard to keep it up to Aunt Amy's exacting standards.

Devon makes it an early night, watching just half an hour of the Anne Lister movie and falling into a deep, dreamless sleep.

∾

On Sunday morning, Devon takes the time to make a beautiful breakfast for herself. Aunt Amy taught her to cook. Breakfast became their favorite shared meal. Devon made dozens of breakfasts for her teammates during tournament weekends, specializing in Colombian recipes from her father's side of the family. She loved creating an island of camaraderie and delicious shared food. Every now and then Devon invites a few of the women to come over for brunch, but now that so many of her wild jock friends are settled into relationships and serious careers, it's hard to get them together. Devon sighs but continues with cooking. Nothing wrong with spoiling herself. Today, she makes a batch of arepas con queso with avocado and tomatoes. She eats slowly and drinks three cups of perfectly brewed Peet's coffee, while reading a biography of Anne Lister. She can't stop thinking about the images and characters in the film. High-voltage electricity seems to be thrumming through her body every hour of the day.

Pushing her last bite of arepa slowly around her plate, Devon suddenly starts wondering about other women who have seen the movie. Still chewing her last mouthful, she grabs her iPad.

Opening a social media site, she enters the title of the movie, and to her amazement finds half a dozen fan groups. She joins one that seems to have a gay vibe to it. Within a few hours, she is welcomed by women from all over the world who share her excitement. She is not alone. There are so many women on here already. Exclaiming, explaining, discovering. Greeting her, asking her about herself.

Devon finds herself sliding from fandom to obsession. Some of the women in the group even live in and around Halifax, where Anne Lister lived.

Devon watches the movie over and over again throughout the day. She is ever more taken by the performance of the stunning actress Celia Denton. Devon looks online for photos of Celia taken when she's not in Anne Lister costume. Without the period wig, Celia has very short silver-blonde hair. Devon is entranced. She digs deeper and finds a series of photos taken a few years ago when Celia was Yorkshire regional fencing champion. Posed in her white uniform, lunging with her épée, her slim, athletic body as taut and focused as an archer's bow. *Oh my God, so hot.* Devon watches a couple more scenes and finally tears herself outside to go for a walk.

Devon feels a bit calmer in the afternoon, but no less obsessed. She reads and reads. She learns that Lister's diaries — those massive journals full of coded references to her very active sex life — are still being transcribed and decoded. That they are on display in the library in Halifax. She explores further and discovers a treasure trove of fan fiction about Lister, some of it quite hair-raising. *I'm never going to get any sleep, am I.*

Devon friends two of the women in the fan group. Claire responds immediately. She is a plump, cheerful-looking woman in her sixties who seems to be the mother hen of the group — she lives in Halifax with her female long-time partner and welcomes all the Anne Lister fans who are now making pilgrimages to West Yorkshire. Claire encourages Devon to come over when she can: "A big gathering is planned for Anne Lister's birthday in April. You should come over, love!"

And then there's a woman a couple of years younger than Devon, who lives in a village near Halifax. She has such a cool name — Larkin. Her profile photo shows a thin, freckled Eurasian face with a wide, devilish grin. Her personality is ebullient, warm. They start texting each other.

Learning that Devon is an artist, Larkin presses her to share a photo of one of her drawings of the movie. Devon puts her off — she doesn't have anything but a few very rough sketches, which she threw into the recycling bin, dissatisfied.

After dinner, Devon paces around the house, tidying up and eventually finding her way into her little art studio. It's getting late and she has to work on a kitchen cabinet installation early tomorrow. But her client's house is not too far away, and Devon persuades herself it will be okay to work in her studio for a half hour or so.

She enters the little room and walks around it, putting away the brushes and paints she left out the last time she worked in here. She notices they are covered with a fine film of dust and feels a pang when she realizes that it's been months since she did any painting. She's been working too many hours, but perhaps the real reason is that it's been a long time since she was inspired.

After cleaning up for a few minutes, she sits on the stool at her art table, her mind blank. Then she returns to the recycling bin and fishes out her sketches of Anne Lister. She smooths the crumpled sheets and stares at them. Hesitantly at first, and then with a surge of energy, she gets her brushes out, fills a jar with water, and starts rendering the sketches in watercolor.

By the time exhaustion overwhelms her, she has created a dozen watercolor sketches of Anne Lister — striding around the Yorkshire countryside, pensively looking into the distance, writing in her journal, shaking her silver-topped cane at an unseen antagonist.

Devon glances at the clock and sees to her dismay that it is three in the morning. She stretches, throws her work clothes, boots, and tools into a pile by the door, and falls into bed utterly empty of thought and feeling.

On Monday morning, Larkin again texts Devon, teasingly demanding to see her sketches. Devon is in danger of being late to work, but she is driven to respond. She looks through her watercolor renderings.

What the heck. She takes photos of her five favorites and sends them to Larkin, her heart thumping ridiculously as she sends them off.

That evening, Devon finds that Larkin has responded with an embarrassing flood of enthusiastic emoji.

- You have to post these on the group! Everybody will LOVE them!
- *Oh, they're just sketches.*
- Come on, please post them!
- *I'll think about it. What time is it there?*
- I'm just going to bed.
- *Well, have a good night.*
- I'll be dreaming of you.

Devon doesn't know how to respond to that, though it sets her heart racing. Then her phone dings again.

- Post them. Please.

5,000 Reasons

Devon is not ready to show her sketches to the world. She sends a message to Larkin explaining that she'll consider it when she's spent more time on them. Larkin sends her a pouting emoji, but follows it up shortly with a row of smiley faces.

Devon thinks all day about Larkin's parting words last night. *I'll be dreaming of you.* She is vibrating with excitement — no, something deeper than just excitement — all the time.

In the following weeks, Larkin and Devon start texting daily, then several times a day, then chatting via text for hours a day. They share life stories, jokes, dreams and hopes. They exchange photos. Like Devon's, Larkin's heritage is multicultural. She's a freelance photojournalist with special expertise in India and Vietnam.

Devon can't stop thinking about her.

They both admit they are nervous to go from texting to a video call. Larkin says:

- If we see each other, we'll fall in love.

- *No we won't. Come on, it's just a video chat.*

- Not yet.

So they talk on the phone first. Devon is nervous to place the call, but relaxes as soon as Larkin answers. The laughing voice that greets her is smoky, the accent Yorkshire but with the slightest flavor of a Southeast Asian accent. They talk for an hour. It is heaven. At one point, Larkin says:

"That music playing in the background —"

"Oh, sorry, I'll turn it off."

"No, lass, I like it but I was wondering — is that Grupo Niche?"

"It's Willie Colón — wait, you know salsa?"

"Oh, just a little," Larkin says. "I love it but I don't know much about it."

They dive deeply into a music discussion and after the call is over, for a few days they send each other links to videos of their favorite songs. Devon loves the music Larkin sends. She starts to wonder how much more perfect this can get.

And then, of course, their curiosity gets the better of them. They have agreed to limit this first video chat to ten minutes. After the first impact of seeing the face of the woman she's been getting to know, Devon is startled by how natural it feels to talk face to face with this distant stranger with the ready smile, the rapid-fire speech, the freckled, catlike face. They spend most of that call discussing their parentage — Larkin's father is Vietnamese and her mother, Welsh; Devon's mother is English, her father, Colombian — and how that, as well as their lesbian identity, set them a bit apart from their peers when they were kids, made them wary, self-reliant.

Also, they discuss their differences. Larkin is appalled to hear about Devon's rejection by her parents. Larkin's own family is supportive and loving, but she finds them smothering and is glad of her frequent long trips for work where she can breathe freely. "I'm still furious at them for almost derailing my career, early on. I had my first big opportunity to do a job for Reuters, in the Philippines, but they absolutely refused to let me go. They hid my passport. I didn't talk to them for months. Granted, I was just a kid, but I hated them for it." She sighs. "We're at peace now, more or less, but I'll never forget that feeling of being caged in."

The conversation is almost too intense for Devon, too confusing. She can barely concentrate on the words, she is so focused on her attraction to this animated, joyful woman and the intoxicating sound of Larkin's voice.

After the brief call, Larkin texts right away.

- Devon, you are gorgeous. That dark hair, the sharp way you have it cut. Your green eyes, those great cheekbones.

- *Are you kidding? Look who's talking. You are stunning. And they're not green, they're hazel.*

- Hope you don't mind me asking, but was your nose broken?

- *Don't mind at all. Broke it in tenth grade, got hit by a pitch.*

- I have no idea what that means.

- *I'll have to teach you about softball. Should I get my nose fixed?*

- Absolutely not. It's sexy AF.

- *You're nuts, but thanks.*

The ellipsis that indicates a text being composed dances across Devon's screen for a maddeningly long moment. Then finally Larkin's message appears.

- I'm falling for you.

Devon stares at her phone, feels the pull of something powerful. Then remembers to breathe.

- *What? You haven't met me.*
- I don't need to. I know my own heart. As Anne Lister would say.

Every few hours throughout the day, as the weeks go on, as the summer edges into fall, Devon's phone sounds the little ping that indicates a new text. She has to turn her phone off to get any work done. But she never stops thinking about Larkin. They get to know each other in ways both trivial and profound. They find many commonalities but also clash around a handful of political and ethical questions. Refreshingly, Devon finds that they can express themselves openly without fear, and accept each other's point of view.

As their mutual trust intensifies, they share their most cherished hopes and dreams. Devon finds herself confessing her lifelong desire to be a "real artist," by which she means to have her paintings displayed in reputable galleries and to be able to make a decent living just from her art. Larkin murmurs that she thinks Devon is a real artist now, and Devon struggles to accept the compliment with grace.

Devon comes to admire Larkin, too, for her idealism and her passion for justice. Larkin is seeking ways to help impoverished women and girls. She tells Devon about some of the women she has interacted with in India, and Devon can tell that Larkin has made a small but significant difference in their lives, mainly by bringing their plight to a global audience through her photographs, but also by connecting them with aid organizations. Larkin gets choked up when she describes some of the dreadful situations she has witnessed. She weeps from frustration that she can't do more to help. Devon is deeply moved.

Although she needs to get up at five for most of her construction jobs, Devon starts forcing herself to stay up till midnight, when Larkin is eating breakfast in England, to send her texts or have a brief video chat or even, on one clumsy and hilarious occasion, phone sex. Devon is woozy from lack of sleep, and high from the almost constant erotic charge. She is amazed to see how much sexual energy she had, lying dormant inside herself. *And we owe this all to a woman who lived two hundred years ago!*

The morning after a long, intense phone call, Devon sleepily answers a text from Larkin.

- *Hi, Lark.*
- When we talked yesterday, did something strange happen to you?
- *Yes. Very strange.*
- Also to me. I could feel a surge of energy all through my body, my heart, my chest, my groin, everything. It lasted for hours afterwards.
- *Wow.*
- Nothing like this has ever happened to me before. What was it like for you?
- *It was as if there was a deep, dark, mysterious pool and we were both in it. It's beyond words, I can't describe it.*
- Has that ever happened to you before?
- *No.*
- I think we should be very careful.
- *You make me not want to be careful at all.*
- We are 8,000 km apart. That is reason to be careful.
- *It's only 5,000 miles.*
- 5,000 reasons to be careful.

There's a pause, then Devon picks up the phone again.

- *And now I'm the one who's falling.*
- (Rolling eyes emoji)
- *Should I stop?*
- Yes.
- *(Crying emoji)*
- No.
- *(Smiling emoji)*
- How do I know, Devon? Do you want to stop?
- *I know I should. This is nuts.*
- Can you, though? Can you stop?
- *No. I'm crazy about you.*
- What would Anne Lister do?
- *She'd cross the Atlantic to get to you. She'd row a boat to get to you.*

- And make love to me?
- *And make love to you all day and all night.*
- Devon. I want you.
- *Larkin. Larkin. Larkin.*

One morning in September, very early, Devon is awakened by a phone call. When she answers, the voice, female and English, is unknown to her.

"Hello, Devon? It's Claire."

"Claire!" Devon exclaims in her croaky early-morning voice. "Hi, how are you?"

"Ooh, listen to your sleepy voice — I'm sorry, love, I just realized how early it must be there."

"No worries, what's going —"

"Devon! You've been hiding your light under a bushel!"

Devon is totally flummoxed and can only mumble a response.

"Your artwork! Your sketches of Anne Lister! They're fabulous! Larkin says you've more!"

"Oh, thanks," she says, weakly.

"Well, do you have more?"

"Yeah, about a dozen altogether, but they're not —"

Claire's voice gets big without, somehow, getting loud. "Please please please would you post them to the group. People'll absolutely love them. We need to see the creative work that's coming out of this fandom."

"But they're only quick sketches —"

"What've you got to lose, love? Come on, post 'em."

"I'll think about it, but —"

"Go on, just do it. I'll be waiting. Bye now."

Claire rings off.

Devon stumbles into the kitchen and pours herself a cup of coffee. She has just an hour before she needs to be on the job site. She hurries into her studio and opens the cardboard portfolio containing her watercolor sketches. She looks at them with a critical eye and chooses eight to post. She takes quick photos of them and, before she can think about it, posts them all with a brief

20

caption — "Some of my sketches." Dumb. No time to fix it.

She texts Claire.

- *Done. Gotta run.*

And then her attention turns to her work, a fairly tricky cabinet installation in Hayward, and she thinks no more about the sketches until that evening, when she logs on after dinner. She finds that her drawings have one hundred and twenty-three likes. The comments are ecstatic, admiring. Eighteen people have offered to buy the original sketches and demand to know the price.

Claire sends just a gif, a cartoon of a very smug-looking cat.

- *Hi, Larkin.*

- My love. So tell me, are you really going to come to the Anne Lister birthday celebration in April?

- *I hope to.*

- Don't tease me.

- *Yes, I will come. I will. I'll figure out a way. I have to see you.*

- What will you do first when you arrive?

- *When I get to Halifax, I'm going to check into my hotel and shower.*

- And then?

- *I'm going to text you.*

- And I'll go to the Minster to wait for you.

- *What's the Minster?*

- The big church in Halifax. Where Anne Lister is buried. And I'll meet you there, in front.

- *I can't believe we will finally meet — I've rehearsed it in my mind so many times. What will it be like?*

- We'll check each other out. And then…?

- *I am going to kiss you. Is that all right? Is it too public?*

- It is all right. No, I don't care if anyone sees us.

- *Good.*

- But you need to know my rules for kissing.

- *Yes, you'd better tell me.*

- I'm joking. There are no rules.

- *I will be gentle with you.*

- No, please, don't be gentle.
- *We will be whatever we are in that moment.*
- How can I live until then? Tell me, please.
- *I don't know.*
- Six months away.
- *I don't know.*

Aunt Amy's Altar

In her studio, squeezed between industrial shelves filled with paintbrushes, sketchpads, and jars of acrylic gel medium, Devon has put up a small wooden shelf.

This shelf is devoted to her memories of Aunt Amy. She thinks of it as a shrine.

There's a framed photo of Devon on the day she graduated from high school, with a proudly smiling Aunt Amy beside her. A few small mementoes — Aunt Amy's turquoise bracelet, a small glass holder for a tea light, and a tiny vase, into which Devon places a few fresh flowers from time to time.

Most of the time, Devon doesn't even notice the little shrine, but in seasons of stress, she comes to sit in front of it for a few minutes. Sometimes she can ask Aunt Amy a question and receive some wisdom. Sometimes she just gets the feeling of her aunt's loving presence, and that's all she needs.

On this foggy September morning after texting with Larkin, Devon lights the little candle, looks longingly at the old photo, and summons her aunt into her memory, as if she were standing by her side. "What should I do about this girl in England?"

Devon sits waiting for an answer. Nothing comes for a time.

But after she sits there for a while, a feeling of warmth arises in her chest. A feeling of light.

As Devon rises and goes to blow out the candle, she seems to hear the ghost of Aunt Amy's voice, calmly whispering, *Trust yourself, Dev. Trust your heart.*

Devon texts Claire and they set up a time to talk on the phone. Claire jumps right in. "So when are you coming over?"

"Um, I'm not sure — some of it depends on — well — "

"Depends on Larkin, does it, love?"

Devon blushes and is glad it's a voice-only call. "Uh…"

Claire laughs kindly. "Larkin and I are great friends. We go walking together every week or so. She looked high the other day — her pupils were dilated, and I know she isn't on drugs — and I wormed it out of her. She said she'd just been talking to you. Pretty exciting!"

"So — you're not telling me I'm crazy."

"No. Larkin is an absolutely lovely lass. I'm sure you are, too, if she likes you so much."

"Yeah, well, I don't know about that. I, uh, want to surprise her."

"Ooh, romantic! Can I help?"

"The thing is, I just can't wait till April to see her. Do you think she'd be all right with that — if I just turned up?"

"I should think so, love. She's up for anything, usually, and she obviously fancies you."

"Well, good. If you don't mind — could you find out if she will actually be around in mid November?"

"Is that really when you want to come? The weather'll be crap."

"I can't get away before then — work stuff."

"'I'll do some detective work and let you know."

"Thanks so much, Claire!"

"Leave it with me. But tell me — why do you want to make it a surprise?"

"I'm not sure — I think — we've spent so much time online, I want to see her when she's unprepared, unrehearsed. Real."

"You'll not be disappointed, pet."

"Oh my God, I can't believe I'm going to do this."

"Come on, love — it's thrilling, really it is. Just think of how much you'll regret it if you don't come."

Devon is silent for a moment.

"What is it?"

"Oh, it's money. I don't know how I can afford the trip."

"Hmmm. Oh, have you thought of selling some of your paintings of Anne Lister?"

"My little watercolor sketches? Not really."

Claire laughs, warmly. "There's your solution. Offer them through the fan site."

"Do you really think they'd sell?"

"No harm in trying, love."

"I guess not."

"Give it a go."

"All right, maybe I will. I can't thank you enough, Claire. Let me take you out for a nice restaurant meal when I get there."

"I will, at that. All right, I'll be back in touch in a few days when I've done me sleuthing. I really hope you'll come, Devon."

When they conclude the call, Devon feels as if she's downed a gallon of coffee. She goes to work vibrating with energy, finishing her part of the kitchen rehab in half the time she and Steve had estimated. Shaking his head in mock awe, Steve sends her home early.

The moment she gets home, Devon posts a "for sale" ad on the fan site, offering her paintings, matted, for what she thinks is a reasonable price. And waits.

Within three days, Devon has sold and shipped all twelve of her paintings, and there is a waiting list for thirty-five more. Within another two weeks, Devon has sold enough to more than pay for her airfare to England and a hotel room in Halifax.

There is no longer a reason for her not to go.

•••《●》•••

PART TWO: Autumn into Winter
Manchester and Halifax, UK

A Landing, A Shadow

When Devon wakes up, her plane is starting its descent into Manchester. Her adrenaline surges as she looks out the window to clouds and a few glimpses of ocean, then clouds again. *Is it really true? Am I going to meet Larkin today?*

Devon turns her phone on as soon as she gets through Customs. There is a text from Claire.

- Landed ok?
- *Yes!*
- Hope you have a good cagoule on.
- *Cagoule?*
- Anorak.
- *Anorak? Oh, rain jacket? I do.*
- Remember when you cross the road, look right then left.

As Devon picks up her bag and walks outdoors, a freezing rain is battering the access road at Manchester Airport, busy even this early in the afternoon. Devon wonders how she will ever find Claire.

A sky-blue Mini flashes its lights and beeps its horn. Peering out from under her rain jacket's hood, Devon recognizes Claire and runs to the Mini. Throwing her duffel in the back, she jumps into the left front seat.

"Thank you so, so much for picking me up, Claire!"

Claire waves off the thanks and starts driving. "Welcome to sunny England," she says, navigating to the exit.

During the hour-long drive to Halifax, as Devon looks out at city streets, then old towns, then bleak moors and lots of sheep, Claire goes over the plan.

"All right, love, Larkin thinks I'm taking her for a drink at the Piece Hall. We're to meet in front of the Minster at five. Only of course, it won't be me, but you."

"I can't believe I'm doing this. What if she hates this kind of surprise?"

"Larkin will absolutely love it. She adores — novelty, adventure. And of course, she's very taken with you."

"Has she talked about me at all?"

"Not to anyone but me, I don't think."

"What has she said?"

"That would be telling," says Claire with a smirk. "Let's just say, after she gets over being gobsmacked, she'll be very glad to see you."

As they enter the outskirts of Halifax, Devon asks Claire if there is a florist on the way. "Oh, there's one right across from your hotel, love."

They arrive at the modest, centrally-located hotel at half past three. After thanking Claire profusely, slipping money to pay for gas (*petrol,* Devon reminds herself) into the glove box, and promising to text her the next day, Devon checks into her room. She flops on the bed for half an hour, then showers and dresses carefully. It's no longer raining, so she puts on her black leather jacket over her white collared shirt and wraps a grey cashmere scarf around her neck.

She inspects herself in the mirror. She looks more or less okay. Her nose looks knobby and she has dark circles under her eyes from her overnight flight. Insecurity sweeps over her in a sickening wave but she thrusts it aside and thinks of Larkin, out there so close at last, and checks herself one last time. "Lookin' good," she tells herself, a nervous dynamo whirring in her stomach, as she combs her fingers through her hair and gives her reflection a reassuring wink.

Then she is out the door and striding down the long carpeted hallway, through the lobby, and out into this strange mud-brown city, where it is cold and already almost dark.

She sees the florist shop and races in, buying a single red

rose from the florist and shuffling her feet impatiently while the cheerful, chatty woman very slowly and carefully wraps the rose in beautiful paper.

Then she is out on the street again and walking fast toward the huge old stone Minster, whose tall clock tower she can see at the end of the street. She bites her lip as she hears the clock chime the hour. She'll be a bit late.

As she rounds the corner, she sees the main entrance of the old church, and at first thinks no one is there, but then she sees a small figure, facing away from her, huddled over a phone underneath the overhang. It is Larkin. Devon recognizes the delicate profile, the slim build.

Taking a breath to savor the moment, Devon thinks, *My life is going to change now.*

She goes through the churchyard gate and walks quietly up to Larkin, who glances sideways at her, then away. Devon clears her throat and Larkin looks at her again, then rapidly surveys the area before returning her gaze to Devon's face.

Devon says, her breath catching, "I have a delivery for a Ms. Larkin Phan." She holds out the rose and Larkin numbly reaches out to take it, looking at the flower and then raising her eyes again to Devon's face.

"What…Devon? Where's Claire? What are you doing here?"

Devon spreads her arms wide. "Surprise!"

"But what — but how —"

Larkin is unable to finish her sentence because Devon has hugged her and is holding her close.

"I couldn't wait till April to see you!" gasps Devon into Larkin's ear. Larkin is smaller than she had imagined, but even through her layers of winter clothes, Devon can feel her wiry strength, as Larkin throws her arms around Devon.

They stand locked together for a long moment, then Larkin grabs Devon's shoulders and pushes her away, searching her face. Larkin is smiling — *thank heavens* — and shaking her head in disbelief. Larkin puts her warm hand on Devon's cold face and whispers, "Kiss me."

Devon looks around swiftly but there is no one nearby, not

that she cares. She leans down, at last — *at last!* — feeling Larkin's tender lips, just the right size — and her tongue, softly caressing her own. After the feverish anticipation of the past few weeks, at last it is really happening, this kiss that she has rehearsed in her mind so many times.

Eventually, Larkin pushes Devon away again and they stare at each other, their faces full of wonder. A shadow comes over Larkin's face for a moment, making Devon's stomach clutch, but then Larkin is beaming at her again, wholeheartedly, and wiping away a tear. She reaches out to touch Devon's face.

"Your beautiful nose."

Devon shakes her head, moves away from Larkin's touch. "No, it's a mess."

"What are you talking about?" Larkin says. "It's the most beautiful thing about you."

"You're joking. It's crooked and—"

"I always think people's wounded places are the most beautiful thing about them."

They smile at each other, wonderingly.

And then the freezing rain starts again.

"Let's go and get a drink and sort it all out in the warm," says Larkin. Taking Devon's hand, she leads her along the pavement.

Devon gapes as they enter the Piece Hall, a vast open-air plaza surrounded by historic three-story buildings. There are large statues here and there, restaurants with tables spilling out into the square. It's lively and bustling. She's seen photos, but it's so much bigger than she'd imagined. Larkin smiles at her amazement, and silently leads the way to a wine bar in the lower level. They sit at a corner table and order pinot grigio. While they wait, Devon realizes how utterly happy and utterly exhausted she is. She looks around at the pretty, cozy restaurant and feels quite at home.

When their wine comes, Larkin toasts: "Here's to finally being together!"

Devon grins foolishly at Larkin, who smiles back as they clink glasses, but there is again a shadow in Larkin's smile that Devon feels she must be imagining.

Larkin leans over the table and holds Devon's hand. "Are you real?"

"Are you?" asks Devon, looking deeply into Larkin's dark-brown eyes.

"So you just couldn't wait to see me?" says Larkin with wonder in her voice.

"That's right," says Devon. She can't look into those eyes any longer or she will cry with emotion. She occupies herself with Larkin's lean, elegant hand, caressing and massaging it in a kind of stupor.

"So now you've seen me," says Larkin cockily, "What d'ya think?"

Devon turns the hand over and traces letters on Larkin's palm.

"What are you doing — writing on me?"

"Yes."

"What did you say?"

"I said I think you're even more gorgeous than I'd imagined."

"Here. Let me write summat to you." Larkin traces ticklish letters on Devon's palm for a long time, an increasingly serious look on her face, and then stops and folds Devon's fingers over her own.

"What did you say?" asks Devon, barely suppressing a yawn.

"I said I'm so thrilled to meet you, my head is all over the place. But also I said that I have some rather bad news."

Devon's heart chills. "You've changed your mind about me — about us," she rasps. "It was a mistake to come." She tries to drop Larkin's hand, but Larkin grasps her harder and won't let go.

"No, no, no," Larkin says. "No, I'm over the moon that you're here. I'm wild about you. I want to eat you up." She goes to kiss Devon, but Devon leans away from her.

"Then what is it?"

Larkin sighs deeply. "The Associated Press called me yesterday and asked if I'd be free to cover the floods in India. Not knowing that you were coming, I said yes. It's time-urgent, obviously, and they offered me a massive bonus."

"Oh, no." Devon is shattered. "Do you have to go?"

"Yeah. It's a huge step up for me to do a job for the A.P. I might not get this opportunity again. I can't afford to turn it down."

Devon sighs deeply. "When do you leave?"

Larkin winces as if in pain. "The day after tomorrow. Midday plane from Manchester." Larkin continues, her head bent over Devon's hand, "Devon, I'm so sorry. But look, I'll introduce you to me mates, so you're not alone after I go. And I'll spend every minute that I possibly can with you until I have to leave for the airport." She looks up and Devon sees a tear in her eye. "I'm really, really sorry. I'd back out of this assignment if I could — but I can't."

Devon takes a long, slow breath and smiles. "Are you available on short notice to visit my hotel room?"

"Oh yes, yes, I am."

"And stay the night?"

"Oh yes, I am. But first, let's get some good Yorkshire scran into you."

"I hope that means food."

Devon awakens to the sound of the hotel room door being opened and closed quietly. Then the smell of coffee. Then the feel of soft lips on her ear.

"Hi," she mumbles as she hurls herself out of bed, getting a quick impression of Larkin standing next to the bed holding two cardboard coffee cups and a white paper bag that looks as if it might hold pastries. She dashes to the bathroom, where she pees for an incredibly long time. Brushing her teeth, she realizes she can't clearly remember much from the time she and Larkin left the restaurant last night. She only drank three glasses of wine — it must be massive jet lag that's causing this mental confusion.

She combs her hair, throws on a sweatshirt, and shyly returns to the room, where Larkin is lying in the bed, evidently naked under the duvet, sipping coffee and smiling at her. "Croissant?" Larkin asks, waving the paper bag.

"Coffee first," says Devon. She takes a long drink. Larkin pats the bed and Devon gets in.

Devon lies on her side, gazing at Larkin. "This is such a cliche, but I honestly don't remember anything from last night after we left the pub. I'm so sorry."

Larkin laughs. "Nothing to be sorry about! I totally understand jet lag."

Devon wiggles closer to Larkin, feeling her body's warmth. "Did anything — did we —"

"You don't remember those three massive orgasms I gave you? I'm hurt — you said you'd never forget."

"I fell asleep as soon as we got here, didn't I."

"The moment you got in bed. Yes."

"Jesus. What a waste."

"But you've had a very good night's sleep now."

"Yes."

"So yer energy's good?" Larkin traces her finger down the side of Devon's face, then gently kisses her nose.

"Who wants to know?"

"I do."

"My energy is very good."

"That's lovely. I just want you to do one thing for me."

"Anything."

"Eat this croissant while it's warm."

Devon now realizes she is ravenous. She tears into the pastry while Larkin runs her fingers through Devon's hair and tells her about the weather (cold) and what her plans are for the day (packing, but otherwise free to take Devon wherever she'd like to go). Devon is practically swooning just from the sound of Larkin's voice.

Devon swallows the last of the croissant and the rest of the coffee. She puts the cup on the bedside table and brushes the crumbs off her fingers. Turning to Larkin, she wraps her arms around the slight, warm body and kisses Larkin's neck. Larkin's low moan vibrates through Devon's body and soul.

Devon bites Larkin's soft, somewhat prominent ear and whispers into it. "Okay, I've done that for you. Will there be anything else, madame?"

Larkin pushes Devon onto her back and climbs on top of her. Staring boldly into Devon's eyes, she whispers, "Yes, I have several more things for you to do, as a matter of fact."

Slowly, carefully, and with awe that she is finally touching the actual smooth warm skin of this woman she's been dreaming of for months, Devon does them.

~

Around midday, they get up, shower, dress — interrupting themselves frequently to kiss and stare at each other in mute wonder — and finally leave the hotel. Outside it is cold but clear. The streets are busy. Devon reminds herself to look right, then left, when crossing the street.

They get into Larkin's car, an old green Toyota, and take the short drive up to Shibden Hall. Larkin is quiet as she drives. Devon starts to ask a question about the view, but Larkin says, "Why don't you just drink in the landscape. You will never again come to Shibden for the first time."

They drive up the hill; looking back, Devon sees a good view of Halifax and the surrounding hills, under low clouds. They drive around a curve and into a graveled parking lot. There are only a few other cars. They get out and walk to a low stone wall. And there is Shibden Hall below them, so familiar from the TV show. *It looks like home*, Devon thinks, and shivers.

Devon throws her arms around Larkin. "Thank you for bringing me here."

Larkin laughs and kisses her. "Are you messing? Thank you for coming all this way to see us."

Hand in gloved hand, they walk down a slope past trees clattering with the last remnants of autumn leaves, until they arrive at the old half-timbered, honey-colored building, now gleaming in a ray of sunshine.

Larkin pulls her camera out of her bag and takes a series of pictures of Devon in front of the revered old building. A sturdily-built woman with short grey hair comes to the door.

"'Ey up! Larkin?"

Larkin runs to hug her. "Steph! Are you working today?"

"Yes, I am. If you can call it work. And who's this handsome lass you're with? Is this the American I've heard about?"

34

"Yeah, this is Devon."

"Howdy," says Stephanie. "I've seen your paintings. What a wonderful artist you are, Devon. Would you like a photo of you together?"

"Yes, please," says Larkin, and shows Stephanie how to use her camera.

Stephanie poses them in various ways, snapping away as she talks. "Volunteering here, I've taken a lot of these photos lately. Pairs of women coming from all over the world, wanting their photo in front of Shibden. Stand a bit closer. Look at each other. Right. Now off into the distance. Good. There you go." Stephanie hands the camera back with a smile.

Inside, they politely rebuff the offers of guides and wander the rooms together. There are only a few other visitors, all women, mostly couples.

Walking from room to room, Devon has feelings that she imagines religious people must have in cathedrals. To think that Anne Lister walked these corridors, lived in these rooms. It is overwhelming. For a moment, she feels dizzy, then Larkin takes her hand and she's grounded again.

In Anne Lister's bedroom, Devon can't resist an impulse to reproduce a scene from the show. She pushes Larkin against the wall and kisses her — at first playfully, then as Larkin pulls her closer, deeply and desperately. Then Devon starts to tremble, and pulls back.

Larkin says nothing, just puts her hand to Devon's cheek and smiles wistfully. "Let's go. You can come back here another day."

Devon asks Larkin to wait in the entrance for a moment. She goes into the little gift shop and buys a small souvenir, slipping the bag into her pocket.

They leave the building and stand outside looking down at the gardens and the little lake for a moment. There is cold sunlight and a colder intermittent breeze. They lean on each other as they slowly walk back up towards the car park.

Larkin says, "I have to go pack bags. Would you like to come with me, or shall I drop you somewhere and meet you later? You can easily walk back into town from here."

Devon turns to her. "I want to be with you every minute I can. Our time is so short."

Something deep and silent passes between them. Larkin takes Devon's hand and leads her back to the car.

~

They stop to buy some groceries and snacks for Larkin's sixteen-hour flight to India. Then they drive out to Todmorden, a little town where Larkin lives when she is in England. She shares a modest second-floor flat with her sister Coral, a nurse.

The flat is cozy, if a bit untidy, decorated with a colorful mixture of Buddhist art and dazzling Indian cushions. The large living-room windows overlook an old stone church and a huge willow tree that Devon thinks must be gorgeous in the spring.

Larkin finds a note on the kitchen counter. "'Pulling a double shift tonight, see you tomorrow.' Fantastic, we have the place to ourselves!"

She makes a snack for Devon and insists that she eat it. Devon obeys, sitting at a well-worn oak dining table. As she chews the sandwich, gazing at the vivid array of colors in the room and the grey landscape through the windows, and also at Larkin, eating quietly beside her, Devon sinks into a deeply peaceful state. She realizes with a twinge that she has not felt so at ease in a very long time.

Devon washes the dishes while Larkin starts packing. When the dishes are done, Devon leans in the bedroom doorway, watching. Larkin is taking a remarkably small quantity of clothes and a remarkably large number of lenses and other camera equipment. Larkin packs efficiently, swiftly, running back and forth to other rooms in the flat as she collects things and brings them to the bedroom. On Larkin's way back from one run to the kitchen to collect some silverware, Devon reaches out and grabs her arm. Larkin tumbles into her, gives her a quick kiss on the cheek. Devon takes the silverware and tosses it onto the bed. She leans into Larkin and kisses her neck. Larkin turns Devon's lips to hers, kisses her, pulls back.

"I'll be finished in a moment, I promise," she whispers.

Devon releases her. In a few minutes, Larkin is packed. Devon helps carry her backpack and roller bag to the door.

They stand, then, looking at each other. Devon is overcome by the beauty of this girl. The sharp angle of her cheekbones, the rich brown of her eyes, the humorous slant of her generous mouth. Larkin walks backward toward the bedroom and Devon pursues her, finally pushing her back onto the bed.

Devon traps Larkin's hands and pins them to the bed. She thrusts a leg between Larkin's. Larkin's eyes half-close and her legs clamp around Devon's.

"What do you want?" whispers Devon, gazing at her.

"I want…you to fuck me. What do you want?"

"I want to fuck you and I want you to stay."

"At least we can do the first part."

"Take off your clothes."

Larkin stands, slowly takes off her clothes. In the afternoon light, at last Devon has the chance to look at her properly. Small, round breasts with large brown nipples. Firm little bottom. Shapely, strong legs.

Larkin stands, neither shy nor flirtatious, enduring Devon's gaze. "Now you," she demands.

Devon strips rapidly and throws her arms around Larkin, smashing their bodies together, tumbling her to the bed.

Remembering from their hasty morning lovemaking what Larkin likes best, Devon holds her down, teasing her nipples with her tongue and teeth as Larkin writhes.

"Kiss me," Larkin begs. Devon continues to caress her tits with fingertips and palms as they explore each other's tongues, teeth, lips. *I could do this for hours*, Devon thinks. *I've never felt like this before.* Her hand floats down, as if of its own accord, to the silky bush between Larkin's legs, and Larkin moans urgently into Devon's mouth. "Fuck me, fuck me." Devon disengages from the kiss and slips two fingers into Larkin's soaking-wet center. She lowers her mouth to Larkin's clit, sucking it into her mouth as she continues fucking her. Within half a dozen thrusts, Larkin is coming, crying out, her inner walls crushing Devon's fingers.

Devon gently withdraws her fingers and lies quietly next to

Larkin as she shudders, gradually calming and lying in a private space all her own. When Larkin turns to Devon, she is smiling but her eyes are full of tears.

"Sorry," says Devon. "I should have made that last longer."

Larkin puts her finger to Devon's lips. "I knew it would be like this with you," she breathes, stroking Devon's face wonderingly. "Like with no one else, ever."

When Larkin makes a move to reach between Devon's legs, Devon gently moves her hand away. "Not now. I just want to hold you."

As Devon pulls the blankets up around their shoulders and wraps herself around the smaller woman, she is overcome with an immense tenderness. She holds Larkin gently, firmly, trying not to think of how short their time is together. Already, the afternoon shadows are creeping across the landscape. As Larkin falls into a light sleep, Devon keeps watch, her heart full of something vast.

Devon gets up after a while, throws her clothes on, and rummages in the kitchen, trying to figure out how to make a cup of tea. Larkin hears her, comes to find her.

They stand holding each other in the kitchen for some time, until Larkin breaks off a kiss and says, "Did you really want tea?"

"I do."

"Look, I just got a text — some of me pals are going to be at the pub in Halifax, and the word is out that you're here. Why don't we go over there and you can have a proper meal."

"But I only want to be with you."

"We won't stay long. It'll be all right. I want you to meet them, so you won't be all alone whilst I'm away. Come on, let's go now, then we'll be back earlier."

They drive back into Halifax through the advancing shadows. The sky is darkening behind the rooftops of the old mill town, and streetlights are on. When Larkin parks the car, they lean together and kiss again. Devon whispers, "Don't let me drink much — I'm already high just from being with you."

Larkin smiles radiantly.

In the low-ceilinged old pub, a table is full of several women. Claire is among them; she sees them first, and leaps to her feet to greet them with a loud "Hello, hello!" and kissing first Devon, then Larkin on their cheeks. Then she organizes extra chairs so they can all sit at the same table.

Devon shakes hands with them all, in a bit of a blur. Tanned, tall young woman with a flop of dark hair: Kim, professional caterer. Laughing Black woman in a colorful headscarf: Miremba, a cabinetmaker from Uganda. Stocky, raucous blonde twins: Evie and Daisy, assistants at Kim's catering company.

Everyone pauses to see this American whose hand Larkin is holding, but when Larkin goes to get a round of drinks, they quickly revert to a passionate discussion about the upcoming Six Nations women's rugby competition. Devon doesn't understand a word but sits back and enjoys the lively ribbing they are giving each other. Sports fans are the same the world over.

Larkin returns with drinks for everyone; Devon is grateful for her pint of lager and takes a healthy gulp. Larkin's hand is in hers again, and though her heart is sore at the prospect of Larkin's departure tomorrow, Devon focuses on this moment, right now, when she can caress this precious hand. A lull comes in the conversation and all the faces turn to Larkin and Devon.

"How long will you stay?"

"Have you been to Shibden yet?"

"Do you follow rugby?"

Claire holds up her hands. "Hey, guys, give them a break. Larkin has to leave early tomorrow. They've only had one day together."

Silence for a moment, then a chorus of dismay. Larkin's protest that she had no idea Devon was coming and had already committed to this job is batted away by her friends.

"Not very romantic, are ya, mate?" Kim says.

Larkin buries her face in her hands and whimpers.

Devon comes to her defense. "She didn't know. I was an idiot to just come over here without checking with her. "

Claire says, "Don't worry, love, you can always come back, can't you — when the time's right?"

"Sure," says Devon, with absolutely no conviction. Her

imagination goes to her pathetic bank account.

Miremba speaks up, in her lilting voice. "Devon, meantime, you'll be here for a week without her? Don't worry, we'll take good care of you. Right, girls?"

Everyone nods vigorously.

Miremba lifts her pint and toasts Devon. "Let's all come back tomorrow evening, shall we, and plan some fun things for Devon to do and see whilst she's here?"

There is a loud assent.

"Don't worry," Claire says to Larkin, "You'll have lots of time together in the future, and meanwhile, we'll look after Devon while you're gone."

Devon manages a smile and says, "Thanks, Claire." She puts her arm around Larkin's shoulders and says, "Come on, Lark. It's not the end of the world." Larkin lifts her head, wipes away a tear, and is soon laughing again.

After a while, they order food. As it arrives, Larkin points meaningfully at her watch. It is seven already and Devon droops, knowing how few hours remain before Larkin will leave.

They eat quickly and depart, after everyone has given Larkin big hugs and well-wishes, and made Devon promise to come back the next evening.

Devon is exhausted but wide awake. It's two a.m. and there is a slight glow of streetlight coming through the curtains.

Larkin is sprawled out on the bed, one arm flung off into space, so deeply asleep that she looks as if she's been felled in mid-flight. Their last lovemaking session, three hours ago, evidently did her in.

Larkin made exquisite love to Devon with her tongue, teasing her to heights of desire that finally caused Devon to explode and then collapse into a boneless heap.

When Devon had recovered, she straddled Larkin and held her down against the bed while Larkin begged her in a desperate voice, "Take me, take me," setting Devon's blood on fire. Responding to Devon's passionate kisses and thrusting, pounding hand, Larkin had two orgasms that almost scared Devon in their intensity and length. After the second one, Larkin had wept and clung to Devon until she fell asleep.

Now, Devon abandons her own attempt at sleep. Leaning up on an elbow, she gazes at Larkin, thirstily drinking in every detail of her face, her slim shoulders, her soft ears, the angles and planes and subtle curves of her. She is stockpiling these memories until she can see Larkin again. The night will end all too soon. She will get up early with Larkin and go with her on the train as far as the airport.

Devon is afraid of the depth of her feelings for this girl. She holds herself back, unwilling to fall in love. They live half a world apart. It's crazy. She knows this. And still she gazes, until eventually her arm tires and she sinks back down, quietly molding her body to Larkin's, until she too is asleep.

Larkin and Devon go outside into the dark early morning and carry Larkin's two bags up the hill a short distance to the train station, where they wait on the platform.

On the cold train, nearly empty of other passengers at this hour, they are almost too tired to talk. They sit as close as they can get, warmth radiating from their shoulders and arms. Devon breathes in Larkin's scent, rubs her hand, looks at its graceful, tapered fingers, the strong tendons — memorizing it all in hopes of being able to draw it later.

Larkin whispers, "I can't believe how much I'm feeling for you."

Devon feels tears spring to her eyes. Huskily, she murmurs, "Don't be silly. We've only just met."

Larkin squeezes her hand harder. "You must come back."

"I'd like to come back for the big gathering in April."

"Five months away. How will I live?" Larkin whispers.

"Well then, come and see me in California on your way home from India."

"Really?" Larkin brightens. "What a wonderful idea." She caresses Devon's hand as Devon tells her to come and stay for as long as she likes, and describes some of the Bay Area sights they can visit together. They set a tentative date of Christmas, or perhaps as late as February.

They are silent for a while, then, and Larkin very quietly says, "You know, I'm quite scared of this assignment. Seeing all that suffering, all the people made homeless in this flood. I've never covered anything this big. And I'm only getting this job because the bloke who was supposed to cover it caught malaria. He almost died."

Devon replies, shocked, "Lark. You didn't tell me that. How long will you be there?"

Larkin looks her in the eyes. "I'm expecting to be there for six weeks or so. You know — I don't just take pictures of these people. I get to know them. I help if I can. I care too much, I suppose. But I feel a sense of — mission, is that the right word?" Devon nods. "A sense of mission to be a true witness to what they're going through. Especially the women and girls. So they know they're not all alone." Larkin sighs. "I'm too tired to explain it properly."

Devon puts her arm around her and holds her close. "It's all right, it's all right," she whispers, not knowing what it all means, but feeling a big space open up in her heart.

They fall silent again, feeling each other's warmth, watching the farms and fields give way to industrial plants, then to urban neighborhoods, then at last, after a change of trains, to the airport.

The black sky is just starting to lighten as they reach the airport. Then they are out on the chilly platform, gazing at each other.

"Have a good flight. Text me."

"I will."

"I have a little thing for you," says Devon, and pulls out of her pocket a small paper-wrapped packet.

When Larkin opens it, she sees the coach-and-four brooch that Devon bought in the Shibden Hall gift shop. She whispers, "Oh, Devon, I love it. Put it on me?" Devon pins it onto Larkin's sweater.

Devon leans close to Larkin. "Whenever you see this, remember that I'm with you. Always. Until we see each other again."

"I hope that'll be soon."

"I do, too. Early in the new year, all right?" Devon says, her heart hurting.

"Let's be brave and hope so, all right?"

"Yes. Let's be brave."

"Kiss me."

Devon does. They stare hungrily at each other for a moment, then kiss again with infinite tenderness and then Larkin heaves her backpack onto her shoulders, picks up her duffel, and is gone.

Devon stands alone on the cold platform for a long time and then numbly goes to catch her train back to Halifax.

Is This an Invitation?

Devon returns to her hotel and sleeps for hours, then goes out to explore the town. It's cold, gritty, rainy. Devon walks on wet sidewalks — *pavements,* she reminds herself — and looks into all the shop windows. She stops in a cafe to get warm and as she toys with her toasted sandwich, she starts to wonder what she is doing there in Yorkshire, now that Larkin has left. Her chest is hollow, empty. Then she reminds herself of Larkin's promise to visit her in California. And then of how eagerly she wanted to see this city.

I mustn't let this opportunity go to waste. She wants to look at these old buildings — buildings that Anne Lister actually walked past, entered, did business in, attended church services in. As she resumes her walk in the darkening town, Devon gets a shiver of excitement alongside her sorrow and questioning. After all, she still has a whole week ahead to explore Halifax and the much-vaunted lesbian mecca of Hebden Bridge right nearby.

At five, she finds her way to the pub again. Claire is already there, and she jumps up to give Devon a big, warm hug. Devon clings to her, chokes back a sob. Claire pats her soothingly.

"She's gone, then? What rubbish timing," Claire sighs. "Come on, get a drink and let's have a laugh. The girls will be here soon. I think Miremba is coming, you met her, the Ugandan. A lovely lass. Amazing, considering what she's been through."

"What has she been through?"

"Oh, you should ask her. Lager again?"

"Yes, please."

43

"Be right back."

Claire is just returning with their drinks when Kim comes in, her anorak dusted with traces of flour, a shy grin for Devon on her tanned face. Daisy and Evie enter shortly after, arguing playfully with each other about the Premier League. They greet Devon with friendly thumps on her back.

As they are all settled at the table, Miremba enters. She is dressed in well-worn work clothes but walks toward their table with a regal gait. Her face is illuminated by a wide grin. Miremba seems ready to burst into laughter at the slightest pretext. She glows with life as she greets each of them. Claire says "Miremba, you remember Devon."

Miremba turns the full glow of her attention to Devon. She becomes solemn. "Did Larkin leave today, then?"

Devon nods.

"Oh, I'm so sorry. What terrible timing. How long will she be away?"

Devon replies, "A month or so. But I'll be going home to the States in eight days."

"What a shame!" Miremba says.

"Yes," says Devon. "I've invited her to come and see me in California, so let's hope that works out."

"Let's hope so, love," says Claire, soothingly. A silence forms as everyone sips drinks.

Kim clears her throat. "Change of subject okay?" Everyone assents. "Guess who I met today?"

They all shrug.

Kim says, "Here's a hint. You all know there's going to be a sequel to the Anne Lister movie. Well, they're going to start filming it in a few months. The craft services people interviewed caterers today, including me. And not only were the staff there to taste our little samples, but a few members of the cast as well." She pauses, coyly. "Actually, *all* the main members of the cast."

Devon, catapulted out of her sorrow, gasps, "You didn't meet Celia Denton!"

Kim smiles. "Not only did I meet her, she liked my scran."

Everyone sighs in unison.

Kim adds, smugly, "She smiled at me and said 'Yum.'"

Evie cries, "You mean we might be working for …"

Daisy jumps in, "Celia Fuckin' Denton?"

Miremba reaches over to slap Kim's back. "That's incredible, girl! Celia Denton!"

Claire says, "Fingers crossed for you, Kim!"

They talk excitedly about Celia Denton, a topic that will never be exhausted. They speculate, as always, about whether she is gay, straight, or bi — she has been seen with people of all genders — and grill Kim about whether Denton had said "yum" referring to the food or to Kim herself.

"You *are* pretty yummy, Kim," says Miremba.

"Oh yeah, I'm sure that's what she meant," laughs Kim.

When there is finally a lull, Devon asks, "I keep hearing about the women's community here — is it really all it's cracked up to be?"

Claire says, "It's been a very tolerant area for a long time, but the Anne Lister phenomenon —"

Kim cuts her off. "Fans, especially women, are coming in droves, from all over the world."

Miremba adds, "Me, for instance!"

Daisy says, "Our sleepy, boring town is jumping."

Claire says, "First they come, alone or in a couple, on a sort of pilgrimage, just to experience for themselves where Anne Lister lived."

Kim: "And then some of them stay."

Claire: "Some of them fall in love with other fans, or with some local lass…"

Evie: "Or with the countryside…"

Claire: "And they settle down here. I am confident that when the second film comes out, we are going to see a load of women moving to the area. When people realize how cheap it is to live here, or start a business here…compared to London, anyway…"

Kim: "You won't be able to take a step without tripping on a lezza."

Devon smiles and takes everyone's order for another round. Miremba jumps up to help. While they wait at the bar, Devon asks about her work.

"I work for myself. There's lots of renovation going on, so I hire myself out to homeowners."

The barman produces the drinks. Devon and Miremba carry them to the table. "I do that kind of work too," says Devon. "What do you do, specifically?"

"A bit of electrical work, a bit of plumbing, but mostly wood — cabinets, cupboards, framing."

The two of them launch into a deep discussion of routers, bandsaws, and drills. Devon finds herself engaged and amused by the vibrant, humorous woman. After a while, Miremba reluctantly says that she has to go home because she has an early job the next morning.

"Will I see you again, then?" she asks Devon, shaking her hand warmly.

"Yes, yes, sure, how about tomorrow?"

"Sorry, busy," says Miremba sadly.

"Next day, then?"

"Same time?"

"Sure."

Miremba winks at her. "Yes, good, we still have to resolve the important question of belt versus rotary sanders."

After Miremba leaves, Kim waves to get Devon's attention. "I wondered, Devon — how do you like it here?"

Devon stammers, "I haven't been here long enough to tell," though secretly she finds the mud-colored buildings ugly and dirty-looking.

Kim laughs. "First impressions might not be the best, especially this time of year. What're you doing tomorrow?"

Devon shrugs. She has no plans.

"I have the day off — why don't you let me give you a tour? You've seen a bit of this city, but our countryside is not to be missed. I'd enjoy showing it to you."

"All right — I'd love a tour. But only if you'll let me buy you lunch along the way."

Kim grins. "Brilliant. Pick you up outside your hotel at ten then, all right?"

Devon nods, grateful for the friendly gesture.

Claire, putting on her coat, says to them, "Right, you two, as you're driving around, keep your eyes open for someplace we could buy as a group."

"What are you on about?" asks Kim.

Claire replies, "I keep saying, if anyone wanted to make a good investment, they should buy one of these old farmhouses, fix it up, and rent it to women who come here to visit Shibden Hall."

Kim snorts. "I don't know if you've noticed, Claire, but we're all just scraping by financially."

Claire replies, "I know. That's why we should get together as a group, pool our resources, and buy one."

Kim says, a dreamy expression on her face, "That's such a lovely idea. Open a bed and breakfast…"

Daisy jumps in, "With scones from our bakery…"

Claire says, "…and eggs and milk from Jess' farm…"

Evie says, "We could make a fortune."

Claire: "So, who wants to organize us?"

No one replies. Claire laughs and says, "Seeing no volunteers, I suppose I should drop the idea. Oh well. Good night, then, everyone!"

As everyone starts to put on their coats, Devon suddenly gets goosebumps all over. She shivers. *Probably still jetlagged*, she thinks, as she says her goodbyes and goes out into the rain to walk back to her hotel.

The day dawns bright and crisp. It is the first sunshine Devon has seen since she arrived, and the city is transformed. While she waits on the street for Kim, Devon drinks in the green of the hills beyond the town. Even the brown buildings look sort of nice in the sunlight.

Kim picks Devon up in the bakery's van and drives her all over the valley. Devon sees old industrial and mining sites, Victorian theaters, Kim's bakery, the gay pub, steep hills, drystone walls, narrow little farms and many, many, *many* sheep. They get out of the car in Todmorden and go for a walk beside the Rochdale Canal, stopping for soup at a friendly little cafe.

She can feel herself beginning to really like the land, the villages, the people she is meeting. It's very strange, the rapport and comfort she is feeling already for this place, so profoundly different from her California home or her Oregon birthplace.

Kim is a lively, funny companion, with a deep knowledge of the history of the region. Everywhere they go, people greet Kim and banter with her. Devon envies her. *To belong to a place the way Kim does, to be known.*

Devon misses at least half the little jokes people are exchanging, due to the Yorkshire accents, but a surprising thought dances into her head. *Kim could be a good friend if I moved here.* Devon gets a flash of how difficult and complicated such a move would be, and the notion of finding a home for herself in this foreign land dances right on out of her head again.

∼

While they are driving back into Halifax, Claire calls Devon and invites the two of them to come to her house for a cup of tea. Kim declines due to work, but drops Devon off at Claire's well-kept, cozy house.

"My wife's in York visiting our son and grandkids for a few days, so the house is mine, mine, all mine!" Claire cackles like a cartoon witch, and invites Devon to sit at the table in the spacious kitchen. A big orange cat promptly jumps onto Devon's lap and purrs as Devon scratches him behind his ears.

While the kettle boils, Devon finds herself responding to Claire's motherly friendliness by confessing her confusion. "I feel like I'm falling in love with this countryside. I keep finding myself imagining moving here. But I have a nice little house and friends and everything in the Bay Area, so…"

"And yet, here you are in England."

"Yes." *Here I am in England. And the girl I came here for has vanished. Fabulous.*

Claire joins Devon at the table and serves tea and some little cakes. She is quiet for a moment, then turns her round, kind face to Devon. "Right, Devon, I know you'll think this sounds absolutely mad, but the fact is, I can be quite intuitive sometimes." She hesitates. "It's almost like I can see flashes of the future." She looks sideways at Devon. "Should I shut up now?"

"No, no," says Devon. "If you have some insight, I'd love to hear it."

Claire gets quiet, sips her tea, looks out at the garden. She puts her cup down and looks thoughtfully at Devon. "This isn't a machine. There's no guarantee. Sometimes the signal comes through very muddled."

"It's okay, tell me. What do you see?"

Claire's brow furrows. "It's not awfully clear — I just see you living around here — being happy."

"With Larkin?" Devon smiles, hiding her painful hope.

"Not at all sure..." Claire laughs ruefully. "Sorry, m'love, it were just a flash. Perhaps a bit of food for thought."

"Okay."

They chat for a while and Devon eats an embarrassing quantity of the delicious little cakes.

"And what are your plans for tomorrow, pet?"

Devon shrugs. "I don't have any plans until the evening. Got any ideas?"

"I wonder — would you like to help me with a little errand tomorrow, and meet another friend of mine?"

"Sure," Devon says. "What's the errand?"

"Well, my friend, Stephanie..."

"Oh, does she volunteer at Shibden Hall? I met her two days ago."

"Yeah, that's her. She's lovely. Her mum died recently, and she's having a hard time parting with her mum's clothes. I offered to take a carload of boxes to the recycling center for her."

"I'd be glad to help."

"Lovely. I think you might be interested in seeing her house — it's just the sort of place I picture for my imaginary bed and breakfast."

"What's her place like?"

"It's just outside Hebden, up the hill, a nice view over the fields. Three stories. And a separate building, it's an old stone barn, right next to the house. She lives in the little barn — she calls it the

Annex — and her mum actually ran the big house as a bed and breakfast some years ago. Now Stephanie has the whole place to herself. I expect she'll move into the big house now."

"I'll be glad to lend a hand," says Devon. "Thanks so much for the tea." She stands.

Claire stands as well and gives Devon a quick hug. "Any time, love. I'll see you tomorrow." She hands Devon her coat. "You'll need to be a bit prepared, pet — Stephanie and her mum decorated the place and it's all a bit…eccentric."

Claire holds her umbrella for Devon as they leave Stephanie's house and wave goodbye to her. They take a long look at the view over fields and distant villages.

They get into Claire's car and drive back into Halifax. They chat about the surrounding area and about Claire's lifelong friendship with Stephanie.

"So, love, what did you think of it?" asks Claire.

"You did tell me the decor was — what did you say? 'Eccentric.'" They laugh — Stephanie's mother, though she never left the north of England, was a fanatical devotee of all things Western, and the house is decorated accordingly. All three floors are festooned with pictures of lariats, sculptures of cowboys. The pepper and salt shakers are miniature Western saddles. There is a John Wayne cuckoo clock in the dining room and cowboy boot vases in the front hall. A chime plays "Jolene" every time the front door is opened.

Stephanie escorted them from room to room, first in the low converted barn where she lives, and then through the bigger house, apologizing affectionately for her mother's taste. Devon can see that the house is solidly constructed underneath the Gary Cooper wallpaper and barn-wood mirror frames. After they had seen everything, from the large bedroom on the top floor to the hot-water heater in the low-roofed basement, Stephanie said conversationally to them, "I'm putting the place on the market in a couple of months, Claire, so if you run across anyone…"

"What? Where are you going, Steph? Not far away, I hope!"

"No, no, lass, I'm going to move into my flat in Sowerby Bridge."

"Oh, I forgot you still had that place. Well, that will be easier to manage than this big house."

"Yeah, I'm quite fed up with fixing the hot-water heater here!"

"Of course, Steph. I'll talk it up — we'll find you a buyer, just wait and see."

The three women loaded up Claire's car with the possessions of Stephanie's mother, and Stephanie, a bit teary, gave Claire a big hug. "Thanks for helping, Claire. It was just a bit much for me to face. Lovely to meet you again, Devon!"

Claire says, driving back to Halifax, "I'm shocked that she's moving, but it makes sense." Dreamily, as if talking to herself, she says, "It's definitely a manageable size for a guest house; and someone could live right next door and see to things easily, without actually being on top of guests." She sighs. "If I were thirty years younger, I'd give it a go. Nice location, isn't it."

"Yes." Though it is just about ten minutes' walk from Hebden Bridge village, it feels as if it's far out in the countryside. The view over the fields was lovely. Devon could imagine it on a spring day, with lambs running around the nearby farms. *I'd love to paint that view.*

They drive to the recycling center and drop off the boxes of clothes. Then Claire drives them back into Halifax. As she pulls up in front of Devon's hotel, Claire turns to her. "I don't suppose you're spiritual at all, are you, love?"

Devon is taken aback by the question. "A little, I guess. I don't really think about that kind of thing very much." She shrugs. "Kind of a boring, down-to-earth gal, I guess."

Claire smiles. "Well, I hope you won't mind my saying this." She takes a breath, looks past Devon and out through the rain-spattered windshield. "I believe that the world calls to us sometimes, maybe just once or twice in a lifetime."

"What do you mean?" Devon is fascinated.

"It's like an invitation — summat is offered to us, an adventure or a challenge, and it's always our choice to accept it or not, but we should consider it very carefully before we decide. It's not an ordinary opportunity — it's a thing that comes in response to our heart, our soul. Summat that wants us to be bigger — to live a wider life." She sighs, exasperated. "I'm afraid I can't describe it very well."

"That's okay, Claire, but why are you telling me this?"

With a little laugh, Claire says, "You may well ask! Well, it's just that I think that mebbe this is what's happening with this bed and breakfast opportunity. An invitation of sorts."

"Yeah, what an amazing chance for someone, huh?" Devon is surprised to find so much yearning in her heart. Envy for whoever could do this.

"Yes," Claire agrees. "Well! Have a nice evening, love. Thanks for the help."

Devon walks to her hotel, and goes up to her room feeling overwhelmed. She kicks off her shoes and lies on top of the bed, her head full of images of everything she's seen today. She falls into a dead sleep and awakens, cold, long after the hotel restaurant has closed. She changes into sweats, finds an energy bar in her suitcase and remembers a little loaf of bread that she picked up at Kim's bakery.

As she eats, a swarm of thoughts buzzes into her head. A flock of crazy, midnight ideas.

To move to England. To buy Stephanie's house. To be immersed in Anne Lister's environment. To explore a relationship with Larkin. To learn a whole new culture. To sell her aunt's house, move across the world, do the mountains of paperwork that would doubtless be involved for her to be able to buy real estate…and surely, she wouldn't have enough money.

There's no way.

But as she settles into bed and starts to drift to sleep again, a question arises, vivid in her mind, as if someone were whispering it into her ear. *Is this an invitation for me?*

•••《●》•••

PART THREE: Winter
Castro Valley, California

A Fall, A Risk

Devon awakens to a California sunrise and stretches luxuriously
— in her own bed again, having landed late last night. *Time to get
back to normal life.*

After breakfast, Devon calls Glo, thanks her for collecting her
mail and watering her plants. They agree to get together over the
weekend. She spends the day unpacking, doing laundry, paying
bills, working on the deck, trying to keep her mind clear, with little
success. She has been texting Larkin every day or two as usual, but
has had only the briefest of replies, and has heard nothing from
her for four days now. She is trying very hard not to be disturbed
about it.

As the late afternoon shadows move in, Devon goes out for
a jog, to reacquaint herself with her home territory. She has an
intense, painful memory of Baxter, who loved going running with
her. She fancies that she can hear his leash jingling and feel his hot
breath on her ankles, and misses him sharply.

She jogs through the neighborhood with its ragged eucalyptus
trees and arid lawns, then up to the hills and her favorite trail. She
can see San Francisco, the Bay, and the tan-color hills that always
make her think of vast sleeping animals. She loves this view, but
is so tired of the dryness here. She realizes that for years, she has
been longing for the green, rainy environment that she grew up in.
A green, rainy environment like Yorkshire. And now she is longing
for Larkin, too.

She jogs until she is sweating and her ankle is screaming, then limps home slowly, trying to think of anything but Larkin, trying not to dwell on the huge loneliness that has opened up inside her.

She takes a long, hot shower. As she is toweling off, her phone buzzes and her heart jumps. There is a photo of Larkin smiling in front of a makeshift fruit and vegetable stand, pointing at a pile of mangoes. The caption says "I would like to feed you this mango very slowly and lick the juice off you for hours."

Devon feels tears spring up. Larkin is so, so far away. She pushes the feeling down and starts to plan her return to work. She contacts Steve, but he tells her there's not much work at the moment, just one or two days this week at most. She realizes that as much as she fears the lack of income, she fears the empty time more — empty time when she will be longing hopelessly for Larkin, and for Yorkshire.

Devon checks her bank balance. Money is tight, but not unusually so. Her usual kitchen rehab work will start to pick up soon, in the new year at least. Meanwhile, she needs to do something to get Larkin off her mind.

Devon busies herself with home repairs and painting her studio. She hikes out to the hills and does a few watercolors there, and some sketches at a winter festival in Oakland. On Thanksgiving weekend, she paints more watercolors of Anne Lister to sell to the fans. Glo calls, persuades her to come to a party with some of their old friends. Devon interacts and laughs, but all she can think about is Larkin. Devon hasn't heard from her in weeks now.

Every day or two, Devon looks online for reports from the flood area, and at last, she comes across a feature with a dozen photos by Larkin. The scenes are shocking, horrible — pictures of destroyed villages, people living in ragged tents, people mobbing aid trucks for bowls of soup. But amid the horror, Larkin has found a few glimpses of humanity and compassion. A little boy covered in mud but grinning because he has found a toy truck in the wreckage. A mother and father embracing a teenage daughter. A smiling group putting the finishing touches on a sturdy-looking plywood hut. Devon's heart dissolves. She prints the photos and sticks them on the wall of her studio.

She's trying hard to hold off on texting Larkin again, but finally, after these weeks of silence, she gives up and texts her.

- *Hey, haven't heard from you for a while. I've seen some of your photos. They are magnificent. It looks intense. I hope you're okay.*

The response comes several days later.

- The squalor and destruction is beyond belief, Dev. Houses destroyed, washed away. And so many women are here on their own, or with small kids, and absolutely unprotected. Starvation, rapes, assaults. I can't tell you how many heart-wrenching stories I've heard. I cry every night. I'm sleeping in a little tent near the Red Cross hospital and just taking photos and doing interviews with these poor women all day, every day. I'm exhausted. I have to keep on documenting this. Having trouble sleeping.

- *I'm looking forward so very much to seeing you again, Lark. I can't wait to show you my favorite places in California. And give you a good rest. Christmas?*

There is no answer. After a few days, Devon resigns herself to the idea that Larkin may be unable to communicate right now. She tries, during the following weeks, to stop hoping for a reply. She even feels guilty for wanting attention from Larkin when she is dealing with such life-and-death issues. Christmas comes and goes with a warm gathering at Glo and Tanisha's, but still no word from Larkin. Her hurt gradually turns into anger. She finds herself yelling at drivers on the freeway, and snarling at Steve when he's too demanding at work.

On a sunny, windy morning in late January, Devon is working in the front yard, raking and pruning, when a sudden gust rips some tiles off the roof and sends them spinning into the street. Devon is furious. *After what I paid for that roof, it should last a decade, at least.*

She calls the roofing company but no one answers. She leaves a scathing voice message, then decides to take matters into her own hands. She storms into the garage and throws tools and supplies into a paint bucket. As she is lugging her extension ladder out to the back yard, her phone pings. Her heart leaps, but it's not Larkin. It's Claire, sending some photos of "the girls" — in the pub, of course — as well as some photos of Stephanie's place. Stephanie is fixing up the kitchen with new appliances and flooring. She will put it on the market in May.

Looking at the photos, Devon finds herself filled with a helpless, grasping, longing feeling. *I could do such great things with that place.*

Devon shakes her head sharply to dispel the feeling and sets the ladder up so she can reach the roof. She puts her foot up to the first rung, when her phone dings again. *I hope it's that goddamn roofing company.* But no, it's a text from Larkin. Devon taps the screen with trembling fingers.

- Dear Devon, I'm writing with a very sad heart to tell you I don't think I will be coming to California at all. I am very involved here, trying to get a shelter organized for some of the women who have lost their homes. I don't know when I'll ever be able to leave. There is so much need. Sadly, I think you and I should call it a day. I care for you very much, but I don't want to lead you on or tie you down. You deserve to be free, and I need to be free so I can stay with these people. You and I had three perfect days. That will have to be enough. I send you love and best wishes, and hope to see you again someday. Always, Larkin.

Devon is numb. She lets the phone fall to the ground. It bounces off the brittle grass. Moving mechanically, she props her ladder against the back of the house and climbs up, the bucket with her tools balanced precariously in one hand.

So there goes that stupid dream, she thinks as she gets her tools out. *It won't be so bad to stay here,* she thinks as she gets the knife out and starts cutting back a damaged tile. *I'll find someone else.* The California sun beams down on her from a clear blue sky. A cool gust washes over the roof. *Think how horrible the weather is over there most of the time.* But as hard as she tries to focus on the tiles, the knife, the brads, the glue — all she can see in her mind's eye is Larkin's face, her head thrown back in ecstasy. *Something I'll never see again.* Her stomach clenches in despair. She drops her hammer and it goes skidding down the sloping roof. She reaches for it, loses her balance, and falls off the roof onto the concrete deck, landing hard on her back.

～

After she gets her breath back, Devon tries to stand and realizes that she has damaged a couple of ribs in the fall. She can't breathe without stabbing pain in the middle of her back. Very slowly, she struggles to her feet. *GOD it hurts.* She makes her way into the house and sits on the couch. She thinks about calling for help and remembers her phone is outside on the grass.

It will be all right to just sit here for a while. She is shaky from shock and knows she is not thinking clearly. She pulls an afghan over herself and falls into a light, delirious sleep.

When she awakens, it is almost dark outside and the house is cold.

She forces herself to get up. Everything hurts. She staggers painfully out into the yard and finds her phone in the grass. Leaning over to pick it up is one of the hardest things she has done physically since she broke her ankle. *Why am I always hurting myself?*

She limps back into the house, sits at the kitchen table trying to remember how to breathe. *I can't manage this on my own.* Finally, she calls Glo.

This morning, Devon is starting to feel a little better. Glo, who has been staying at Devon's for almost a week, has made breakfast, and will be sticking around for another hour. Glo puts the plates in the dishwasher, waving away Devon's offer of help. She pours them both another cup of coffee and sits.

"So your question that you want me to answer for you is….?"

"Should I go to England?"

"As in, move to England."

"Yeah."

"What do you think I'm going to say?"

"I don't know, Glo, that's why I'm asking you."

"What do you think you should do?"

Devon sips her coffee, trying to get in touch with her heart. Glo sits patiently, waiting without speaking. Eventually, Devon sees the outline of what she really wants.

"I think I should go to England. At least for a couple of years.

If I can. And see what it's like."

Glo nods. "Why?"

"Because…when I was there I felt truly at home, and…" Her voice trails off.

"You felt truly at home. And…?"

"And I just loved it, Glo! I loved the countryside — I thought it was ugly, at first, but after a few days I wanted to paint every field and every hill! — and I loved the old buildings and the way people talk. Bus drivers call you 'M'love'!"

"And…?"

"And I really, really liked the women — they were so friendly and funny and nice and quirky. And I think, I really think, more and more women will be moving there. From all over the world! It's going to be an amazing community."

"And…?"

"Grrr!"

"Come on. Dig deeper."

Devon thinks hard for a moment.

"And — just the way Aunt Amy gave me a home, a wonderful home, when I was kicked out, I'd love to do that for other women. I had her to save me, but what about the women — especially the young lesbians — who don't have an Aunt Amy? Maybe I can be that for them, at least in a small way. Maybe I can get a house that I can set up as a B&B. A temporary resting place. A place where they can get — I don't know — support. I'm not a counselor or anything, but you know I like fixing up old houses, and I love making breakfast for people."

"Beautiful breakfasts," Glo comments.

"And just to be part of a community with all those women — it's my dream. You know it is."

"You have been wanting that kind of community for years," Glo agrees.

"I sure never thought I'd chase the dream to another country."

"What about Larkin?"

"That's over. Well, if she comes back, we maybe could negotiate a friendship. Or even date each other, I don't know. But I'm sure not counting on it. I don't feel like dating anyone right now, I'm

60

too busted up. I think it would be a good place for me to heal."

"But…?"

"What do you mean?"

"There's a 'but.'"

"Well, yeah. Money. I'm doing pretty well selling these paintings, but at this rate, it'll be four years before I can even make a down payment on a house there. It's hopeless." Devon slumps.

Glo bursts into laughter.

"What's so funny?"

"You are. Complaining about being a pauper, while sitting on a goldmine."

"Goldmine?"

"California real estate? Hello? Do you have any idea how much this house is worth?"

"It's not in the greatest shape."

"Do you have any idea? No, you don't, do you?"

"Well, no, I don't. I've owned it for three and a half years, since Aunt Amy died…but I never thought to find out how much it's worth."

"What? Didn't you have to pay property taxes?"

"Aunt Amy left money to cover that. The accountant pays the taxes. I can't believe I've never looked up how much it's worth. I just figured I'd live here for ever."

Glo pulls out her phone and gets onto a real estate site. When she finds Devon's house, she laughs again and hands the phone to her.

Devon gasps. She had no idea. The house is valued at a ridiculous figure. She could buy two or even three decent sized houses in Halifax for that amount. Or one pair of twin semi-detached houses to set up a B&B…and invest the rest to live on while the business got off the ground. Her head spins with the possibilities. But she passes the phone back to Glo.

"I could never sell Aunt Amy's house."

They sit in silence for a moment.

"It's a huge step," says Glo.

"A huge risk," says Devon.

"You might really regret it," says Glo.

"Yeah, but…" says Devon. She pauses, chewing her thumbnail.

"But..?"

Devon says, "But I might regret not going for it, even more."

They sit in silence for a minute. Then Devon says, as if to herself — "I've got to ask myself, what would Anne Lister do?"

Glo says, encouragingly, "Well, what would she do? What was she like?"

"Brave. Adventurous. Selfish." Devon suddenly feels her arms prickle with goosebumps. "And she liked fixing up her buildings and grounds."

"Hmmm," says Glo.

"Hmmm," replies Devon.

"Claire, hi, it's Devon — oh no, is it too late to call?"

"No, it's…um…too early but that's all right, love, what's going on? When are you coming back to see us?"

"I just need to know — has Stephanie sold the house?"

"No — are you interested?"

"I might be."

"Really? Do you still have her number?"

"Yes."

"Well, phone her! Not just at this moment — it's only 4:30 in the morning —"

"Oh, I'm so sorry!"

"— But in a couple of hours."

"Yes."

"Will you tell me what's going on?"

"After I've talked to her. Thanks so much, Claire!"

Hey team, one of our own is moving to Britain and I'm throwing a surprise farewell party for her. No gifts, but please wear your softball uniform — whatever part of it still fits, ha ha — and come prepared to tease her about cricket and rugby. Details below. Let's celebrate Devon's departure in style! — Glo

Devon! I heard a rumour that you're coming back to live here! Is that true? Are you gonna open a guest house? I have so many potential customers for you! And fresh-baked bread cakes and scones for your breakfasts! Can't wait to see you! Cheers, Kim (of Kim's Catering)

Devon, I've finally received the last of the paperwork — and so now the house is yours. Yee-ha!! We must celebrate! Please let me know the moment you arrive. I'll be more than happy to help you get it up and running. Best, Stephanie.

Devon grunts as she puts the very last box of trash into the bed of her truck. *And now for the hardest part.*

She goes into the little house for the last time and slowly, carefully, reverently, packs Aunt Amy's altar into a small box. Then she walks from room to echoing room, remembering all the interactions with her aunt during the years Devon lived there with her. In each room, she murmurs thanks and appreciation. In each room, she cries.

As she steps out of the front door for the last time, the small box cradled under her arm, Devon turns back and, tears pouring unchecked down her cheeks, says one more time, from her heart, *Aunt Amy, thank you. I'm incredibly sad to leave the house. But you're coming with me, wherever I go, always.*

Resolutely, Devon locks the door and drops the keys through the mail slot. She wipes her eyes and climbs into her truck, the precious box at her side, and sets out to Alameda, where Glo will take possession of the truck and hand it over to its new owner in a couple of days. *I'll be in England by then*, Devon reflects incredulously, as she pulls onto the freeway. *I sure hope I know what I'm doing.*

Miss Lister's Guest House Floor Plan

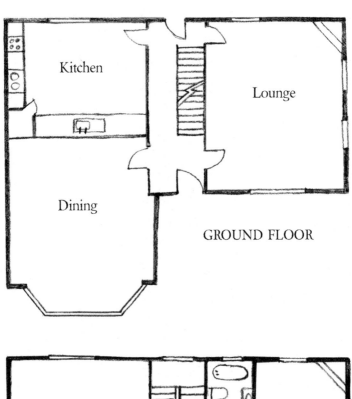

Kitchen

Lounge

Dining

GROUND FLOOR

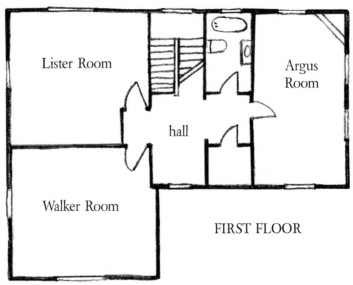

Lister Room

Argus Room

hall

Walker Room

FIRST FLOOR

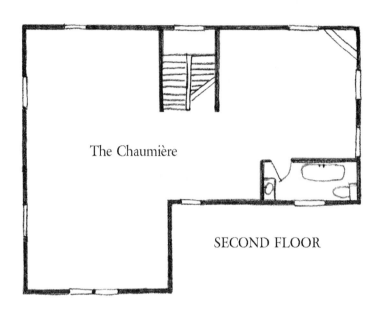

The Chaumière

SECOND FLOOR

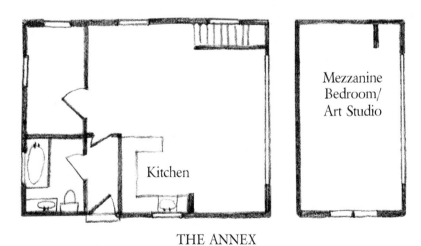

Kitchen

Mezzanine
Bedroom/
Art Studio

THE ANNEX

PART FOUR: Summer to Early Autumn
Yorkshire

I Have Many Skills

- *Miremba, hi, this is Devon, do you remember me? The American? I was here in November and we met at the pub with Claire.*

- I remember you very well, Devon. You have the nice broad shoulders and the nice green eyes.

- *Hazel.*

- The nice hazel eyes, then.

- *Well. If you say so.*

- I do. You're back in England?

- *Yes, I've bought a house in Hebden and I'm fixing it up to be a guest house. A bed and breakfast. And there's a little converted barn next to it that I'll live in.*

- Wonderful!

- *I need some help and I remember that you're a skilled carpenter.*

- I have many skills. Yes, carpentry is one.

- *Are you available at all? I've announced that the Grand Opening will be in September and there's still so much to do. Two and a half months don't seem nearly enough.*

- I think I'm available. Let me check and I'll get back to you tomorrow, all right?

- *That would be great.*

- Bye for now, then. And congratulations!

The next day is cool and rainy. Devon has been working all morning in the guest house bathroom on the third floor — what they call the second floor here, for some reason. Now in the mid-afternoon, she is finally finished with the tiles.

She estimates that the Annex — the low stone barn where she will live — is about halfway to being habitable. It's cozy and has a great view over the fields. She is sleeping there now, on a brand-new bed. And she figures, perhaps optimistically, that the guest house is about a quarter of the way complete. She is starting to panic.

Her back is acting up, sore and bothersome. She takes a brief break to make a cup of tea and look at the guest house kitchen. She can get the counter done today if she starts right now. She stretches and gears herself for more strenuous labor.

Devon is wrestling a big section of particleboard into place in the kitchen when she hears a truck pull into the courtyard, followed by a loud knock at the door. She curses under her breath but shouts, "Come in!" as she heaves the board onto the edge of its frame. She twists her head around, and sees Miremba, smiling in the doorway. She wears a bright multi-colored headscarf and a grey hoodie, and carries a tote bag.

"Hi!" Devon grunts.

Miremba, dropping the bag, jumps forward to help Devon lift and push the heavy board into place.

"Wow, thanks! I'm super glad you're here," says Devon, grinning at Miremba. "Would you please please come and work with me?"

"Always glad to help a sister," says Miremba with a broad, friendly smile.

"Hungry?" asks Devon.

"Always glad to eat something." Miremba's expression is mildly suggestive. Devon is amused.

As they sit over sandwiches and tea back in the Annex, they look at Devon's sketched plans for the guest house, discuss terms, and agree to a good, union-level hourly wage. Miremba doesn't disguise her admiration of Devon, looking her over obviously but somehow not at all rudely, as they talk — and smiling, if anything, more broadly. Devon finds herself smiling more, as well. Suddenly the job seems achievable.

"When shall we start?" asks Devon.

"How about now?" Miremba takes off her hoodie, revealing a red T-shirt stretched tight over beautifully muscled shoulders and arms. She straps on a tool belt over her jeans. Devon finds something moving in her core that she hasn't felt since her time with Larkin. She pushes it out of her mind. *Inappropriate!*

Devon starts their work together giving orders, but it becomes clear after about ten minutes that the Ugandan woman knows far more about carpentry than she, and Devon steps back as Miremba gracefully takes charge.

They chat lightly as they work, and Devon learns that Miremba left Uganda two years before, when the government was again cracking down on "the gays." She has been living in England on an expired student visa, doing jobs for cash and traveling on a circuit of Northern towns where she knows lesbians and has friends in the construction business. It sounds as if Miremba has been steadily employed, and Devon can see why. Within an hour, the countertops are in place. Within another two hours, wiring the outside lights — a job that Devon thought would take half a day to complete — is also finished. Miremba knows shortcuts, tricks, techniques, tolerances of various materials, voltages — she is a one-woman construction crew.

At six o'clock, Devon is exhausted and declares an end to the work day. "You sure?" asks Miremba. "We can still cut that lino tonight for the kitchen floor."

"No, we can't. I'm done for the day and so are you."

"Okay, boss, if you're so tired."

Devon laughs at her and goes to find her wallet. She pays Miremba and adds a tip. Miremba counts it and hands the twenty-pound note back. Devon waves it off. "You've earned a tip."

"No," Miremba says. "The wage we agreed on is fair. Anyway, you don't need to pay me till the whole job is done."

"Call it a bonus, then," Devon wheedles.

Miremba frowns and shakes her head. Devon takes the note back and Miremba smiles her sunny smile again. "How about a beer, boss?"

"Here? Or down at the pub?"

"Oh, let's go to the pub," says Miremba. They put their tools away for the night and walk down the hill through a cool drizzle to the bright, noisy pub.

"Let me buy you dinner, I mean tea, at least," says Devon, and Miremba cheerfully agrees.

While they are eating, Devon asks Miremba where she will be staying while she works on Devon's house. "I'm staying at the hostel," says Miremba.

"Will you work with me for the next two months?"

Miremba grins. "Of course, I'd be happy to."

"Well, then, why don't you be the first customer at the B&B. I just bought sheets and blankets. Let's fix up one of the beds for you."

"Devon, that is an *excellent* idea!"

They clink their pints and take a great gulp. Looking at each other over the top of their glasses, they laugh about nothing in particular.

Devon and Miremba have been working hard on the B&B for three weeks, and Devon can scarcely believe how much they have accomplished. Miremba is a fantastic worker — an imaginative problem-solver; strong; cheerful and patient, even when the water heater broke and the guest house had only cold water for three days.

They watch TV together in the evenings, sharing a takeaway from the Indian or Chinese restaurant, or head to the pub. Devon privately thinks the local Chinese food is horrendous, but they are both so hungry they eat everything in sight with no second thoughts. Then they retire to their bedrooms — Devon in the Annex, Miremba in the B&B.

Every night as she gets into bed, Devon thinks of Larkin. Sad, longing, angry thoughts that have not seemed to lose their power as the months have gone by. But now, exhausted as she is, Devon finds herself brushing the memories of Larkin aside with ease, as images of Miremba fill her mind. She touches herself as she wonders what Miremba looks like under her overalls and sweatshirt, what her small, firm breasts feel like, how her lips might feel between Devon's legs.

In the brightness of day, though, Devon shoves these thoughts away. Miremba is, after all, her employee — though she really doesn't feel like one. She feels like a co-worker and, increasingly, like a friend. Their racial, economic and cultural differences are realities — real barriers — between them, but these are dissolving rapidly as they attack the remodeling projects with all their energy and an engagingly competitive spirit. Hearty laughter echoes off the bare walls with increasing frequency. And more than once, Devon catches Miremba looking at her with a particular kind of smile that might be affectionate and might be lustful.

They work together sometimes, but just as often they are in different rooms, finishing separate projects. In between, they share their life stories, and Devon learns to her horror of how bad the anti-gay crackdown in Uganda has been. Miremba was attending a trades training program in Leeds, studying domestic electrical installation, when she heard from her friends back home how oppressive the new laws were. Miremba's family — her parents and two sisters — encouraged her to stay in the U.K. as long as possible.

"So," she says to Devon while they are drinking bottles of lager on Devon's front steps one hot evening, "I have overstayed my visa. I am here on borrowed time. I hope that if I keep moving from place to place, the authorities won't catch up with me. I've applied for asylum, but it is taking for ever to hear back about it." She shrugs and takes a sip of beer. "At least I am managing to save a lot of money," she smiles.

"What will you do with it?" asks Devon.

"I send much of it home to my mum. But I'm saving the rest. I want to be in business for myself. Get licensed. Buy a van, specialize in kitchen renovations."

"You'll be very successful at that," Devon says.

"I hope so, boss."

"I'll recommend you to everyone I know."

"Thanks, boss."

"But only if you quit calling me boss."

"Okay, Miss Devon."

"That's worse."

"Ha!"

73

"So, Miremba — do you think we can be finished in another ten days?"

"I think so, all but the painting of the walls in the second floor room."

"I think so, too. Well, it's time to start promoting the place. I thought we might have an open house for the Grand Opening. Would you be up for that?"

"A party?"

"Yes."

"That's exciting, Devon."

"Yes, isn't it?"

They sit peacefully together, looking up at the bright summer stars.

It's going to be sunny and hot on this Thursday morning in late August. Miremba leaves the B&B, walks the few steps to Devon's front door and enters with her own key. She goes to the kitchen, where she turns the sound system on to upbeat pop, starts the coffee maker, and puts bread into the toaster while Devon, entering in shorts and a rumpled T-shirt, yawns a hello and starts to scramble eggs and fry ham. "Like an old married couple," says Miremba, bumping hips with Devon and giggling at her embarrassment.

After they've eaten, they sit over their second cups of coffee and plan their day. Devon is feeling cautiously elated because they are so close to finishing. Miremba echoes her optimism.

"Devon, we only have that plastering to finish today, right?"

"Yeah, and hanging the sign, and then the plastering is really the last project. When we've finished that, we'll be done."

Miremba is silent, and a rare pensive look has come over her face.

"What's up?"

"Well, if this job is finished, I'll be moving on tomorrow then. I have a job in Leeds waiting for me. I was supposed to be there three days ago."

Devon feels hollow all of a sudden.

"Tomorrow? Damn. I'll really miss you. It's been so great

working with you. Spending time with you."

"I'll be back to visit," Miremba grins, "I'll come for the Grand Opening, and to make sure you're not abusing that poor hot-water heater."

"If you need anything — a reference — a place to sleep —"

"I'll be in touch. Don't worry about me, boss."

"You've taught me so much." Devon feels shaky.

Miremba smiles at her. She puts her hand on Devon's arm and strokes gently, then rises and stretches. Devon's arm tingles from the touch.

"Come on, Devon, if we sit here all day, we will never get that bloody job done."

"Right, let's get to it. And we'll have a blowout at the pub tonight to celebrate, okay? On me."

"Sure."

Devon goes to her sitting room and gets the beautiful wood sign that she commissioned a local artisan to make. In vivid black paint over pale natural wood, it evokes the days when Anne Lister traveled around the country in a fast coach. The horses, the coachman with his top hat and whip, and the shape of the coach itself all generate a sensation of adventure. Above the picture, the sign says simply "B&B." Miremba fetches the stepladder and then Devon climbs up to hang the sign ceremoniously from the black steel cross-arm that they installed yesterday. The sign looks splendid, and it sways gently in the light breeze.

"It's gorgeous," Miremba says, and Devon has to agree. She could stand and look at it for hours, but they have to get that damn plastering done.

As they get to work on the top floor of the guest house, Devon remembers why she left this until last. It is unpleasant, dirty, intricate work, repairing a botched plastering job that first needs to be chipped away and then painstakingly reconstructed. As the morning wears on, the sun rises in the unusually cloudless sky, and they get hot. They open both windows of the big bedroom, which look out on the green valley where a scattering of sheep graze under a brilliant blue sky. Devon brings in her electric fan and sets it in a window at the highest setting. But by lunchtime, they are both stripped down to singlets and shorts. Every now and then, Devon steals a glance at Miremba's smoothly sculpted arms and legs, speckled with plaster and slick with sweat.

Devon lifts a bucket of plaster, swings it over to her stepladder, and gasps, bending over in pain.

Miremba lays down her trowel and strides to Devon's side, putting her arm around her shoulders. "What's the matter?"

"My ribs — just a bit sore."

Miremba takes the bucket, sets it down. "Sit, boss. Sit down now, please." Devon sits on a crate and Miremba fetches her a couple of painkillers with a glass of cold water. She moves the fan so it blows directly on Devon's face. As Devon takes the pills and drinks the water, Miremba lightly strokes her shoulder. Devon can feel the heat radiating from Miremba's torso, which is so close to Devon's face right now that she could turn her head and bury her face in Miremba's breasts. For one moment, they are both still, with the pulsing rhythm of the electric fan the only sound. Even through her pain, Devon can feel a fierce wave of desire wash through her.

Miremba carries on the work, keeping an eye on Devon. After a few minutes, Devon staggers to her feet and renews her work, more cautiously.

"What are you doing?" Miremba asks.

"I'm feeling much better. I'll take things easy."

Miremba grunts skeptically but Devon resumes her work with no problems, though the afternoon heat is intense. They work as quickly as they can. Finally, all that remains to be done is a final cleanup around the edges of the patched areas.

As they work, Devon finds herself telling Miremba about her fall from the roof, the end of her affair with Larkin. Miremba clicks her tongue against her teeth sympathetically but says nothing until Devon says, "I've talked your ear off. It's your turn. You've never told me about your love life. For all I know, you're a virgin."

Miremba's laugh is sharp, then she is quiet for a moment and Devon wonders if she has overstepped. But then Miremba tells Devon about a lover back in Uganda, a woman who loved Miremba but was too afraid to stay with her in the capital when the government crackdown was rumored to be underway, and so went back to her home village, leaving Miremba bereft.

"So you and me, we are both lonely little goats," Miremba says.

Devon nods solemnly and then throws her head back and cries, "Baaaa!"

They bleat together like goats as they carry their equipment downstairs and clean their tools.

Finally, they go back up and look around at all they have accomplished. They high-five each other and rotate around looking at their work.

Devon says "Now what?"

Miremba has her back to Devon. She has a smear of white plaster on her shoulder. It's incredibly sexy, the white streak of plaster on the brown skin. Without thinking, Devon reaches out to rub it off. She can smell Miremba's sweat, clean and sharp.

Miremba turns and grasps Devon's hand. "Plaster," Devon says weakly. "On your shoulder."

Miremba looks her in the eyes and speaks softly. "I'm leaving in the morning, boss, so whatever is going to happen better happen tonight, if it's going to happen at all."

Devon pulls her hand away. She can feel herself blushing. "How about a shower and then a cuppa?"

Miremba nods gravely.

"I have taught you how to make a proper pot of tea, so this is acceptable. I will take the first shower, then." Miremba goes into the bathroom and runs water, leaving the door wide open.

Breathing heavily, her mind in a swirl, Devon rushes down to the kitchen, fills a kettle, and puts it on the new gas stove to boil. Then she climbs back upstairs and passes the bathroom. The door is still open, and she can see Miremba dropping her clothes and headscarf on the floor and leaning over the tub to adjust the water as it shoots down vigorously from the just-installed shower head.

Devon stands for a moment, feeling guilty, voyeuristic, admiring the muscles sliding under the glistening skin, the powerful butt, the strong legs. Devon can't stop a small moan from escaping her lips. Miremba hears her, turns, smiles and beckons, and steps under the shower.

As if hypnotized, Devon tears her sweaty clothes off and, her heart pounding, steps into the hot falling water. Miremba's back is to her. Devon still hasn't seen Miremba's front. She has imagined what her breasts look like but now she doesn't have to imagine, as Miremba grabs a washcloth, fills it with water and soap, and hands it back to Devon.

Miremba leans both hands on the wall of the shower. Devon gently runs the soapy cloth over her back.

"Harder, boss. I won't break."

Devon accepts the challenge. Spluttering a bit under the strong hot spray, Devon scrubs Miremba's back as hard as she can, and then, reaching her left arm around Miremba's waist to hold her in place, she curves her right hand around to wash her breasts. Looking over Miremba's shoulder, Devon can see the dark, prominent nipples harden and stand up like little thimbles. Miremba groans. She grinds her butt into Devon's crotch.

Devon turns Miremba around and looks into her deep brown eyes, blinking in the spray. As if at an unheard command, they both lean into a deep, hot kiss. Miremba's tongue occupies Devon's mouth. Her generous lips caress Devon's for a timeless, soaked moment, then they move their heads apart and stare, breathless, at each other.

At that moment, the kettle downstairs starts to whistle loudly.

"Oh, God," says Devon. "The kettle will melt." She jumps out of the shower, throws a towel around herself, and runs downstairs to the kitchen, where she pulls the very hot kettle off of the burner and stands, drying herself off. Then, instead of heading back upstairs, she sets about making a pot of tea.

Miremba, toweling her short, springy hair, comes down the stairs and into the kitchen. "Hi," she says, walking to Devon and holding out her arms for an embrace. Devon grabs her arms and, looking at the floor, says miserably, "Oh, Miremba. I just...can't. I'm so sorry. I want to, but..."

"Oh," says Miremba sadly, dropping the embrace and resuming her hair-toweling. "Is it because of Larkin?"

"I guess so. I mean, it's not like she's my girlfriend, or that I owe her anything at all — "

"I know, I know," Miremba says softly. "She's your woman. She has your heart. Whether she knows it or not." She laughs, sadly.

"Dammit," says Devon. "Just dammit. You're so hot, and you're so damn nice."

"And very good with my hands, don't forget that," smiles Miremba.

"I really like you."

"Don't worry, I understand," says Miremba, with a massive sigh.

They drink their tea quietly, and go to their separate rooms to dress. As evening is falling over the courtyard, Devon returns to the B&B and yells up the stairs, "Want to go to the pub? I promised you a blowout."

"I remember, boss!" shouts Miremba, and in a moment, she comes downstairs, wearing the same red T-shirt and grey hoodie she wore when she first arrived. Without thinking, Devon steps over to her and embraces her. They stand hugging for a long moment and then, with a sigh and a little laugh, they break apart and walk down through the cooling dusk to the pub.

In the morning, Devon gets up very early and silently makes arepas con huevo for Miremba. It takes a long time, but the end result — the crispy corn cake with the fried egg inside — is worth it. *I hope it shows her how much I care for her.*

She puts it on a tray with a cup of coffee and a flower in a tiny vase, tiptoes carefully across the courtyard and up the stairs, and knocks lightly on Miremba's door. "Room service," she calls out, entering the room with the tray. Miremba sits up in bed, blinking.

"What's all this?" she asks.

"I wanted to give you a little treat before you go."

"Very, very nice, Devon," says Miremba, genuinely pleased. "Will you join me?"

They sit on Miremba's bed, sharing the food and discussing ideas about their businesses. When they've finished, Devon gathers everything onto the tray. "I am truly going to miss you, Miremba."

Miremba moves over to one side of the bed, holds the blanket up to make a tent, and beckons Devon over. "Come here, you lonely little goat."

Devon puts the tray on the floor. She climbs into the bed and Miremba enfolds her. They breathe together, a deep trust and affection floating between them. Devon feels tears coming and doesn't fight them.

"We did great work together, didn't we?" Devon says eventually.

Miremba smiles loftily. "Yes. You are very lucky to have Miremba in your life, aren't you?"

Devon strokes her face. "Very lucky. I wish you didn't have to go."

Miremba gives a sad smile. "You knew from the beginning I'd be moving on."

"It doesn't make it any easier."

"I'm sorry. It's hard for me, too. You're a bit of all right, you know, boss."

"You'll come back for the Grand Opening."

"Of course."

Miremba takes Devon's hand and runs her lips over it, giving Devon shivers.

"You'll take care of yourself, and call me if you need anything, Miremba, right?"

"Of course."

Devon feels her heart crack open again and the huge loneliness flood in. She pauses, breathing the tears away and focusing on caressing Miremba's curving cheek. "Miremba."

"Yes?"

"What does your name mean?"

"Peace," says Miremba, gently biting Devon's hand and then standing. "It means peace."

∿

The Grand Opening

Not much baking seems to be going on at Kim's bakery when Devon stops in. Kim, Evie, and Daisy are huddled around a table, drinking coffee and laughing their heads off.

Kim looks up and greets Devon. She is still giggling. She points at the paper-wrapped packet under Devon's arm.

"Hello, love! Ooh, are those the flyers for your open house?"

"Yeah," says Devon, smiling at the contagious laughter still rippling through the room. "What's so funny?"

Kim says, "We're just having a bit of a laugh…"

Daisy chimes in, "About the new Anne Lister film."

Evie says, "You mean the Celia Denton film." The three of them sigh, and then talk all at once, at the top of their lungs.

Devon somehow manages to discern that the cast and crew of the first movie about Anne Lister will be returning to Halifax in a few months to shoot the sequel.

"I heard January!"

"No, no, it's definitely February."

Kim grins widely. "And, Dev, they rang up and told me that they're considering Kim's Catering to provide all their delectables. We're one of their top three choices." Daisy and Evie are practically jumping up and down with excitement.

Devon is elated. "That's so exciting! What do you need to do to get hired?"

Kim replies, "Oh, they'll do some sort of sampling thing. They said they want to use a local firm, so we have a few months to perfect our offerings — right, you two? And by the way, don't you have some sausage rolls to finish up?" Evie and Daisy roll their eyes and get back to work.

Kim pours a mug of coffee for Devon and takes her back to her untidy little office. They sit down to talk.

"Let's see the flyers!"

"Right," says Devon, pulling one out of the packet. "I just picked them up from the printers." The flyer is a brightly-colored half-page sheet. It invites everyone to celebrate the Grand Opening of Miss Lister's Guest House. It promises "Delicious snacks provided by Kim's Catering," among other delights.

Kim looks admiringly at the flyer. "You designed this?" Devon nods. "Very nice indeed. I can't wait to see the place."

"Come up any time, Kim, really. I'd love to show you around. And I thought you might pop a few of these flyers into your deliveries, if that's not too obnoxious."

Kim smiles. "Glad to, pal. I've a feeling this'll be just the start of lots of chances for us to work together."

They review Devon's order for hors-d'oeuvres trays for the open house and decide to double the number of trays, given the response Devon is getting on social media.

Kim whistles. "This must be costing you a fortune, mate."

Devon winces, then shrugs. "It is. I just hope that I can fill the place up during the Anne Lister research conference. If I can do that, and the guests have a good experience — well, you know how the grapevine operates. I hope for a steady stream of Lister fans year round."

Kim stands. "We'll do our best to have some really good snap for you. Speaking of which, I need to get back to me sausage rolls."

When Devon drives back to the guest house, it's almost dark and there is a delivery van in the courtyard. The driver hands her a flat, rectangular package.

She takes it into the Annex and turns on the lights. The stamps are Indian; the postmark indicates that it was sent three weeks ago. *Larkin.* Devon's heart rate speeds up. She puts it on the kitchen table and gets a beer from the fridge. Drinking the beer quickly, she stares at the package as if it is a bomb that might go off if mishandled. She drains the bottle, finds a sharp knife, and takes a deep breath.

She cuts the tape off the package and pulls off layers of packaging. She finally peels off the last swath of bubble wrap to reveal a photograph mounted on hard cardboard, about one and a half by two feet in size.

The background of the picture shows a muddy village square, with a broken-down hut in the foreground. The focus of the photo is a barefoot young girl, perhaps eleven, thin as a whip, clad in a ragged sari. She grins at the camera as she pulls her right foot back to kick a soccer ball made of rags and string. The grin is devilish, delighted. The background of the scene is dark and dirty, but her face is radiant with joy and bathed in a golden sunset light. Devon gazes at it for several minutes before she notices a letter that came in the package. She sits to read it, feeling a pang when she recognizes Larkin's handwriting.

"Dear Devon, This is Nandita. As you can see, she has a great spirit, and is going to be a football star. Already, she can score at will against the best goalie on the boys' team. Her mother is in the little group organising the effort to build a safe shelter for the girls and women in this village. I'm doing my best to help them. My assignment is over, but I am staying on to document this project and to chip in where I can.

"I know that you are creating a safe space for women there in Calderdale and if you like this picture, I would be honoured if you'd put it up for your open house, if it gets to you on time. I hope that Nandita's spirit, as well as dear old Anne Lister's, blesses you and your guest house.

"I miss you so very much and hope we can be friends, and see each other when I come back to visit my family. I don't know when that will be — there is so much work to do here. I hold you in my heart and wish you peace. Always, Larkin."

Devon's bruised heart feels like breaking all over again. Carefully but resolutely, she re-wraps the picture and takes it up to her studio. She stashes it in a corner where she will not have to see it. Maybe someday, she will be strong enough to hang it up in the guest house. But not yet. Not yet.

The Grand Opening is about to start, within the hour. Devon was unable to sleep much the night before, in fear that no one will come today. She busies herself in this last bit of time before the open house is due to begin.

Miremba has come for the day to help out. *Thank goodness she was working nearby.* Devon puts her in charge of welcoming visitors, and Daisy and Evie in charge of setting up the snacks and drinks, while she takes Kim on a quick tour.

"So," Devon says nervously, "Here's the ground floor — you've seen the kitchen. Here's the dining room and the lounge…"

Kim exclaims appreciatively. "I've been here several times in its previous incarnation — I love the simplicity and the fresh colors, but I must say, I miss the lariats."

"Har, har," replies Devon, and leads the way to the second floor (*no, first floor,* she reminds herself). "The Anne Lister Room…the Ann Walker Room…and the Argus Room." They are all nice-sized rooms with big windows and queen beds. The walls are all off-white; there are a few framed pictures of Anne Lister, Shibden Hall, and stills from the movie on the walls. Curtains and duvet covers are in rich, coordinated colors. "We haven't finished decorating, obviously," she says.

Kim responds, "Minimalist, I like them fine how they are."

Finally, they reach the top floor and Kim takes two steps into the spacious room. Her breath catches and she whistles. On the wall is a framed watercolor by Devon depicting the cozy little moss-covered hut in which Anne Lister entertained her lovers. "So this is the Chaumière Room," Kim says.

"Yeah. It was originally three rooms," Devon says. "We knocked down the walls."

"It's just amazing."

"Thanks," says Devon shyly, "I thought there should be one big room explicitly devoted to…"

"Grubbling?" says Kim, using Anne Lister's word for fingering.

"I *was* going to say romance. But sure, grubbling."

Kim admires the simple, dark red furnishings and the ensuite bathroom with its large, claw-footed tub. There is a king-size four-poster canopy bed at one end of the room, with a view out over the fields and valley. At the other end is a sitting area with a comfortable-looking loveseat ("It unfolds into a nice double bed") and two armchairs. A partial wall separates the two halves of the room, making it more like a suite than a single room. A small fireplace completes the picture.

"Get up on the canopy bed, would you?" says Devon.

Kim obeys and crooks an eyebrow. "Is there really enough time for you to have your way with me before guests arrive?"

"Shut up," Devon replies, putting a small remote control into Kim's hand. "Push the button," she says. Kim does so, and the fireplace lights up with a gas flame.

"This is absolutely epic," Kim says, stretching luxuriously.

"Ooh, what a comfy mattress, an' all. Bloody hell, I wish I lived further away."

"Why?" asks Devon.

"Because I'd love to come and stay here sometime. If I ever had someone special to spend a night with."

They hear women's voices from far below. Kim reluctantly gets up from the bed. As they start to go back downstairs, Devon pats Kim on the shoulder. "You never know," she says. "Tell you what, if you ever do find someone special enough to bring here, I'll give you a twenty percent discount."

"Forty."

"Thirty."

"Thirty-five and I'll throw in a half dozen éclairs."

"Done."

Downstairs, half a dozen women are milling about, eating canapés, chatting excitedly. As Devon enters, she notes with satisfaction that Miremba is greeting everyone warmly and making sure they each take business cards and flyers.

Kim pulls Devon aside. "Would you like me to take some of them upstairs so you can stay down here?" Devon gratefully agrees.

"Time for the grand tour!" shouts Kim. "See the bedrooms! See the Chaumière!"

Giggling and jostling, the visitors follow Kim up the staircase. Devon goes to see Miremba and they hug with delight. "It's happening, boss!"

The deep rumble of a motorcycle shakes the windows and Devon steps out to the courtyard to see a tall woman on a red Kawasaki 650 pull up and park. The woman swings a long leg over the bike and stands grinning at Devon as she pulls off her helmet, revealing a slim, handsome face and long blonde hair. "Hi!" says the woman. "Are you the American?"

"Guilty," says Devon.

"I've been wanting to meet you! I'm Perry."

"Oh, the poet!"

They shake hands as Perry throws back her head to laugh. "At last! My fame precedes me!"

"I saw a poster at the cafe on St. George's Square about your poetry reading. Next Saturday, is it? Nice photo of you."

Perry smiles modestly. "Come along if you like, but don't expect owt grand. At least their coffee's good."

They stand talking motorcycles for a minute. A van pulls in, barely squeezing into the last parking space. It is painted with a portrait of a collie and the words, "Refreshing Paws Mobile Dog Groomer." A large woman gets out of the van. Perry greets her and says, "Devon, this is Jess. If you want to know anything at all about dogs, talk to Jess."

"'Ey up, lass!" Jess says cheerfully, shaking Devon's hand. Jess is broad-shouldered, red-cheeked, short-haired, and dressed in tough work clothes. Loud barks issue from the back of the van. "Quiet, Tesla!" shouts Jess.

"Sounds like a big dog," Devon observes, as she leads them into the guest house.

"Oh, aye, he's a mastiff," Jess says.

"Fucking giant," comments Perry.

Right after they enter the guest house, another group of half a dozen women arrives, and Devon is kept busy. Perry and Jess go upstairs.

After a while, Perry comes back down and approaches Devon, her eyes comically wide. "What an amazing job you've done with Cameron's place, Devon!"

Devon gestures toward Miremba, who is at this moment doubled over laughing with a couple of women. "Miremba did half the work and had more than half the ideas."

"Well done," says Perry. She never seems to stop smiling, and radiates a contagious joy. Devon finds herself wondering if Perry has a girlfriend, then remembers hearing that she doesn't. A thought tries to sneak in, but Devon dismisses it — *she's probably mobbed all the time.* And indeed, women seem to turn and stare at Perry whenever she's in a room.

Perry moves closer to Devon and leans over toward her. "Devon, I'm here on behalf of me two pals, Lindsay and Dawn. We're all working on transcribing Anne Lister's diaries. They both live pretty far away and they asked me to scope out your guest house to see if they'd like it."

"And...?"

"They'll love it, of course! They're coming for just two nights, then they'll be back for the research conference in October. So I'm ready to make the reservation for them."

Devon is taken aback. "You mean now?"

"Yeah, mate."

Devon can't help waving her hands in the air in glee. "Our first reservation! Whoo hoo! All right, come with me..." She leads Perry into the kitchen, where the reservations book is, and takes down all the information. "Any preferences as to room?"

Perry shrugs. "They're not romantically involved."

Devon says, "Then I recommend the Lister and Walker Rooms on the first floor. They're right next to each other. Privacy and convenience."

"Let's do it," says Perry with a big grin, handing over her credit card. After the transaction is completed, and Devon is staring at the reservation book in disbelief, Perry slips a postcard into Devon's hand. "Here's the details about the poetry reading next week," she says. "It'd be fun to see you."

"I'll do my best to be there," says Devon. "And tell your friends they will be very honored guests."

"You're on!" says Perry, giving Devon a quick, strong hug. "Well, I'm off — I have three jobs and I'm always late for one or other of them! Congratulations on a wonderful addition to our community. I think you're onto a total winner." Perry grabs a handful of flyers as she leaves, and promises to distribute them widely.

By the time the open house is over, and the last visitors have been gently but firmly shooed away, Devon goes to Miremba and they share a long, relieved embrace.

Beers are distributed in the kitchen. Devon and Miremba sit down with Kim and her staff. Everyone is tired, but beaming.

Kim lifts her bottle. "To the successful launch of Miss Lister's Guest House!" They cheer and toast, and then dig into the leftover snacks. Devon is ravenous. They all talk at once, excited and delighted by the enthusiasm of the visitors.

Miremba looks at the visitors tally she kept throughout the day. "Seventy-eight people!"

Daisy says, "Everyone seemed to love it."

Kim says, "Now that word is out, I wouldn't be a bit surprised if you have guests continuously from now until the end of year."

"And beyond!" Evie says. They all drink to that.

Dawn, Lindsay, Perry: Summer

The pub in Halifax is full of people watching a football match. The noise is deafening. Two women are sitting at a table in an adjoining room that is slightly quieter. They have no interest in the football match.

"What a scrum!" shouts Perry cheerfully as she squeezes her tall, black-leather-clad body through the crowd around the bar and deposits two glasses on the table. "Orange squash for you, Dawn. What a surprise."

The quiet little Scot with the frizzy blonde hair smiles and takes the soft drink with an inaudible word of thanks.

Perry pushes a pint of bitter over to Lindsay. "Pint for you, Lin." Lindsay, a wiry tomboy with straw-colored hair that stands straight up, removes the toothpick from her mouth, and grins. "Cheers, Perry."

The three new friends clink their glasses together.

"A toast!" says Perry. "May I, on behalf of all the Halifax women, welcome you, Dawn, and you, Lindsay, to Yorkshire. May the three of us become firm friends in real life, as we have online."

"Hear, hear," says Lindsay, and the three of them clink their glasses together again and drink.

"How's the B&B?" asks Perry.

Lindsay rolls her eyes. "It's just wonderful! Don't you think, Dawn?"

Dawn agrees. "Devon's a lovely host. And she makes a scrumptious breakfast."

"That's grand, glad to hear it," says Perry. "Oy! Just think!" she says, exuberantly. "We're going to learn how to read Anne Lister's secret codes!"

Dawn says, shyly, in her light brogue, "Well, there's no

guarantee that we'll even pass the decoding test. I've heard it's quite challenging." As always when she speaks up in a public setting, Dawn instantly feels intensely uncomfortable in her skin — itchy, hot, as if her clothes are too tight and made from steel wool. She focuses on her fizzy drink.

Perry says, "So I'll see you at the transcribers' information meeting tomorrow at three?"

Lindsay and Dawn look at each other. Lindsay says, "We have a meeting in the morning with a woman from the West Yorkshire Archives. We're hoping to get started on the codebreaking right away."

Dawn adds, "It's a brazen attempt to butter her up, or bribe her, or whatever works."

Perry raises her glass to them. "Good for you!"

Lindsay asks, "Perry, you've lived here all your life — have you known about Anne Lister for long?"

Perry replies, "Sort of, you know, one of many historic figures in the background, but I was only aware that she was a lesbian and about the secret diaries fairly recently. And when they shot the film here — and even more when the film was released — all of a sudden, this quiet place turned into the sapphic capital of the Western world."

Lindsay asks, "Did you enjoy the movie?"

Perry waves her hands about dramatically. "Oh my goodness. It's one thing to visit Shibden Hall, and read a bit about Anne Lister's escapades, but to see Celia Denton portraying her…" Perry pretends to wipe sweat off her brow.

Lindsay breaks in, "Kissing little Ann Walker up against the wall! That's the way to do it!" Leaning forward, Lindsay says, "Do you lot know about the fanfic?"

"The what?" asks Perry.

"The fan fiction. People are writing stories about the film and posting them online — free."

"What sorts of stories?" asks Perry.

Lindsay grins slyly. "Taking the love scenes a bit further than can be shown on screen. Quite a bit further, in fact." She wiggles her eyebrows.

"Hot?" asks Perry. Lindsay nods emphatically.

"Where are they?" Perry demands, thumping the table. "Show us immediately!"

Lindsay pulls out her phone and opens a website. She shows it to the group. "Look, there are 18 stories about Anne Lister already — no, 20 — two new ones since yesterday."

Perry turns to Dawn. "Do you know about this stuff, too? Am I the only one in the dark?"

Dawn, flushing hotly, replies, "I've heard of them, yes."

Perry shakes Lindsay by the shoulder and says, "Come on, give us a taste, then."

Lindsay says "Yeah? All right, give me a moment." As she scrolls, Perry turns to Dawn. "What have you been up to since you arrived?"

Dawn blushes again, as she seems to every time she looks at Perry, and says, "Och, I'm such a nerd. I've been mostly in the library, looking at the old documents about Anne Lister."

Perry says, "That's not nerdy. You're a researcher, right? So naturally you like that stuff."

Lindsay breaks in. "All right, I found a pretty good one. Are you ready?"

Perry and Dawn nod.

Lindsay looks around to make sure they are out of earshot of other customers. "All right…well, this particular story isn't set in Anne Lister's actual era. It's what they call an Alternate Universe story. In this one, Ann Walker and Anne Lister meet in the Wrens during World War Two. This story happens a few years later — Anne Lister is an art appraiser —"

"Jump to the juicy part," says Perry, pretending to slaver.

"She hasn't written the really juicy part yet, but I think this is the bit that comes just before it." She scrolls for a moment, then winks at them. "Ready?"

"Yes, yes!" they chorus. Lindsay reads.

Running as fast as she has since basic training, she rushes down the lane, blind to the rain, to the wet pavers beneath her shoes, to the sodden landscape, to everything except the shape of the terrain as she at last nears the copse, straining her eyes to discern among the trees the dove-grey raincoat and black umbrella that she hopes to see any moment, and then she rounds the last bend and there, from a small rise, she looks down and can see that raincoat, that umbrella, striding away from her, and she pauses to catch her breath and then runs down the hill. Ann shouts, with the last of her breath, "Anne!" The umbrella turns toward her. Ann runs ahead, gasping, and Anne Lister strides to meet her, holding the umbrella out to shelter her.

Ann rushes under it. Breathing hard, she grasps Anne Lister's lapels. They stare at each other, Ann no longer afraid, but trembling with the weight of the change that is about to happen in both their lives.

Summoning enough breath to speak, she tightens her grip on Lister's lapels. "Anne Lister, may I kiss you now, pl—"

Anne Lister doesn't wait for the end of the sentence, but bends Ann backward, sweeping her into a deep, passionate kiss, crushing her ribs, enveloping her, turning her head to make the kiss even deeper, kissing her thirstily, kissing Ann as she has never been kissed or even imagined being kissed — and then eventually pulling back, as Ann gasps. Putting her lips to Ann's ear, she breathes, with a catch in her voice, "When do the servants leave?"

"Well, go on," orders Perry. "Why are you stopping?"

Lindsay grins and sticks her toothpick back in the corner of her mouth. "There isn't any more yet. The author admits in the comments that she's a terribly slow writer. But she promises she'll publish the rest of it soon."

"Who writes these things?" asks Perry.

Lindsay shrugs. "I don't know. There's no money in it. The authors are fans like us, I expect. This one calls herself Louise Alexander, but I'm sure that's not her real name."

Larkin chimes in, "You're a writer, Perry — maybe you wrote it."

Perry laughs. "I'm a poet, not a writer of erotica. But I'll tell you what.." She winks and leans in. "I'd love to meet that author."

Lindsay says, emphatically, "Oh, so would I!"

Dawn, who has been silent until now, is even redder in the face than she was before. In her quiet voice she asks, "Really? What would you want to say to her?"

Lindsay snorts. "*Say* to her? *Say* to her? I'd skip the conversation and bang her so hard she wouldn't know what day it was." She drains her pint. "Whose round is it?"

"Mine, I think," says Dawn, rising. "Same again?"

If anyone is watching her, they might notice that her gait is a little wobbly as she walks to the bar.

PART FIVE: Autumn
Yorkshire

The Trees at Shibden Hall

After cooking breakfast for three departing guests, making the beds and cleaning every inch of the guest house, Devon packs her old green art-supplies satchel and drives to Shibden Hall.

She bought the car, a used Nissan, last month. After the initial terror of driving on the wrong side of the road, she has adjusted to a point where it feels nearly normal, except on roundabouts, which she finds terrifying and always needs to circle more than once, cursing continuously.

It's sunny today but quite cool. She walks down to the Hall, spreads her car blanket on top of a stone wall, sits on it, and sketches several views of the grand old mansion and the grounds — feeling, as always, closer to the indomitable spirit of Anne Lister as she sketches there.

Leaves on the trees are just starting to turn orange and red, and she tries to capture their shapes and hues with her watercolors.

As so often happens, the act of sketching affects her like a powerful, benign drug. Everything else — her anger, her longing, her worries about money and love — fades into the background and all she can think about is the colors of the leaves, the texture of the stones that make up Shibden Hall, the shapes of the scudding clouds.

People pass by and she barely registers the sound of their feet on the gravel. But now, she hears a new set of footsteps, coming closer, then stopping. A throat is cleared. Devon looks up, disoriented, to see a friendly, smiling face under a grey buzz-cut.

"Hello, Devon."

"Hi, Stephanie!"

"You're sketching."

"Yes."

"You're cold."

"Oh. I guess I am, a little."

"Brought you a mug of tea." Stephanie holds it out to her.

"Wow, how nice of you! Thanks so much!" Devon takes it gratefully.

"I won't disturb you — just wanted to know how things are at the house."

"Absolutely great, thanks. I sure appreciate your leaving it in such excellent shape."

Stephanie smiles. "I'll let you get back to your sketching. Just drop the mug in the office when you're finished, eh?"

"Sure thing," Devon replies.

As Stephanie walks back towards Shibden Hall, Devon takes up her waterbrush and again stares at the trees, feeling warmed not just by the mug in her hand but also by Stephanie's friendly gesture. A cool breeze rises, and Devon works until her fingers are too stiff to hold the brush properly. Then she packs up her kit, goes into the warm Hall, and returns the mug to the office. She lingers, and chats a bit more with Stephanie. They make a date for her to visit the Guest House within the next week.

At home, Devon looks over her work and feels discontented. The colors are not as vivid, as affecting, as she'd like. Watercolors just can't convey the power of those rich reds and oranges.

She goes up to her studio and searches for her acrylics. The tubes are old and cracked. She throws them into the garbage.

Impulsively, she gets back in her car and drives to the best art supply store in the area. She spends an incredible amount of money on a full complement of acrylic paints, some good canvas squares, brushes, and a portable palette.

After supper, she can't resist trying out her new supplies. On the kitchen table, she props up this morning's watercolor sketch.

She squeezes some paints onto the palette, and finds a brush that feels right in her hand. Taking a deep breath, she starts painting the trees with her richly-tinted new paints.

Three hours later, she emerges as if from a fervid trance, tired and happy. Her painting isn't bad. Not bad at all. She props it on the counter and washes her brushes in the kitchen sink. As she gets into bed, she realizes that for the first time in ages, she is not obsessing about Larkin.

She falls asleep thinking about the trees at Shibden Hall.

Dawn, Lindsay, Perry: Autumn

It is an almost-sunny Saturday in Halifax, and Lindsay would love to be outdoors, preferably on her mountain bike, but here she is in this fusty and overheated meeting room at the Piece Hall on day two of the Anne Lister research conference. Lindsay sighs, stretches, and reaches into the breast pocket of her plaid flannel shirt for a fresh toothpick to chew.

Lindsay glances over at Dawn, her temporary housemate again at Miss Lister's Guest House, and feels a surge of gratitude for her. Dawn is a skinny little thing, but very amusing to be around, with her sly Scots sense of humor and her air of unfeigned innocence. Based on the slang expressions for sexual activities she has already had to explain to Dawn in their brief acquaintance, Lindsay is starting to wonder if Dawn has ever had a girlfriend. And also creeping into Lindsay's imagination is a wish to be Dawn's first lover — an impulse she quickly dismisses. Lindsay is here to learn more about Anne Lister, not to get a crush on someone who lives so far away.

Right now, Dawn is twirling a lock of her frizzy blonde hair while listening intently to the lecturer, Dr. Janice Finley, a local historian with a specialty in locating the graves of Anne Lister's and Ann Walker's friends, lovers, and relations. Lindsay decides she had better tune in to the lecture, as well.

As she starts to pay attention, Lindsay notices Perry on the other side of the room, raising her hand and asking a question about local birth and death records. Lindsay's focus on the lecture evaporates. Perry is really something. She wears a form-fitting black leather jacket and looks effortlessly sexy. Lindsay believes in the superiority of regular bikes, but she does like a nice ride on a motorcycle…As she drifts into a reverie, she notices that about half the women in the class are looking not up at the slides, but sideways at Perry.

∽

Dawn, too, has noticed Perry, but now she is riveted by Dr. Finley's slides of the graves she has discovered, and takes copious notes in her favorite pale-blue Letts of London notebook.

As the lecture comes to an end, Dr. Finley is encouraging the attendees to search for the missing graves of several friends and associates of Ann Walker's. She hands out paper copies of a map showing the cemeteries where the graves might be found, and concludes: "History isn't something only experts do. It's something you can do, as well. Ann Walker's story has so many gaps — it needs all of us to do whatever we can to fill in those gaps. If you find anything at all, or have any interesting theories or leads, I'd love to hear about them; you can contact me any time." And with that, the lecture is over.

Dawn checks the schedule for the afternoon offerings and concludes that she can skip them all — she is galvanized by the historian's challenge to go out and discover something on her own.

Dawn gathers her things and walks outside into the Piece Hall's huge central square. She checks Dr. Finley's map against the map on her phone, and chooses the cemetery in Lightcliffe for her afternoon exploration.

Someone jostles her elbow, and she looks up to see Lindsay, with her vertical hair — how does she manage that, Dawn wonders — and smiling face with a toothpick in the corner of her mouth.

"Hello, mate," says Lindsay. "What are you up to?"

Dawn decides to lie. "Feeling awfully stuffy in that lecture hall. Thinking of going for a walk to get the cobwebs out."

"Very Anne Lister of you," Lindsay replies. "I'm tempted to

take the afternoon off, as well, explore a bit."

At this moment, Perry lopes by, grinning at them, her helmet under her arm. Lindsay and Dawn wave at her, then notice each other staring and giggle.

"Well, see you later at the guest house, eh?" says Lindsay, and they part.

Dawn trots to a nearby tea shop and waits impatiently as a sandwich is made and wrapped for her. Then she hurries to the bus station and hopes it doesn't rain again this afternoon.

Dawn gets off the bus at Lightcliffe and walks to St. Matthew's Churchyard. She pauses by the tower — all that remains of the ancient church where Anne Lister and Ann Walker worshiped together. She stops again for a moment at the small marker that commemorates Ann Walker herself.

The graveyard is quite large, and relatively well tended. Parts, though, are overgrown, and many old gravestones list to one side. The grass between the headstones is long and still wet from last night's rain, and Dawn's trainers quickly get soaked. She barely notices, so intent is she on her quest. Some granite headstones, though dating back to the 1770s, are still legible and in good condition; but most, made of crumbly slate or the local honey-colored sandstone, are well worn by the elements, the names barely legible. Feeling very fortunate that the rain has held off, and also feeling very hungry, she pulls her sandwich out of her bag and chews on it as she meanders slowly around the small graveyard.

Consulting the professor's map, Dawn spends the better part of an hour surveying the parts of the graveyard where associates of Ann Walker are buried. Some of the headstones are sunken so far into the ground that they are barely readable; others are overgrown with weeds.

Two grave markers attract Dawn's close attention. One marks the grave of Ann Walker's housekeeper, Lydia Wilkinson, who married a George Fenton and is buried with him. The other, much smaller, is completely enveloped by vines. Dawn's heart beats faster — putting together a handful of clues, she has surmised that Lydia might have had an older sister, possibly named Nelly, who died in childhood.

Looking around nervously but seeing no one, and reflecting that in any case, no one seems to have cared about this grave for decades, Dawn lays her rain jacket and bag on the turf, kneels on her jacket, and grasps a handful of vines. The vines are tough and unyielding but she manages to pull them far enough to see a few letters that are carved on the grainy granite. Wishing she had brought gardening gloves and some tools, Dawn grasps another handful. Behind her, someone clears her throat. Dawn spins her head to see a hand holding a knife.

The hand — and presumably the knife — belong to Lindsay, who is grinning widely.

"Would this come in handy?" she asks.

"Oh, Lindsay. Thank you." Dawn takes it. She knows she is blushing, but then, this is an almost constant state for her. "I couldn't resist."

Lindsay laughs. "Neither could I! I went to the afternoon lecture but found myself running out and jumping in my car after ten minutes. Who do you have here?"

Dawn is a bit disappointed that someone else has discovered her treasure. But she explains, and shows Lindsay her notes. Lindsay grows excited. "Yes, that seems possible! Good for you! Can I help?"

"Of course," says Dawn, feeling more generous now, and soon they are working side by side, pulling the tough vines out and hacking at them with Lindsay's pocket-knife. Lindsay says, "What if this really is Nelly Wilkinson's grave? What a discovery! You'll be famous!"

Dawn says wryly, "Aye, that's my great goal in life."

They have half the headstone cleared now and are about to be able to read the name on it when they hear the crunch of feet on gravel. They continue to pull at the vines but look up when they hear a woman's voice — a rather deep voice — saying, "Oho, what have we here?"

They turn to see Perry, helmet under arm, smiling at them.

Lindsay says, "Oh, nothing."

Dawn shoves Lindsay and tells Perry, "We think it's Nelly Wilkinson's grave."

Perry whistles, then laughs and says "Who?"

Dawn explains. Perry looks intrigued and drops her helmet onto the turf. "Can I help?" Lindsay and Dawn look at each other and shrug. "Of course," says Dawn.

"Especially if you have a knife," adds Lindsay.

"I do have a knife," says Perry, reaching into her jeans pocket and pulling out a bulky Swiss Army knife. She kneels and starts cutting vines.

"Who discovered this?"

Lindsay says, "Dawn did."

"Good on yer," says Perry, and then they work in silence for a few minutes until at last Perry stands and pulls the cut vines off of the headstone, revealing the worn and just barely legible name and dates: "Eleanor Wilkinson, Departed this Life Second Day of May, 1832, age 14."

Lindsay says, doubtfully, "Eleanor? Not Nelly…"

"Nelly is a nickname for Eleanor! And those would be her dates!" exclaims Dawn.

Lindsay claps Dawn on the back. "You've made a real discovery!"

Dawn blushes. "She's such an obscure person, it's not a big discovery, really."

"Don't be silly! It all adds to the historical record! Very well done," says Perry, giving them both a high-five and pulling them up as they clamber to their feet.

"You've both helped a lot," says Dawn.

"Let me take some photos," says Perry, pulling her phone out of another pocket.

Lindsay says to Dawn, "You should pose alone."

"No, no, you need to be in the photo too," insists Dawn. "And Perry, as well." They kneel next to the headstone and point to it, and Perry snaps a series of group selfies, with the headstone featured prominently.

Perry texts the photos to them. Looking at the photos on her phone, Dawn feels exuberant, as if she's found King Tut's tomb or something. She laughs silently at herself.

～

Once the euphoria of the discovery has started to ebb a bit, Lindsay notices that it is teatime and getting dark, and says, "Anybody hungry?"

Perry says, "Yes, always!"

Dawn adds, wiping her forehead expressively, "And I'm fair trauchled, as well."

Lindsay laughs and says, "If that means exhausted, I'm with you."

Perry adds, "We should have a drink to celebrate this find, what do you reckon?"

Lindsay says, "There's a pub near our guest house. They do a nice burger."

Perry, picking up her helmet, says "Oh, how is Miss Lister's working out for you?"

"It's wonderful," Dawn says.

"Thanks so much for telling us about it," adds Lindsay.

Dawn says, "Why don't we have a drink at the pub and do some carry-out back at the guest house?"

Lindsay adds, "Yeah, Perry, be our guest for tea."

Perry grins slyly and says, "I accept your invitation. I'm very curious to see what kinds of shenanigans you can get up to over there."

Dawn says, "So far, the shenanigans have been consisting entirely of sleeping and eating breakfast…"

Lindsay chimes in, "But you never know!"

Dawn finds herself reddening again but continues, "So if there are going to be shenanigans, Perry, perhaps you will need to initiate them." She can feel herself having one of her most horrible blushes and is glad it's getting dark enough that the others won't notice. She swipes at an invisible gnat.

They gather their things and walk to the entrance of the cemetery. Lindsay turns and says in the direction of the grave, "Sleep well, Eleanor."

"Sleep well!" Perry and Dawn chime in. They stand still for a quiet moment before heading to the car park.

Perry follows Lindsay's car to the guest house, and leaves her motorcycle there as they decide to walk down to the pub.

Since the pub is too crowded and hot to carry on a conversation, the three of them leave as soon as their food is ready. Laden with boxes of palak paneer and chana masala, they walk back uphill to the guest house. There, they spread out their meal on the kitchen table and have an enjoyable conversation about all things Anne Lister.

While they are talking, the heavens open and a downpour starts. Perry gets up and walks to the window. She grimaces.

Dawn follows her to the window. "That doesn't look like much fun for your ride home."

Lindsay joins them. "Why don't you sleep here tonight, Perry."

Perry looks at them. "Really? That would be all right?"

"I'll phone Devon now."

After getting permission from Devon to use the Argus Room for a nominal charge, Perry gladly agrees to stay there for the night. Lindsay and Perry have another drink. The three of them relax around the fire.

Perry is especially interested in the decrypting work that all three of them are engaged in. "Why are we spending so much time and effort on it?"

Lindsay says thoughtfully, "She had this whole secret life — her affairs — imagine what a scandal it would have been if it got out."

Dawn adds, "She must have been terribly lonely with it all. Her journals were her only confidante. And so she wrote it all in code and now that I'm learning to decipher it, it's just as if Anne Lister herself is talking to me, as if I was her closest, most intimate friend."

Perry nods, and comments thoughtfully, "Deciphering the code — it's a lot like deciphering a woman, isn't it. Learning all the little clues and hints that make up who she is. Learning her history, things like that."

Lindsay, who is a little tipsy, says, "What if we each had a secret journal? What would be in them?"

"That's a secret," says Perry.

"Oh, ha ha," replies Lindsay. "I know what would be in mine."

"What?" asks Dawn, intrigued.

Lindsay shoves a toothpick into the corner of her mouth, folds her hands behind her neck, and says, "Fantasies, I suppose. The secret fantasies that you'd be too embarrassed to tell anyone."

Perry says, "Kinky stuff, you mean?"

"I suppose so," says Lindsay. "Well, not necessarily kinky, just out of the ordinary."

"Tell us one, then," urges Perry.

Lindsay looks at her. "I'll tell one, but you both have to as well."

Perry grins. "All right."

Dawn looks as if she wants to disappear into the couch cushions. "I'm not at all sure, to be perfectly honest."

Perry says, "That's all right, no one will force you to do anything. Lindsay, you're going first then, right?"

Lindsay agrees. "So, I'm in some sort of club with half a dozen other women, and we fulfill each other's fantasies on our birthdays, but we never know how or when it will happen. It's my birthday and I'm walking along the street, not doing anything in particular, when they pull up in a van, and two of them drag me into the van and put a blindfold and handcuffs on me. So, it's — it's scary, because I don't know what to expect, but it's also safe, because I know everyone. That's about it."

Perry nods slowly. "I love that! Maybe we should try it sometime! In a similar vein, one of mine is that I've just won a big poetry slam in London, and two of the other poets come back to my hotel room to help me celebrate, and we start drinking and reciting bits of poetry to each other and then we're all in bed together, giggling our heads off and having quite the slap and tickle." She smiles. "I could go on with details, but you get the gist. Dawn?"

Dawn surprises herself. "I find motorcycles very sexy, actually, so when I see a cute woman on one, my thoughts rather turn to riding behind her with my arms wrapped around her waist, and not knowing where she's taking me." She pauses. "Not very exciting."

Perry looks at her and raises an eyebrow. "I ride a motorcycle," she says.

"Och, I hadn't noticed," Dawn responds, deadpan.

Perry stands and stretches luxuriously. "Well, what about it?" she asks, draining the last beer from her bottle.

Lindsay and Dawn look at each other, then back at Perry.

"What about what?" Asks Dawn.

"What about bringing one of our fantasies to life?"

"Which one could we…" Dawn trails off.

"Not the motorcycle," Perry cautions. "It's still pelting down out there. And we don't have a van. That leaves…"

"The threesome," says Lindsay. "Well, we could."

"That's the spirit!" says Perry. "What's stopping us? I mean, really? At the end of this weekend you two will go off to your homes. No emotional hangover. We can do it in the spirit of friendly adventure. Don't you think it would be fun? I mean, no worries if not, but this is a rare opportunity, you have to admit."

Lindsay, grinning all over her face, says, "What would Anne Lister do?"

Dawn says, "I'm sure she wouldn't hesitate. But that doesn't mean we'd all be brave enough."

Perry says, "But why would we need to be brave? We're all friends."

Dawn says, "I'll be very brave, then, and share a secret. I'm a virgin. I wouldn't have the foggiest what to do. So, no."

Lindsay exclaims, "That's no reason to say no!"

Perry says, firmly, "Any reason at all is a good enough reason. If she's not totally enthusiastic about it, then she doesn't consent, and the idea is a non-starter. Don't you agree, Lin?"

"Yes, of course," Lindsay says. "But come on, Dawn, it's an adventure. You might never have this chance again."

"No," says Dawn firmly. "Just no."

"That's absolutely fine," says Perry. "Forget it, it was just a drunken idea. We should probably just call it a night and go to bed."

They put things away and go upstairs one at a time. There are some giggles as they get settled in their rooms, but the walls are thick and they are very tired, and very soon a peaceful silence falls, along with the rain, on Miss Lister's Guest House.

~

Dr. Finley looks up from her notes at the lectern, with a big smile. "This concludes our symposium," she says. "And what a wonderful surprise it has been to hear about Lindsay and Dawn's discovery in the cemetery." The attendees applaud, as Lindsay and Dawn smile modestly. Dr. Finley sends them all off with an exhortation to continue their research and to come to the next codebreakers workshop, which will be part of the next Anne Lister birthday gathering in April.

The attendees go to the next room for the farewell reception and stand around in noisy groups eating canapés and sharing their plans for their next research ventures. Dawn and Lindsay stand sipping tea and not saying much. Dawn wishes she could magically be on the train back to Perth and not have to deal with goodbyes. And she wonders how to determine if Lindsay is interested in continuing their connection.

The night before, as they were preparing for bed, they had run into each other on the first-floor landing and shared a spontaneous, laughing hug. And then, such an odd moment, as Lindsay had looked intensely at Dawn, a deep look, with a depth of — what? Not lust, or at least not only lust, but a deeper desire, a more insistent craving for connection. Lindsay had reached out her hand, touched Dawn's arm, seemed about to speak. Perry had come up the stairs just then, and the moment was gone. Dawn is still wondering if she'd imagined it.

How do you decipher an actual, living, woman?

A black-leather-clad arm thrusts between them. The attached hand holds a plate of tiny quiches. It belongs, of course, to Perry.

"Quiche me quick, I'm off back to my job," says Perry with a goofy grin. Dawn takes the plate while Lindsay hugs the taller woman. Perry thumps her on the back and says, "Great to see you." Lindsay replies, "Same here, Perry. Be good, now."

Perry grins and turns to Dawn. She takes the plate away from her, putting it on a nearby table. Dawn looks up into the flashing,

106

smiling blue eyes and has a second of connection and then Perry kisses her on the cheek and gives her a firm, close hug. "Goodbye, Dawn, see you again, I hope," Perry whispers into her ear, before kissing her again. Then Perry is gone, leaving a strangely empty place in Dawn's heart.

Lindsay puts her hand on Dawn's elbow. "Are you going back to the B&B at all?"

"No, I'm all packed," Dawn says. "My bags are in the lobby here."

"Oh, too bad," Lindsay replies. "Catching the train soon, then?"

"Yes, in forty minutes," says Dawn. "I'll get home in five and a half hours. How long will it take you to get to Bristol?"

"Four hours, if I'm lucky," says Lindsay, looking sad all of a sudden. "So I suppose this is goodbye, then?"

"I suppose so," says Dawn. "But we can stay in touch, I suppose, if you'd like to?"

"Oh yeah, you bet," says Lindsay. Her expression is unreadable. Dawn has a powerful desire to touch Lindsay's cheek, but suppresses it and simply hugs her quickly.

"Must run," says Dawn. She heads toward her suitcase, which is leaning on the wall.

Lindsay calls after her, "Can I give you a lift to the station?"

Dawn replies, her voice threatening to break, "Oh no, thanks, it's so close by. See you!"

Lindsay calls, "See you in April, if not before!"

"Right!" calls Dawn, not daring to turn and look at Lindsay again.

Dawn grabs her bag and walks quickly out to the street, setting off on the short walk to the train station. She feels as if her insides are being left behind, and the tear that threatened to fall, now does. *How do you tell if you have any future with someone?* she wonders as she strides away into the early dusk.

Painting the Moors

Devon has seen Lindsay and Dawn depart with regret. They've been lovely guests, appreciative and fun. She turns her attention to her empty guest house and takes up her chores with quiet efficiency.

Devon has mastered most of the basic tasks of running the guest house, and no longer panics when the hot-water heater goes out. Every week brings new learnings — the name of the most reliable plumber to fix a leaky bathroom pipe, where the best local source of organic beef is, the best pubs in Halifax and Hebden Bridge.

Even when the challenges come thick and fast, Devon manages to keep her guests reasonably happy. Most of them don't seem to mind if breakfast is late or there is a bit of a wait for fresh towels — they all seem quietly thrilled to have a room in a guest house where there is no awkwardness at all about two women sharing a bed, and where the landlady lives right next door and is friendly without being intrusive.

Devon has the maintenance and housekeeping tasks down to a routine that takes her no more than two hours a day. The dim, cooler afternoons are empty, and starting to be a challenge for her.

Her thoughts turn unavoidably to Larkin. Longing and hurt eat away at her heart. She knows in her rational mind that Larkin didn't actually reject her. She knows that Larkin made a decision that had little to do with Devon.

But to her heart, Larkin's choice feels like rejection. In the past, experiences of rejection have brought a descent into depression, and so she fights mightily against the melancholy that so often overwhelms her on these darker afternoons.

Sometimes, for a day at a time, she finds herself wretchedly homesick for the sun-drenched hills and sparkling waves of the Bay Area, as well as for her friends there.

Though Devon has met quite a few interesting women here in England, she can't shake the conviction that Larkin is her soulmate. Larkin's sense of humor; her sly, seductive smile; her passionate feminism; her skilled fingers...Devon can hardly bear to think of her without an aching bitterness that doesn't seem to be easing with the passage of time.

The only solace she's found is to go on long rambles over the moors and through the old villages. All the walking reminds her of her hikes back in the Berkeley hills with Baxter. What a sweet dog he was. Sometimes the loneliness and anger wash over her so powerfully when she is out for her countryside walks that she finds herself furiously throwing rocks into the bracken, until she is sweating and spent.

But the colors and shapes of the scenes through which she storms gradually work their way into her bruised heart. The subtle natural beauty of the moors and hills, which initially formed just a backdrop to her brooding, at times now makes her eyes tear up with awe.

Yesterday, which was sunny, she was sitting on a rocky ledge overlooking a broad vista of fields with their flocks of sheep, glistening streams, and little bridges, and found the colors piercing her heart. *I need to paint these scenes*, she realized, with a surge of urgency that felt like hunger. When she returned home, she got her satchel out, organized all her art supplies, and resolved to take it with her everywhere.

This morning, a day of cold, intermittent rain, she huddled under a tree atop a hill, sketching a far-off stream and a stone church until her hands were numb.

Now, at home in the late afternoon, with a mug of tea beside her and the fire blazing, she paints the scene with care, checking frequently against the reference photo on her phone to be sure that her color choices are as faithful to the original as possible.

When her little painting is dry, she props it up on her kitchen table. She looks at it critically and notices where she could do better next time. Sipping her tea, she feels deeply content, her sadness and rage held at bay for the time being.

She takes her teacup to the sink and washes it, and notices that she is whistling a tune — something she does only when she's happy.

Oh wow — I'm finally starting to feel like an artist again.

109

Honour and Stephanie: Autumn

Honour smelled Stephanie — or at least, her cologne — well before she actually saw her.

The woodsy scent reached Honour when she was, at long last, standing in Anne Lister's bedroom, feeling light-headed from the astonishing magic of knowing that her heroine had slept here, in this low-ceilinged room with the view over the Shibden grounds.

Shibden Hall was not crowded on this chilly October day. Miraculously, Honour had the room all to herself. A powerful, surprising feeling of reverence, almost sacredness, had swept over her as she'd entered the room — a feeling she had experienced only once before, when singing the *Magnificat* by Thomas Tallis in her church choir.

She took a moment to look out of the window and gaze at the view that Anne Lister herself had seen from this very place thousands of times. She felt almost faint, and took a few deep breaths to steady herself.

That is when the scent reached her. Honour suddenly felt like a bee sensing the first flower of spring. Jo Malone, was her guess. Who was wearing this divine scent?

Footsteps were approaching and Honour pulled herself out of her reverie, smoothed the skirt of her navy tweed suit, patted her messy bun to make sure it wasn't *too* messy, and composed her face to meet whoever was approaching.

The scent grew stronger and even more alluring, and a sturdy woman with short grey hair, bright blue eyes, and a handsome, weatherbeaten face strode into the room.

The woman smiled warmly and said, "Hello, love, I don't mean to disturb you — I think I left a brochure in this room…Yes, here it is." Honour replied with a quiet murmur and the woman left the room with an apologetic grin and an admiring glance. Honour instantly missed the scent of the cologne, though a trace lingered for a moment.

Half an hour later, Honour had seen every room in Shibden Hall at least twice and was starting to feel a bit hungry. She went into the gift shop and was browsing the key rings and postcards when she smelled the cologne again. It came from someone standing chatting quietly with a handful of people in the reception area. Honour didn't even need to look; she knew it was the same woman. Honour never forgot a scent.

Honour was intensely aware of the woman's proximity. She paid for her souvenirs, buttoned up her coat, nodded to the small group in the lobby, and walked outside. It had warmed up a bit and the sun was starting to penetrate the clouds. She took a moment to look down over the grounds and the little lake. *I'll come back in the summer*, she thought, sighing at the necessity of the drive home.

She walked slowly up the slope to her car and got in. She closed her eyes for a moment, savoring the fact that she was still on Anne Lister's home turf. She heard footsteps crunching on the gravel from the other end of the car park and her eyes snapped open. She couldn't linger too long; Nora was expecting her home for supper and it was a long drive back to Carlisle.

She started the car and began to drive slowly toward the main road — and there was that handsome woman, walking by herself through the car park.

On an impulse that surprised her, Honour stopped her car and lowered the window.

"Excuse me!" she called. The woman smiled at her again and stopped. Honour tried to keep her voice steady. "I hope you don't think I'm bonkers, but I noticed your scent and wondered if you'd tell me what it is."

Without a word, the woman walked over to Honour's Corsa and shot her left wrist out, holding it through the car window so Honour could smell it. Honour touched the offered wrist lightly, sniffed deeply, and let it go, looking into the bright blue eyes that were twinkling at her.

"It's a Jo Malone scent," the woman said in her husky voice.

"I knew it!" said Honour. "It's absolutely luscious. What's its name?"

The woman shrugged. "Do you know, I'm not absolutely sure, love. It came in a package with another one and I like them both so I just dab myself with whichever is closer. I'm so glad you like it."

Honour said, "I do, very much. I'd like to get some for myself."

"I could text you the name, if you like."

"Oh, I'd love that! I'm Honour, by the way."

"I'm Stephanie. Pleased to meet you." Stephanie pulled her phone out of the inside breast pocket of her green wool jacket and offered it to Honour. "If you'd give me your digits…"

"Of course," said Honour, and took the warm phone. She entered her information and handed it back.

Stephanie typed in a short text and Honour's phone vibrated.

"Thank you so much," said Honour, mesmerized by Stephanie's eyes.

"Are you visiting from elsewhere?"

"Yes, Carlisle. This is my first time at Shibden."

"Pretty amazing, isn't it? I volunteer here on my days off from work — I teach adult learners, mainly men. It's a nice change to be here." Stephanie hesitated. "Would you by any chance be free for a spot of food? I'm headed for Woolshops."

Thinking with irritation of Nora, Honour said, "Oh, I'd love to, but I need to head homewards."

Stephanie sighed, then smiled. "Oh, well. Have a good drive home."

"Thanks. Nice to meet you!"

"Same," smiled Stephanie. "I'll text you the info."

Honour waved and drove away.

The rain started before she even reached Denholme. All the way up the A629, Honour was kicking herself for not accepting Stephanie's invitation. "What's the matter with you?" she berated herself. "She seemed so nice. What harm could have come to you?" She sighed and resigned herself to a dreary drive in the rain.

It's a lovely morning in Halifax, with puffy clouds and a bright blue sky. Stephanie is distracted from her curriculum planning by thoughts of Honour.

Two weeks have passed since their encounter at Shibden. They have texted quite a few times in a lighthearted way, discussing scents and many other things. Honour is a chartered accountant who works in a small firm. She has mentioned someone named

Nora once or twice in passing and Stephanie presumes she is a housemate, or perhaps a work colleague.

There is a warm, rather sexy tone to their conversations, unless Stephanie is imagining it — it's been a long time since her last relationship, and she's a bit creaky. And an even longer time since she's experienced satisfying sex, since Stephanie's ex never wanted to make love to her, though she was perfectly happy to receive Stephanie's attentions. Stephanie sighs.

But as her correspondence with the lovely Honour continues, they seem to be developing a repartee, a gentle air of teasing that definitely feels flirtatious. They've shared personal information: Stephanie admitted to her lifelong addiction to Western movies and music, and Honour to her love of Renaissance choir music.

Stephanie wonders where this might go, what would happen if she told Honour how attracted she is. She can't stop imagining what it would feel like to unpin that lovely smooth chestnut hair and see it tumble around Honour's shoulders. It is all much more interesting than the lesson on Fundamentals of Electrical Engineering she is meant to be planning.

Perhaps a bit of exercise will help.

Stephanie takes her midday break early and goes for a brisk walk through the city streets. She passes a florist shop and a minute later finds herself turning on her heel and returning to it. It is a flood of delicious scents, bright colors, steamy air. She chooses a nice mixed bouquet, asks for a short message to be printed on the card, and orders it to be delivered to Honour's workplace the next day.

The next morning, Stephanie can't resist writing to Honour:

- *Something might be delivered to your office today.*

Honour replies a few minutes later.

- What's going on?

Stephanie has never been any good at all with surprises.

- *I hope you like narcissus.*

Honour replies immediately.

- OH NO, you haven't sent me flowers! It will be an absolute disaster! Sorry but can you stop them?

Stephanie, her pulse racing and her face flushed with embarrassment, replies that she will try. She calls the florist immediately. "I've made an awful mistake and someone will be in trouble if those flowers are delivered. Any way to claw them back?"

The woman at the florist is instantly responsive. Stephanie thinks this might not be the first time someone has regretted a flower order. "I'll get in touch with my driver right away and I'll call you back."

"Thank you so much." Stephanie's stomach knots with tension while she waits for the call. It comes mercifully fast.

"I managed to reach the driver just as he entered the building. He didn't deliver the flowers."

"Oh thank God." Stephanie waves away her offer of a refund. "Please, give the flowers to someone nice. I can't thank you enough."

She texts Honour:

- *Canceled the flowers. Sorry about that. I thought you'd like them.*

Honour replies:

- Thank you — both for the flowers and for being willing to cancel them. So sweet of you! But I work in a small office and if I'd received flowers, it would have been the gossip of the day. And also, my housemate, Nora, is my boss, and it would have been awkward.

- *At least I had the sense not to sign the card.*

- What did the card say?

- *From a friend who appreciates you.*

- Aw, that's lovely. I really like that a lot. I'm glad you appreciate me, but I've really no idea why you should.

Stephanie stares at her phone for a moment, then types,

- *Is it all right to flirt with you a bit?*

There is no reply for quite a while. Stephanie's hand, clutching her phone, starts to sweat. Then the little dots show that Honour is composing a reply. Finally it comes:

- Yes, please. I think I'd like that.

Stephanie leaves work feeling very lucky that she was able to rescue the flower situation — and decides not to take more risks with Honour today.

The next morning, as she is having breakfast, Stephanie's phone buzzes and there is a text from Honour.

- Hello? I was told there'd be flirting.

Stephanie smiles and proceeds to flirt. Over the next couple of weeks, the flirting evolves from friendly chatter to more suggestive questions, then to intimate descriptions of what they would like to do with and to each other if they were to meet again. Stephanie is quite astonished — and very aroused — to read some of the graphic language coming from this outwardly ladylike woman. They start to discuss, rather vaguely, the possibility of getting together in person.

After a few days of this, Stephanie feels emboldened to ask a relevant question.

- *So you are single, right, lass?*

There is a long delay in replying. Stephanie starts to fear that she has destroyed the delicate structure of this new connection.

Then, at two a.m., she gets a reply:

- I'd love to meet up with you. It will need to be a secret, I'm afraid. I'm technically single, but my ex, Nora, and I never moved apart after our breakup six years ago. We were always good friends — we should never have become lovers, we both know this. At least, I do. So we are just housemates, and quite compatible day to day. She owns the house, and I pay her rent. It's a much, much nicer place than I could afford on my own. But she has become very dependent on me for many things. She has no social life of her own, and often invites herself along when I go to parties and things — and of course, women we meet think Nora and I are partners, so you are the first woman to flirt with me for ages! And then, we work together as well. She's my boss, actually. That's why I was alarmed about your lovely gift of the flowers, and I'm so sad about that. Somehow, I always feel the need to report to her on where I am and who I'm with. I suppose I should do something about it, but one gets into ruts, and our lives are so intermingled now that it would be awfully difficult to separate them. Anyway — I am starving for — well, passion. Desire. I would, quite frankly, love to explore this with you, if you're willing to consider having a fling with someone who might never be truly available.

Stephanie writes back immediately:

- *Thank you for the explanation. I would be more than happy to explore with you. Would you like to return to Halifax for a few days — a weekend?*

The next day, Stephanie hears again from Honour. She has invented a pretext to return to Halifax — "a choral music workshop at the Minster" — and they agree to set a date soon.

Stephanie looks around at her sitting-room and kitchen, and decides that Honour's visit deserves a special setting. Her own house has too many distractions, from two loud cats to battered old furniture. Not to mention all the saddles, lariats, and cowboy hats that have been brought here from her mum's B&B and not properly put away yet. It's all too much, and too messy, for romance.

∼

Devon is taking advantage of a very quiet weekday afternoon to dust the whole guest house and do major laundry when the phone rings. "Miss Lister's Guest House."

"Hi, Devon, this is Stephanie, got a mo?"

"Sure."

"I'm actually close by, could I stop in for a bit? I'd like your advice on something."

"Of course. I'll put the kettle on. Come to the Annex."

They sit in Devon's bright lounge and share local gossip and news. They are on their third cup of tea by the time Stephanie works up her courage to broach a sensitive topic.

"I met this lovely woman at Shibden Hall…"

Devon wiggles her eyebrows. "Tell me! What's she like?"

Stephanie smiles dreamily. "Oh, well…she's elegant and beautifully dressed — feminine, mature, a real womanly woman, if you know what I mean, with the most gorgeous chestnut hair…"

Devon pretends to be swooning. "Sounds luscious."

"Luscious, that's the exact word." Stephanie looks into her teacup as if hoping to discover hidden treasure there.

"And…?"

"And we've been chatting for weeks. It's getting…"

"Hot and heavy?" Devon suggests, grinning.

Stephanie groans. "Very hot, love, and pretty heavy. I really want to invite her to come and spend a weekend here but there are a couple of questions…" She falls silent, looking out the window.

"Go on, Steph, tell me if you like. I might not have any answers, but at least I can listen."

Stephanie takes a deep breath, stirs her tea, exhales. "I suggested going up to visit her, and she kept hesitating, but I finally found out that she's…entangled with an ex. They live together and even work together."

"Oh boy."

"She insists that she's single. But she just can't tell this woman, Nora, that she wants to see me. Anyway, I'm inviting Honour down here. My place is just too much of a tip, but I thought of booking the Chaumière here for a weekend."

Devon pats Stephanie on the arm. "Perfect! And for you, Steph, no charge."

Stephanie smiles, touched by the gesture. "Oh no, I'd pay, that's not the issue. It's this bloody Nora. I mean, is this adultery or not? Should I wait to see Honour until they completely break it off?"

Devon furrows her brow. "I don't know, really. What do you think?"

Stephanie says slowly, "I don't think it is really adultery. I mean, it's Honour's business anyway, isn't it?" She sighs. "I just wish it were all a clear, clean break, you know?"

"What would be the fun in that?" They both laugh. "But seriously, Steph, I think you need to ask yourself if anyone is going to get hurt."

"I don't think so."

"What about you? Will you be hurt if you and Honour get together and then she goes back to this Nora?"

"Well, perhaps I would, but I'm going into it with my eyes wide open, so I'd be prepared, right?"

"Not so sure we can ever really be prepared." Devon leans back in her chair and looks Stephanie in the eyes. "What do you want, Steph? What do you *really* want? What's your heart's desire?"

Stephanie sits silently, delving into herself. Her eyes close. She finds her answer. "I want her," she says softly. "I fancied her from the moment I saw her in Anne Lister's bedroom."

Devon laughs. "Get outta here, is that really where you met?"

Stephanie smirks. "Aye. And we've been getting so close in

all these texts and phone calls. I feel I know her better than some people I've known for my whole life. And I want her, Devon. More than anything or anyone I've wanted in many years. I feel a deep, real connection between us, as if we're fated or something. Do I sound like an utter barmpot?"

Devon guesses at what "barmpot" means, and shakes her head. "You want her."

"Aye. Yes. I want her. To be specific, I want a dirty weekend with her here at the guest house."

Devon laughs. "What would Anne Lister say?"

Stephanie thinks. "Oh, there's no doubt at all. She'd say go after her and have a good time and sod the consequences."

Devon gets up, reaches over to a cabinet, and fetches a large red ledger. She leafs through it. "How about the first weekend in November? There won't be anyone else staying here."

Stephanie gulps. "That's just — ten days away?"

"Yes," smiles Devon. "Shall I pencil you in?"

Honour accepts Stephanie's invitation. Over ten days of anticipation, their correspondence becomes more intimate and trusting. They share their most secret desires and build a fantasy scenario between them. Twice, they have quite amazing phone sex based on this fantasy.

Stephanie, with a new-found confidence, challenges Honour to have some courage and enact their shared fantasy in person. Honour, after a brief hesitation, agrees, and now the excitement has intensified a hundredfold.

Every day now is full of joyful expectancy. Just two days till Honour arrives! Stephanie whistles while she works and finds herself grinning at nothing. The students who normally drive her round the bend are now as easily ignored as gnats. She greets strangers on the street with a hearty "Lovely day!" even when it's raining.

Stephanie feels young again, and alive down to her toes. Preparing for the rendezvous, she fairly percolates with joy, doing the specific shopping she needs to do, getting her hair cut specially.

As Laura cuts her hair into a shapely style she calls a "stint," she asks Stephanie, "What's up for you this weekend? Something sexy?"

For once, Stephanie can answer with a knowing smirk. "Well, since you ask, love, I'm hoping so!"

"Oooh, who is she?"

"A lady from the north country," Stephanie says slyly.

"Have a wonderful time, Steph!"

Stephanie struts out of the beauty parlor feeling fabulous. Perhaps her delight is seasoned with a dash of apprehension about Honour's entanglement. But Honour is a grown-up woman and if she feels the need to stay attached to this Nora person, that's her business.

Out in the street, Stephanie sends a quick text to Honour.

- *I've just got my hair cut and can't wait to feel your fingers running through it. What's left of it.*

- Oooh, I can't wait, either!

- *Are you still on board for our adventure?*

- Yes.

- *Special items arranged?*

- Special items all arranged. I've never done anything like this!

- *Neither have I! Feeling a bit shy and a lot excited!*

- I'm feeling a LOT shy, but ready.

- *Well, good. Drive safely, love.*

Finally, the day arrives. Stephanie leaves work a bit early to move her bags into the guest house and prepare.

Honour drives through a downpour and some heavy weekend traffic, but hardly notices anything around her. She is fixated with a burning intensity on what it will be like to finally touch Stephanie again — touch her properly this time.

After all the years with Nora — years of stifling custom and boredom — to at last be embraced and, she hopes, ravished, by a big, handsome woman — she is wet just thinking about it. She looks around at the other cars on the crowded motorway and wonders how many other frustrated women are headed off for their own "dirty" weekends.

And also — and she blushes to think of it — she is melting as she thinks about the special activity they have arranged for their second night together. She realizes that it is not too late to turn back, that she can stop before she takes this potentially very embarrassing plunge.

Then she remembers the scent of Stephanie's perfume. The rough, straightforward texts telling Honour how beautiful she is and how Stephanie is going to push her up against a wall and kiss her neck. The blue of those eyes. Honour nearly goes off the road. She turns on Radio 4 and forces herself to pay attention to a programme about vegetable gardening.

Honour drives carefully through Hebden Bridge and up the hill. She spots the swinging sign with the stagecoach on it. She realizes she is breathing shallowly, and instead of pulling in to the courtyard, drives on. She proceeds along a curving country road for a mile or two, calming her breathing, and then turns and drives back. She pulls in this time, parking in the courtyard and looking up at the attractive three-storey stone building. She gets out of the car, feeling a bit stiff after her drive. Heart thumping, she gets her bag out of the boot and walks to the door. There is a card taped to the door that says "Welcome, Honour! Ring bell!" with a rough sketch of a bunch of flowers.

So she rings the bell.

Right away, the door swings open and a tall young woman in jeans and a green sweatshirt opens the door. "Welcome to Miss Lister's Guest House! I'm Devon. Please let me take your bag."

Honour gives it to her. Devon ushers her in, saying "Here's someone for you, Steph!"

Stephanie, smiling joyfully, steps into the foyer. Devon disappears up the stairs with Honour's bag.

And then they are standing there.

"Hello!" says Stephanie, looking at Honour as if she's admiring the crown jewels.

"Hello!" says Honour. "I'm sorry for this to be the first thing, but…"

"The loo is just at the top of the stairs," says Stephanie, and shows her the way.

Devon comes back down and says, "All right, Steph, I'm out to my place for the night. You have the house to yourselves. Have a blast!" Stephanie thanks her profusely and Devon leaves.

When Honour comes back down, Stephanie is waiting for her in the lounge. Stephanie spreads out her arms, grins cockily. "Would you like a bit of a cuddle, lass?"

Honour would. Conquering her shyness, she steps into Stephanie's embrace. For a long moment, they hold each other and sway together. Stephanie's body is warm, and bigger than Honour had realized — taller, broader. She smells deliciously, intoxicatingly, of the same Jo Malone cologne. Honour presses her cheek against Stephanie's and sighs deeply. Though she is fizzing with excitement, she also feels a depth of safety and relief that in an instant reveals to her how much she has been missing. How much tension, how much longing, she has been carrying for such a long time.

Honour runs her fingers through Stephanie's hair. "It is very short. I like it," she whispers.

Stephanie murmurs in her ear, "I thought you'd never get here." Honour murmurs back, "You feel like home."

Then Stephanie gently but firmly presses Honour against the wall, looks her in the eyes — that blue! — and kisses her with such tenderness and hunger that Honour has to cling to Stephanie's shoulders to stay standing.

Stephanie could keep kissing this beautiful woman for hours. Honour is returning her kisses with fervor, with passion. Stephanie wants to know every inch of her. Honour is surprisingly strong, and Stephanie remembers that Honour is a devoted gardener. Stephanie runs her hands up and down Honour's back, cradling her buttocks, kissing her neck. Honour moves her hips against Stephanie, sighs in her ear.

After a while, Stephanie pulls back, laughing. "Let me look at you." Honour obediently allows herself to be looked at, resisting feelings of insecurity about her weight.

"You're a goddess," whispers Stephanie, lightly tracing Honour's curves with her hands. There are tears in Honour's light-brown eyes. Her lipstick is smeared and Stephanie uses a thumb to tidy it.

Stephanie touches the clips restraining Honour's hair. "May I?" she whispers. Honour nods. Stephanie releases the clips and Honour's hair cascades, a thick glossy brown waterfall, to her shoulders.

Honour shakes her hair out and grins impishly as Stephanie stares. "You like?"

Stephanie sighs with deep satisfaction. Honour moves in for another kiss but Stephanie stops her. "Wait, please, while I can still think clearly — are you hungry?"

Honour says, reluctantly, "A bit."

Stephanie takes her to the kitchen, where there is a big tray of sandwiches and cakes, supplied by Kim's Catering. She puts the kettle on and they are soon eating at the kitchen table and talking nonstop while also somehow managing to hold hands.

Honour finishes her plate and Stephanie picks it up. "Anything else, madame?" she asks, and Honour replies "Oh yes, please," in a tone that makes it clear that she's not talking about tea.

As Stephanie clears the table, Honour's phone rings. She goes to fetch it from her handbag in the sitting-room. She talks so quietly that Stephanie can barely hear her. "Yes, love, all's well. You know you don't need to worry. The roads were fine. The B&B is lovely. See you Sunday about teatime, I'd think. You too, love. Have a super evening. Miss you, too. Bye."

Honour returns to the kitchen, where Stephanie is drying her hands on a towel. She looks sad, Stephanie thinks, but Honour looks at her and smiles ruefully. "The ball and chain."

Stephanie asks, "Is everything okay?"

Honour hesitates. "I suppose so. I mean, she's fine. I've been away for choir workshops plenty of times."

"But…?" Stephanie prompts, putting the towel on the rack and leans on the counter, her stomach tense, prepared for a blow.

"But, well, I've never — seen another woman while I was away. This is new."

Stephanie's heart is fluttering. "If you're having second thoughts —"

"No, no," Honour says emphatically, striding to Stephanie and taking her hand. "No, I'm here to be with you. That hasn't changed. There's just this other thing here as well, a bit. I know it's weird."

"It's all right," says Stephanie, relaxing somewhat.

Honour puts her arms around Stephanie's neck and whispers into her ear, giving her goosebumps. "Forget all about that, Steph. I want you." She bites Stephanie's earlobe.

"Are you sure?" Stephanie responds, flirtatiously, her knees shaking a bit.

Honour looks her dead in the eyes. "I've never been more sure of anything. Please can we…"

Stephanie cuts in — "Get on with it?"

Honour laughs. "Yes, for God's sake, can we get on with it?"

Stephanie wakes early on Saturday morning and lies unmoving, relishing the warmth of the body beside her, the rattle of a light rain on the window, the luxurious comfort of this big bed.

Stephanie turns and very gently puts her arm around Honour, who is still fast asleep. Stephanie buries her nose in the luxuriant chestnut hair and wonders how on earth she will bear to let Honour go home tomorrow afternoon.

As she very quietly gets up, puts on a terry robe from the bathroom, and goes downstairs to make tea, Stephanie thinks back over last night with absolute delight and a sense of wonder verging on disbelief.

Last night, their pent-up desire was such that Honour had an orgasm while Stephanie was still just undressing her. Later, Honour woke Stephanie with a passionate kiss, and Stephanie responded with an extended session of teasing fingering, which had Honour begging for release and then gasping in extremely loud ecstasy for what seemed like five minutes. Stephanie was very glad they had the building to themselves. *Such a treat.* Honour had then fallen fast asleep, and Stephanie, holding her gently, had followed suit soon thereafter, deeply contented.

Stephanie makes tea and carries a cup upstairs to Honour, who awakens slowly, groaning and mumbling adorably as Stephanie gently kisses her cheek. Honour mumbles, "I fell asleep before I had a chance to make love to you."

Stephanie shushes her gently and goes into their ensuite. As she washes, she notices with delight that among the bottles of shampoo and lotion in the well-equipped bathroom are bottles of lube and a big bottle of massage oil. How very thoughtful, she thinks, her mind running wild yet again. She tiptoes quietly through the bedroom, where Honour is still lying with an arm flung out into space. Stephanie smiles and goes back downstairs to warm up the breakfast that Devon left for them.

On this rainy day of shy smiles and spontaneous embraces, they eat breakfast scandalously late, sit on the couch in the lounge for a while cuddling and kissing, and then at about two in the afternoon, when the rain finally subsides, they get dressed and drive into the village. They buy some delicacies for their tea, and cache the packages in Honour's car. Then they go for a walk through the village and along the canal towpath. There are few people out here, though the ones they pass give them friendly looks and the occasional greeting.

They walk along the path for half an hour arm in arm, in a peaceful silence, and then Stephanie works up her courage.

"Um, Honour, so, how are you feeling about…"

"Our fantasy?"

"Yes, I want to be sure you're really on board and not just saying so to indulge me."

"Are you joking?" Honour squeezes Stephanie's arm. "I'm so looking forward to it!"

Stephanie is elated. "Really?"

"Yes, really. I can't imagine anything more exciting, honestly. And I'm glad we…got to know each other properly last night, first."

"It was a beautiful night for me, Honour."

Honour drops her voice to a whisper even though there is no one in sight. "Oh, for me, too. You're the lover of my dreams."

Stephanie is so excited she can hardly walk straight. She manages to say the truth that is in her heart: "I feel incredibly lucky to be getting to know such a beautiful, gracious woman."

Honour just smiles and squeezes Stephanie's arm. They proceed in silence for a few minutes, then Stephanie says, "Well, shall we meander back to the B&B?"

"By all means, let us meander."

By the time they are back at the guest house, dusk is setting in and the air has cooled considerably. They go up to their room and find that Devon has made the bed, tidied up, and left a small vase of fresh flowers on the bedside table. They turn on the gas fire and hold a quick conference to outline the enactment of their fantasy. Honour can't get through the conversation without giggling. She apologizes and Stephanie responds, "Ah, lass, if we can't laugh at ourselves, let's not do it at all." At last, they agree they are ready to start.

Honour closes herself into the bathroom. Stephanie gets one of her bags and some other items from the closet, and goes downstairs to change. Stephanie's heart is racing as she goes into the cold bedroom — the Anne Lister Room, she notices with a grin as she sees the portraits on the walls, amused by the fact that it was formerly her mum's sewing room — and changes into her outfit. She waits the agreed-upon ten minutes, adjusting her costume and looking at herself in the full-length mirror. At last, the chime in her phone goes off, raising her heart rate once again. She looks at herself in the mirror once again and whispers to herself, "Yee-ha!" She heads up the stairs to the Chaumière.

Honour has finished checking herself in the mirror. Her hair is up. She has, with some difficulty, laced herself into a sexy red corset that pushes her breasts up and together, creating a rather spectacular cleavage. On her legs are black fishnet stockings; her feet are in elegant little black slippers. She has a black velvet choker around her neck, and a feather boa draped around her shoulders. She runs to put one more lick of scarlet lipstick on her lips, and picks a pink carnation from the vase to tuck into her cleavage. She hears Stephanie's steps on the stairs and becomes aware of how incredibly aroused she is. Her whole body is throbbing with anticipation. She drapes herself on the loveseat and tries to look seductive as Stephanie knocks on the door. "Come on in," Honour says in her best Western drawl.

Stephanie struts in, grinning. She is in complete cowboy gear, from her black Stetson and neckerchief to her sky-blue shirt with its elaborate embroidery and mother-of-pearl buttons, to her vintage Levis and shiny black cowboy boots.

"Why, hello there, cowpoke," says Honour. "You're looking extremely handsome."

Stephanie removes the Stetson and bows graciously. "Why, thank you, ma'am. I hear tell that a cowpoke might get some lovin' comfort at this establishment. Is that correct?"

Honour suppresses a giggle. "Some lovin' comfort, indeed. What's your name, good-lookin'?"

Stephanie replies, "You can call me Oakley, ma'am. And who do I have the honor of addressing?"

"They call me Miss Kitty. Won't you join me here on this settee?"

"I don't mind if I do, ma'am," says Stephanie, and, placing her hat on a chair, sits down next to Honour. She doesn't know what to do with her hands, so she fiddles with her big brass belt buckle.

Honour looks enticingly at Stephanie. "You've paid for my services for the entire night, Oakley, so why don't you tell me what I can do for you, to help you relax from that long cattle drive?"

Stephanie gulps. And says, "Why don't you come and sit on my lap, little lady, and we'll take it from there."

Honour stands and moves over to Stephanie, putting her hands on Stephanie's shoulders and straddling her. "Like this?" she whispers, lowering herself onto Stephanie's thighs.

Stephanie has forgotten how to breathe. She leans forward to sniff the carnation tucked into Honour's cleavage. "Nice flower, ma'am," she manages to say. Honour pulls the flower slowly from her bosom and pushes it behind Stephanie's ear.

"Thank you, ma'am," Stephanie whispers hoarsely. She is on fire. *I can't remember when I've ever been so turned on.* "Would you take those clips out of your hair, please, ma'am?" Honour complies, slowly pulling the clips out and shaking that glorious chestnut hair so that it caresses Stephanie's flushed, delighted face. Honour tucks the clips into Stephanie's breast pocket.

"And would you kindly remove your choker, ma'am?" Honour does, and tosses it wantonly into the air. Stephanie reaches up to caress Honour's snowy neck and then she slides her hands to Honour's breasts. The stiff material of the corset prevents her from feeling very much. "Does this thing come off, ma'am?"

Honour looks at Stephanie through her eyelashes. "I believe if you reach around, you'll find a bow."

Stephanie fumbles around, her face distractingly close to Honour's breasts, until she finds the bow. She unties it, and then it is a matter of gradually loosening the ribbon that criss-crosses the back of the corset. After a minute of effort, she sits back to see that the corset is almost loose enough to come off. She pulls again at the ribbon, and the corset comes away, revealing a tight, almost transparent white cotton camisole that barely contains Honour's generous breasts. With a low moan, Stephanie pulls Honour to her, kissing Honour's neck and palming her breasts. The flower behind Stephanie's ear falls, unheeded, to the floor.

Honour is highly aroused already, rocking her hips on Stephanie's thighs, sighing with desire. Stephanie reaches around and discovers that Honour has nothing on down below. She can't resist the impulse to pinch the generous round buttocks. Honour hisses, "Yes, yes." She kisses Stephanie ravenously, as Stephanie continues to pinch her bottom.

Eventually, breathing hard, Honour pushes herself back and says, "Oakley, you paid handsomely for my time tonight. I want to be sure you get your money's worth. You said you'd tell me what you want."

"Oh, yes ma'am, I did say that." Stephanie is sweating a little now.

"Well, what do you want?" Honour asks.

Stephanie says, "Well, as you may recall, some of it was written in that message I sent you by, uh, Pony Express. Remember?" Honour nods.

"But right now — I want you to stand up." Honour does, feeling absolutely brazen as Stephanie leans back on the couch and looks her up and down. "Now take off the rest of your clothes."

Honour removes the cami, and her garter belt, and her slippers. "Leave the stockings on," says Stephanie with an unfamiliar harshness in her voice. Honour's knees are weak.

Stephanie stands and wraps her arms around Honour. They kiss passionately. Stephanie runs her hands all over Honour's body, paying special attention to her breasts, until Honour, grinding her crotch against Stephanie, whispers, "Please…"

"What's that? Do you want something, little lady?"

"Yes, I do want something," says Honour slyly, pushing Stephanie's hands off her, stepping back from her, and walking to the side of the bed. She holds up a bottle — Stephanie recognizes it as the massage oil bottle from the bathroom — and says seductively, "I seem to recall that you said you like to have a good hard rubdown after a long cattle drive."

"Yes, I seem to recall that I said that, but…"

"So I'm here to give it to you, cowpoke. Get over here and get undressed."

Stephanie's eyes widen. *I thought I was going to be in charge of this fantasy.* She feels a little uncertain and unsteady as she pulls her boots off. *If Honour is planning to make love to me, I hardly know what to do, it's been so many years.*

She has some trouble with her Western belt and its massive buckle, and finally when she gets it off, she flings it across the room in frustration. Then her jeans come off. She looks at Honour.

"Okay to keep my socks on, ma'am?" Honour laughs.

"Absolutely not. I want you buck-naked, and no more stalling," Honour commands.

Gulping, Stephanie peels off the rest of her clothes and follows Honour to the bedside.

Honour has placed two of the huge bath towels on the bed, with three strategically placed pillows on top of them. Honour directs Stephanie to lie down on her front, and she does so.

She shivers a little — it's still cool in the room, and she's more than a bit nervous. She adjusts the pillows a bit and waits.

Honour walks away for a moment and puts on some slow

instrumental music on her little portable speaker, and turns off the lamps. Then she goes to her suitcase and puts on a red silky thigh-length kimono. She turns the gas fire up to maximum and returns to the bed.

Honour warms up some massage oil in her hands. There is no light in the room now except for the fire and a few electric candles. The firelight plays over Stephanie's body and Honour admires her narrow hips and flat — but not too flat — bottom, as well as the strong-looking shoulders. She has been brushing up on the massage techniques she learned during a short course a few years ago and has a plan. She chortles to herself.

Stephanie, her voice a little shaky, starts to speak — "What are you fixin' to do, ma'am?"

Honour shushes her and whispers into Stephanie's ear, "Shut up and relax, cowpoke, while I take you to heaven."

Stephanie hums in ecstasy at the first touch of Honour's warm, well-oiled hands on her shoulders.

As Stephanie very gradually relaxes and gives in to Honour's firm, deep kneading, twisting, pinching, fanning, and slow, delicious strokes up and down her body, she drifts into an altered state where time disappears.

Honour turns her over onto her back and massages Stephanie's front, with special attention to the tense muscles above Stephanie's small breasts, which she touches lightly. She moves on to the arms until Stephanie feels soft and floppy.

Then Honour says, "On your front again, Oakley."

Stephanie turns over slowly, with a deep sigh of contentment. "I feel a little like a flapjack on a griddle, ma'am," she jokes.

Honour spanks her just hard enough to get her attention. "Shhh." Honour gives a thorough massage to Stephanie's feet and legs, and eventually reaches Stephanie's buttocks. She gives them a very slow, deep massage until Stephanie's glutes relax completely. Stephanie moans.

Honour goes to get the other bottle, and gets a nice quantity of lube on her hands.

"Get that other pillow, cowpoke, and put it on top of the pillow under your hips."

As if hypnotized, Stephanie obeys and resumes her former position.

"Legs apart," Honour orders, and when Stephanie has spread her legs, Honour climbs onto the bed and kneels between her legs. Honour admires Stephanie's elevated bottom and gently but firmly pushes Stephanie's thighs further apart.

Honour places a lubed-up hand between Stephanie's legs. Stephanie tries to say something, then stops with a gasp as Honour finds her sweet spot and very, very lightly rubs it. Honour puts her other hand firmly on Stephanie's bottom and holds her in place. Honour flutters her fingers for a few minutes, making Stephanie writhe with delight, and then sinks two fingers slowly and deeply into Stephanie's center, causing her to cry out. Soon, in response to Stephanie's moans, Honour has developed a rhythmic pattern that she hopes says *I could do this all night* instead of the truth, which is *This position is killing me, please hurry up.* Stephanie comes suddenly, with a surprised roar and a powerful series of aftershocks that pound Honour's hand almost painfully. Honour very slowly withdraws her fingers and gazes, smiling, at what she has created.

Stephanie lies like a felled tree until Honour, feeling impossibly smug, gets up, stretching her legs gratefully, pulls the extra pillows from under Stephanie's midsection, and climbs into bed, draping the duvet over both of them.

Stephanie turns to face her. She looks at Honour from close range and touches Honour's cheek with wonder in her eyes. "Can we return to real life now?" she asks. "I'm too...thoroughly pleasured to be a cowpoke any more tonight."

Honour smiles and nods. "Of course." Honour notices, now, small tears in Stephanie's eyes. Honour kisses the tears away lightly.

Stephanie closes her eyes and sighs from deep, deep inside herself. "That was the absolutely best fuck of my whole entire life. What a complete surprise. Thank you so much."

Honour says quietly, "It's been a long time, has it, love?"

Stephanie nods and for a moment looks very sad. Then she opens her eyes again and smiles with delight.

"Worth the wait, I hope?" Honour whispers.

"Oh my God, oh my God, yes," Stephanie says emphatically. They kiss slowly and sensuously, exploring the new territory of trust that has opened to them.

Stephanie makes a move to make love to Honour but Honour pushes her hand away and says, "No, love, this evening is just for you."

Stephanie shakes her head in disbelief. They hold each other for a while, as dusk turns to darkness. Stephanie's stomach growls and she remembers that they haven't had a proper meal for quite a while. She hears a quiet snore and gently kisses Honour awake. "Hungry at all, love?" Honour murmurs assent. They get up, thread their way through the discarded clothes that litter the floor, change into their night clothes and dressing gowns, and go downstairs to construct a meal out of the good things they bought in the village that afternoon.

In deep contentment, Stephanie and Honour sleep through the night. But now they are up and Honour is showering. Stephanie's heart feels achey and already bereft. Honour will be leaving in half an hour.

Honour emerges from the shower and Stephanie gives her some privacy by carrying her own bags down to the foyer. On impulse, she dives into her backpack and tears a page out of the notebook she always carries. She writes a brief note to Honour and tucks it into her pocket.

Stephanie goes upstairs again as Honour is zipping up her suitcase. "Let me carry that down for you," she says, and Honour smiles gratefully.

They hold hands and say goodbye to the Chaumière. "What a magical time we've had here," says Honour. Stephanie kisses her hand, then sighs, picks up Honour's bag, and follows her downstairs.

"I hate to see you go, love," says Stephanie as she drops Honour's bag in the foyer.

"And I hate to go. Thank you for the loveliest, loveliest time imaginable."

"Shall we see each other again?" asks Stephanie with a tremor in her voice.

"Oh, I hope so — I mean, yes, yes, yes — by all means," says Honour passionately, throwing her arms around Stephanie. They exchange tender goodbyes and kisses, then at last Honour picks up her suitcase. "I'm stronger than I look, you know," she winks. Stephanie picks up Honour's handbag and, while Honour is putting her suitcase in the boot, Stephanie slips her note into the handbag and puts it in Honour's car.

Honour drives off, waving goodbye through the window. Stephanie closes up the guest house, leaves the key in Devon's mail slot. She feels like she ought to say good-bye and thank you to Devon, but she can't bear to talk to anyone just yet. She drives home to her cats.

Honour arrives back home on time, to her great surprise. She has little memory of the past two and a half hours — her memories of making love with Stephanie are so vivid and intoxicating that she has been driving on autopilot the whole way.

She and Nora are just sitting down to tea on Sunday evening when Honour's phone in the pocket of her jumper vibrates silently. She knows from the vibration pattern that it is a text from Stephanie.

She excuses herself from the table and rushes to the WC. Stephanie's text reads simply, "Miss you," followed by a row of heart emojis. Honour's heart swells.

She returns to the dinner table without replying to the text, except for a kiss emoji. She looks at Nora as they eat their meal, trying to see her as if for the first time.

Nora is her perfect companion, really. She's nearly as attractive as when they met twenty years ago. They share many interests — lawn bowling, singing, growing vegetables in their allotment, and watching reruns of "Scott and Bailey." They never fight or even argue. Their life together is safe and predictable, though Nora seems to be becoming more fragile, timid, and dependent every year. Honour feels responsible for Nora in a way that she knows is irrational, but there it is. She is horrified at the possibility that Nora will ever find out about Stephanie. It would destroy her.

On the other hand, as she does the washing up, Honour falls into a reverie, replaying in her mind some of the most beautiful moments with Stephanie. Perhaps she *can* keep this up. Perhaps there will be a whole series of imaginary choral workshops in Halifax. She smiles to herself but is apprehensive, as well. Nora's voice breaks in.

"Do you have any Rennies, Honour?"

"Oh, do you have heartburn again?"

"A bit, yes."

"I have a few in my handbag."

"Thanks, I'll look for them," says Nora, and Honour returns to thinking about Stephanie — her lips, her eyes, her clever, clever hands…

Nora shrieks from the living room. "What's this? Who is Oakley?" Nora feels a lightning bolt of anxiety shoot through her. She quickly rinses the suds off her hands and dashes into the living room. "What are you talking about?"

Nora is waving a piece of paper. "This is what I'm talking about!" She reads from the paper in a voice dripping with acid. "'My darling woman, how I long to taste your lips again before too long.' Good God." She stares at Honour. "You didn't go to a conference, did you?" Honour numbly shakes her head. "Did you have an affair with this...Oakley?"

Honour shrugs helplessly. "A weekend fling."

"Was this a woman you met through that bloody Anne Lister group?"

Honour nods. Nora tears the paper into tiny shreds and storms upstairs to her room, weeping loudly, and slams the door.

Honour picks up the little scraps of paper from the carpet and holds them in her hands, wondering if it's worth it to try and piece the message together, but deciding against it and reluctantly throwing them away. *How could I take this risk? She'll throw me out and I'll have to find a new place to live. Or I'll stay and she'll make my life a living hell.*

Honour goes to bed eventually and tries futilely to sleep. The intense joy she had felt with Stephanie has dissolved in a cloud of guilt and self-loathing.

I can't live with this tension. I know how Nora can be. She'll hold onto this for months unless I break it off with Stephanie. I'll have to do that. It's over.

And yet the last image she sees in her imagination as she finally succumbs to sleep is Stephanie's bright blue eyes.

⁓

Stephanie is at the office at midday on Wednesday, absolutely unable to focus since she has not heard a word from Honour except for the kiss emoji on Sunday night. Stephanie's texts have gone unanswered.

She forces herself to concentrate, and is writing a quiz for her first-year apprentices when her phone beeps. It's a text from Honour. She opens it with trepidation.

"Dear Stephanie, I'm so grateful for our time together, you have no idea. But I've realized that to continue with you would place an unbearable strain on my life as it now stands. It's not a perfect life, but then whose is? Nora found your note and now I am just going to be in hell for months.

"My whole living situation depends on maintaining domestic peace. So I won't be open to the idea of seeing you again, at least not for a long time. I don't mind the occasional text, but preferably they will be few and far between. I do hope this doesn't hurt your feelings too much. Believe me, if I weren't otherwise connected, I'd be courting you for all I was worth. But I've made a mistake — I'm not cut out to be a wanderer, apparently. Thank you a million times for being so wonderful. Goodbye. Honour."

Stephanie feels as if someone has driven a huge, spiky icicle through her heart.

⁓

It's midday and Stephanie goes out for a walk around the neighborhood. Her hunger has fled and she walks in a daze of pain and confusion. In her pocket, her phone buzzes again. It's Devon.

- Hey, Steph — are you by any chance missing a nice leather belt with a big brass buckle, depicting a bucking bronco?

- *Yes, that's mine!*
- Want to pick it up this afternoon?
- *Yes please. I get off work at three.*
- Come on over, pardner! I'll be in my place.

When the knock comes on the Annex door, Devon quickly puts Stephanie's belt on over her work clothes. She opens the door, strikes a pose with her thumbs in the belt, pretends to spit, and says, "So, the Yorkshire Kid is back."

Stephanie tries to smile but can't. Devon immediately brings her inside and hands her the belt. "You look a little depressed, pal," she says.

Stephanie tries the smile again. "I'm okay."

Devon doesn't know what to do. "Hey, guess what I just bought."

Stephanie shrugs.

"Come on in and I'll show you."

Devon pulls Stephanie into the kitchen, plops her into a chair at the table, and quickly puts a small bowl of chocolate ice cream in front of her. Stephanie stares at it. Devon points at the ice cream, then at her own mouth. "Eat…good," she says encouragingly. Finally Stephanie takes a spoonful of the ice cream.

"What happened, Steph? Weekend romance didn't go the way you hoped?"

"Oh, no, it went perfectly," Stephanie says quietly. "It was the best thing that's happened to me in years." She takes another spoonful. "It's what happened when she left. She got home and this woman she lives with read a love note I'd put in Honour's bag." She sighs deeply.

"Oh, crap," Devon says.

"Yes, crap. And now she says the woman — Nora — is all upset, so Honour has to break things off with me."

"I thought they weren't involved any more."

"Well, Honour lives in Nora's house, and they work together, and do all kinds of things together. They're as involved as can be."

"Except romantically."

"Yeah."

"Sounds very screwed up. My sympathies. I know you really like her."

135

Stephanie drops her face into her hands. "I really, really, *really* like her. I thought maybe we could build something together. Oh well." She spoons up the last of the ice cream and puts on a simulacrum of a happy face that breaks Devon's heart.

Devon thinks for a moment. "Are you much of a walker?"

"Not like some of these hill-climbing lasses, but yes, I like a good ramble. Why?"

"Because I've been wanting someone to keep me company on the moors. What if we went for a hike on Saturday?"

"You and me?" Devon nods. Stephanie brightens. "That would be lovely, mate."

"I could use a friend, myself," Devon says.

Stephanie tuts. "Of course you could. That business with Larkin."

Devon says, "Yeah, so we could go for a hike or a ramble or whatever, and throw rocks, whaddaya say?"

Stephanie laughs whole-heartedly for the first time in days. "I love it."

"And why don't we gather a few friends together at the pub?"

"Oh, I'd be too embarrassed to tell anyone about this."

"You don't have to tell them what happened, we can just say we need some company. Don't be alone too much with this."

They work out details for their Saturday hike, and Stephanie leaves. By the time she gets back to her flat, Stephanie has started saying positive thoughts to herself. *I've been rejected before, and survived. An evening at the pub with pals will help, even if I don't tell anyone why I'm blue.*

Stephanie feeds her cats, sighs a few deep sighs and then resolutely focuses on doing her laundry, steadfastly ignoring the stabbing, icy pain in her heart.

～

A Cold Day at Shibden

The Guest House is empty. On this rainy Wednesday morning, Devon has done all her chores, lifted weights in her little home gym, and gone for as long a walk as she could stand in the wind and rain. Now, after lunch, she sets up her easel and painting supplies, but finds she is completely uninspired, and too restless to settle down and do anything creative.

On impulse, she drives to Shibden Hall, as she has quite frequently in these cold, wet weeks. She chats with the volunteers. They empathize about the depressing weather, and remind her that the Hall will close for the winter at the end of the month. She feels even more downhearted when she hears this. She wanders morosely from room to room, trying to summon the spirit of Anne Lister as she gazes at the furniture and decorations of the rooms her heroine once inhabited.

She buys a cup of tea and a scone and sits in the small tea room, achingly remembering her visit there with Larkin almost a year ago. She pulls out her sketch pad but is unable to draw. Then she finds herself writing out her feelings. She writes page after page on her rough watercolor paper, surprising herself with the volume and intensity of her emotions.

She writes a letter to the spirit of Anne Lister, as she imagines Lister standing near her, dispensing wisdom.

Devon jumps when she feels a touch on her shoulder. It's one of the volunteers, a kind-faced man with a white beard, gently telling her that the Hall will be closing in a few minutes. She's shocked to see that it is quite dark outside.

As she walks up the hill to the car park, her agonized monologue is running over and over around a well-worn track: *I was an idiot to leave California.*

But when she gets home, she decides to turn her despair into a little art project. She warms up her art studio and makes a paper statuette of Anne Lister, striding through the countryside. She takes the statuette downstairs and puts it on the shelf where she has located her Aunt Amy shrine. Then she looks over all the despairing notes she wrote at Shibden Hall, summing up the essence of each one and making a concise list on a small piece of handmade paper:

I'm lonely.

I'm homesick.

I miss Larkin.

I want a dog.

I need ....

And here her mind goes blank. She sighs and adds the slip of paper to the shrine and sets the Anne Lister statuette on top of it. She feels ridiculous, but then a peaceful sensation starts warming her heart and she gets the distinct conviction, as if Anne Lister herself had whispered a reassuring word into her ear, that just writing down what she longs for is a very important step. And the unmistakable feeling that things will look brighter before too long.

～

Imara: Autumn

Imara prides herself on doing everything without breaking a sweat. Her friends constantly marvel at how well she does — and how little she works. "It's all about managing," she says. She learned a lot from her parents, Punjabi immigrants who climbed from poverty to owning three successful restaurants. But she also realized early on that because they insisted on doing everything themselves, they never had much time for Imara and her two brothers, let alone for any kind of fun.

Imara has therefore developed a lifelong obsession with efficiency. At university she studied not only her primary interest, art history, but also industrial engineering and business management. It has paid off for her.

She manages her home-based medical billing business by using subcontractors, so she manages to have plenty of time for tennis, cycling, and visiting art galleries. At forty, she still has a tight, loyal circle of pals from uni, as well as a few ex-lovers who have become friends.

She manages her spacious flat in Manchester and all her personal business by hiring specialists. Her house cleaner, massage therapist, and auto mechanic all like working for her, because Imara is direct and clear about her expectations, and, though sometimes brusque to the point of rudeness when her expectations are not met, she is usually fairly considerate. And she really does pay well.

Imara also manages her two lovers without breaking a sweat, unless you count the sweat that comes from a vigorous afternoon lovemaking session. After experiencing various dramas and complications that came from conducting her romantic life close to home, she now manages it better by relocating it to this nearby city.

And so every two months, Imara goes to a hotel in Halifax for a few days, to manage the branch of her business that's located there. And to manage her two girlfriends, who don't know about each other.

On Wednesdays, she sees Alice, who does Imara's taxes and her books. Alice is reserved and businesslike while working, but a lot of fun during her off-hours. Alice is not the most brilliant conversationalist, but her temperament matches well with Imara's — Alice treats their affair lightly, with fondness but no demands. Imara is confident that when the time comes for her to break it off, Alice will transform into a friend fairly rapidly. It's quite perfect.

On Thursdays, she sees, and has her hair done, by Laura, who has her own salon. Laura is everything Imara is not: passionate, impractical, spontaneous, dramatic. Lately, she has been hinting that she wants Imara to fly them to Portugal for a week. Imara loves the way Laura does her hair, and her wild, hot lovemaking, but is becoming tired of Laura's operatic scenes whenever they have to say goodbye. Imara senses that their time together may come to an end before too very long, and is starting to think about how to find a good new hairdresser. She doubts that Laura will transition peaceably into the friendship zone, and rather dreads the ensuing melodrama. But it's not an immediate concern — maybe for the summer quarter.

Fridays, Imara focuses on the business. On Saturdays, Imara takes the day for herself, and on Sunday she returns to Manchester.

Usually, Imara stays at a nice hotel in the center of Halifax. But she has heard good things about a new place over in Hebden Bridge, Miss Lister's Guest House, run by an American woman. The privacy would definitely be an advantage over the hotel, and Imara enjoys a change of pace. So, even though she dislikes most Americans, she decides to try it on her next trip to the Halifax branch.

∾

On this Wednesday evening, Imara checks into the guest house, telling Devon that she is expecting a "friend" later in the evening, to which Devon smilingly agrees.

To her surprise, the American woman is gracious and efficient. The guest house, though a little on the minimalist side, is quite lovely, and just as private and discreet as she needs it to be. Imara welcomes Alice into the guest house when she arrives at nine, and bids her a drowsy farewell at midnight.

～

Imara has a solid sleep and a lovely bath, then dresses in a business suit and heads downstairs. When she reaches the ground floor, Imara can hear Devon making breakfast in the kitchen.

Imara's eye is caught by the tasteful, richly-colored furniture in the lounge, and then by three small but exquisite landscape paintings on the walls. She finds that she can't drag herself away from them. She recognizes some local landscapes in these pictures, but more than that, her trained eye sees a rhythm in the compositions, a depth in the colors, and some sort of magical essence that demonstrates that the artist has a deep love of the subjects. The artist must be local, she thinks — but she can't recall ever seeing anything else they have painted. She is leaning over one of the canvases, trying to make out the artist's signature, when Devon steps into the room, wiping her hands on a tea towel.

"Oh, good morning, Imara. I was just coming to announce breakfast. I have some very nice bacon from a farm down the road."

"That's fine, and a cup of coffee."

"You bet," says Devon, heading back to the kitchen.

"Oh, um, Devon — I'm curious about these paintings."

"Do you mind coming into the kitchen? I'm just cooking."

Imara follows her into the kitchen and Devon pours her a cup of coffee that turns out to be, surprisingly, almost as good as Imara's own special blend.

"The paintings…?"

"The three oils in the lounge. Or are they acrylics?"

"Acrylics."

"They're quite interesting."

"Oh, yes?" Devon leads her into the dining room and serves up a beautifully plated omelette. Imara sits and holds up her cup for Devon to refill.

"Yes. Do you know the artist?"

Devon smirks as she pours the coffee. "Yes, I do. Quite well."

"She — or he?"

"She."

"…is quite gifted. I've seen thousands of paintings of the moors but these are rather unique."

"In a good way?" smiles Devon, pouring herself a cup of coffee and sitting down across from Imara .

Imara nods, her mouth full. When she can talk, she says, "I'd like to talk to her. If she doesn't have an agent, I might be able to connect her to a gallery in Leeds that a friend of mine runs. Does she have a lot of paintings like those?"

"She has what in the States we call a shit-ton of them."

"I'd quite like to see them."

Devon thinks for a moment, clearly amused. "How's after breakfast work for you?"

Taken aback, Imara checks her phone. "Can't be today. Hmm, bit busy this week. Maybe Saturday?"

"That should work," Devon replies.

They agree on a time, and Devon wishes Imara a good day. As soon as her guest is gone, Devon laughs to herself while she washes the dishes.

The next morning, which is Thursday, Imara warms up her own breakfast from covered dishes Devon has left for her, and goes to get her hair cut by Laura. As usual, the cut is quite satisfactory, as is the afternoon rendezvous in the cozy flat behind Laura's salon.

Imara works industriously all day Friday.

She wakes early on Saturday, and since she has a free day, she dresses in her walking clothes and goes out for a saunter around the village. It's a brisk, windy day and the wind whips Imara's scarf around her face.

As she walks, she mulls over her current lovers. There are small annoyances — Laura's devotion, Alice's limited conversation topics — but mostly she finds it all quite decent. She gets affection and sex with no complications. She spends a lot of money on both of them, between dinners at the best area restaurants and the occasional special treat, like a piece of jewelry or a silk scarf she's found that would suit them. Everyone always says that Imara has exquisite taste, and she has to admit, it's true.

The wind is getting to be a bit much, so she turns downhill towards the village center with the intention of stopping at a cafe to while away the afternoon in the warmth with a novel. Most immediately, she really needs a ladies' room.

She goes into a cafe on St. George's Square and orders a latte, then trots up the stairs to the loo. On the wall, she sees an intriguing flyer: there will be a women's poetry reading here tonight at seven. There are photos of the three poets who will read, and one of them is pictured sitting on a huge motorcycle, wearing aviator sunglasses; her blonde hair is lofted in the wind. Vibes so strong Imara can practically feel the rumble. Perry. *Hmmm.* Imara thinks about wandering back down here this evening.

While she is finishing her coffee, an alert sounds on Imara's phone. It reminds her of her appointment with Devon. She pays her bill and walks briskly back uphill to the guest house.

Devon is dusting the furniture in the lounge. "Don't let anyone tell you that the B&B business isn't glamorous," she says as Imara enters.

Imara smiles briefly, then walks over to the nearest of the three paintings.

"Will you tell me the name of the artist, or are you going to keep on being cagey?"

Devon smiles. "Sorry, I didn't mean to be cagey. I was just a bit embarrassed."

"Why?"

"I'm the artist."

"You are?" Imara takes a step backwards and looks incredulously at her hostess. "Well. They are really good. I'd love to see the rest of them."

Grinning to herself, Devon takes Imara next door to the

Annex, and up to the studio on the first floor. There are a couple of dozen small canvases of scenes painted on the moors.

Devon sets up an easel and puts the paintings on it, one at a time. Imara looks at each one carefully, asking an occasional question but otherwise not commenting. Devon feels a bit vulnerable, especially since Imara's questions show that she is an educated connoisseur.

At last, Devon comes to the end of the paintings. "That's it."

Imara looks at her. "What are your plans for these?"

Devon shrugs. "I don't really have any plans. Right now, I'm just enjoying painting them," she says. *They are keeping me alive.*

"They're far too good to keep to yourself."

"Thanks," says Devon, a bit embarrassed. "I just haven't thought about showing them."

"Well, you should," smiles Imara. "You're a real talent." She checks her watch. "Oh, I have to get moving — I'm going to the poetry reading tonight."

"So am I," says Devon. "See you there, I expect."

Devon finishes her chores feeling warmed by Imara's smile and her educated compliments. *Maybe it's time to start taking myself seriously as an artist.*

Imara dresses carefully in a flowing green dress that looks deceptively casual but shows off her slight, delicate figure to its best advantage. She drives down to the cafe on the square a bit before seven so she can get a good seat. She needn't have worried — there are only about twenty people here, in chairs that have been arranged in front of the cafe's tiny stage. Imara takes a seat a few feet from the stage, and looks around casually, hoping to catch a glimpse of this Perry person.

And there — that must be her. Tall, Nordic, with long blonde hair pulled into a low pony-tail. Dressed in a form-fitting black motorcycle jacket, black jeans, and with a bright yellow scarf around her neck. Talking and laughing with three women who appear to be fans, they are looking at her with such admiration.

And no wonder, thinks Imara. She's not conventionally beautiful, this poet, but she has attractive, strong features, and she radiates charisma, charm, whatever one wants to call it. Imara shifts in her seat and realizes she is a bit aroused. Interesting. Another person enters the room and Imara sees that it's Devon. They wave at each other, but Devon sits at the back.

The emcee, a chunky young woman wearing a baseball cap, comes out, checks the microphone and introduces the evening's program. Perry will read last. Imara pays some attention to the first two poets, who are quite good, but also quite clearly straight. When Perry is announced, a rustle goes through the audience, an anticipatory excitement.

Perry, who has taken off her leather jacket to reveal a well-worn navy wool sweater with leather elbow patches, strides to the microphone and smiles confidently at the audience. "Who ever would have dreamed there'd be so many poetry fans in Hebden Bridge, turning out on such a windy night?"

A woman in the audience calls out "Perry fans, more like!" and there is a spate of applause and laughter. Perry shakes her head and smiles, not in the least embarrassed.

Imara listens with half an ear to Perry's poems, she is so struck by the woman's self-confidence. It's the sexiest thing about her. Even sexier than her lanky frame, lopsided grin, and sharp jawline.

When Imara finally tunes in, she is moved by the delicate, insightful poems — about love, about the moors, about the intense joy of riding motorcycles, even a surprisingly touching sonnet about sheep. This is a real talent.

Imara joins in the enthusiastic applause at the end of the reading. The audience members mill around and a large proportion of them surround Perry. Imara waits for a long time until they have dispersed. Perry and Devon have a rather long, quiet chat that ends in a comradely hug, and Devon leaves.

At long last, Imara is face to face with Perry, who has just picked up her leather jacket.

"Hello," ventures Imara.

"Hi," says Perry, looking her up and down with a smile as she shrugs into the jacket. "I haven't seen you before."

"I'm here every now and then," Imara replies, looking her directly in the eyes. "I liked your work."

"Thank you, mate," replies Perry, but it's clear that she's heard this too many times tonight for it to make any impact, and she turns a little toward the door.

"Would you be my guest for dinner?" Imara continues.

Perry turns back. "Well — when?"

Imara shrugs. "Right now."

Perry laughs. "I'm absolutely ravenous, now would be pretty terrific." She hesitates and looks mock-askance at Imara. "You're not an axe murderer or anything, are you?"

Imara smiles shyly. "I'll tell you over dinner. Where would you like to go?"

Perry looks her up and down again. "You're not dressed for a long walk, so it had better be somewhere close."

They settle on an Italian restaurant that's five minutes' walk away. On the way over, and throughout the elegant meal, they share basic details. Perry works as a bar back in three different pubs, putting in as many hours as she can, saving money. She lives in Todmorden and is, as far as Imara can tell, unencumbered by pets, girlfriend, or family. Her motorcycle, which for some reason she calls Fred, is in need of some parts that are a bit too expensive for her right now. Perry is also involved with the team of codebreakers who are deciphering Anne Lister's journals. *Hmm. Interesting.*

Imara reveals little about herself, except to subtly convey that she is successful and wealthy.

"Oh, it must be so nice to have some money — I never seem to have a penny to spare," Perry says cheerfully.

"Yes, I've been very fortunate," says Imara. "I like to share with my friends in whatever way I can."

Perry takes this in without comment, but Imara thinks Perry is intrigued in spite of herself.

They finish the meal, but Imara orders two more glasses of wine, and Perry doesn't argue.

Imara says, "Your motorcycle — it needs some parts?"

Perry looks sad. "Yes, poor old boy, he needs a carburetor. It's all right, I can manage with buses for a week or two and then I should have enough for the part, and I do the labor myself."

"Good for you," says Imara. "I wish I knew how to fix things."

"It does come in handy," Perry agrees. "But would you like to see my true love?"

Imara is taken aback, but says, "All right."

Perry pulls out her phone and shows Imara a photo of a motorcycle. "That's a 1958 NSU Super Max. A collector in Bremen is keeping it for me. I've been saving up for three years and now I have almost enough to go and get it. Soon." Briefly caressing the photo, Perry puts her phone away again and smiles at Imara.

Imara smiles back. "Well, in the meantime, what do you do for fun?"

"My whole life is quite fun, but one of my passions is walking on the moors. This is the most beautiful part of the whole country and I'm out in it every time I have a few hours off. Everything fades into the right proportion when I get away from town and up on the fells."

"Do you hike alone, usually, or…?"

"One or two mates, sometimes, but usually alone, yes."

Imara hates any form of outdoor exercise and has never actually been out on the moors, no matter how many times her old girlfriend, Larkin, tried to lure her out there. But she says, "Would you ever consider taking a new friend with you? For, perhaps, an easy hike to start with?"

Perry sips her wine and uses the glass to hide her barely restrained private smile. Imara thinks, *she knows exactly what I'm up to.* It's a bit disconcerting — usually, Imara moves subtly enough to distract her prey until the time is right to strike.

"And you would be the new friend, I take it?"

"I'd like to be, yes." It's not often that Imara feels a bit off-balance when engaged in a seduction. It's a novel and not entirely unpleasant feeling.

"I'm going on a wee ramble tomorrow afternoon. Perhaps you'd like to come."

Imara is irritated — Sunday is her day to drive home and get ready for the work week. "What time tomorrow?" she asks.

"Noon."

"You couldn't do any earlier?" wheedles Imara.

"Working all morning, I'm afraid," says Perry. She stretches and yawns.

"I could manage noon, I suppose…" Imara says.

"Or next time you're in town," suggests Perry nonchalantly, pulling her wallet out of her pocket.

Imara reaches across the table and taps Perry's hand to stop her from opening her wallet. "Put that away." Perry complies, shrugging cheerfully.

"Thanks, Imara."

Imara pays the bill and takes a big breath. "I'd love to join you tomorrow if I won't put a cramp in your plans."

Perry nods. "It's supposed to be a beautiful day." She smiles. "I think you'll love it."

"Brilliant," says Imara with trepidation in her heart but a smile on her lips. "What should I wear?"

Perry shrugs. "Oh, you know, the usual — you have hiking boots?"

Imara nods.

"A mac, bring a sandwich and a bottle of water. Sticks, if you've got 'em." Perry yawns. "Awfully sorry, I'd better get going. Early job tomorrow." She rises and picks up her helmet.

Imara stands as well. She really wants a kiss for all she has invested in this evening.

But Perry just grins at her, thanks her for dinner, and claps her on the shoulder. "Meet you in front of the Old Gate Pub, then, noon?" Imara nods. "All right, see you then, cheers," Perry says, and lopes off.

Imara sits back down and thinks about the things she'll have to look for in the shops tomorrow morning.

Hiking boots, for one.

Perry calls a halt on top of a hill. Imara flops onto a rock and never wants to move again. They have been hiking for an hour and a half. For the first twenty minutes or so, Imara was engaged by the views — the black bracken, the rolling moors — but for the past hour the hike has been purgatorial. Several spots on her feet feel as if they have been stung by malicious bees.

Perry has every appearance of enjoying herself tremendously, taking deep breaths of the cold air and surveying the views with delight, pointing out distant bridges and the occasional lapwing or red grouse. Imara is simultaneously annoyed by her own stupidity in agreeing to the hike and incredibly attracted to Perry. Pain and desire fight each other for domination in her body.

She begs for a rest, and Perry obligingly finds a spot on a flat-topped boulder that's big enough for both of them to sit.

Perry takes out her thermos and offers Imara a cup of tea. Imara gladly accepts, while silently taking stock of her feet. The left foot is on fire, especially her little toe and the back of her heel. Her right foot has its own special delights, with the big toe and ankle-bone both rubbed raw.

Perry points out Stoodley Pike, the incredibly ugly war memorial monument that dominates the landscape. Imara endeavors to look interested, but is in too much pain. Perry notices. "I say, are you all right?"

Imara attempts to look nonchalant, but fails. "Well, no. I think I have the beginnings of a blister or two." *Or ten,* she adds silently.

Perry looks concerned. "Let's have a look. May I?" She kneels in front of Imara, and if Imara wasn't in agony, she would be able to imagine all sort of lovely outcomes for this particular posture, but instead Perry is gently taking off Imara's boots.

"Your boots look brand new," she exclaims. "How long have you had them?"

"About…twenty-two hours. Bought them yesterday," Imara confesses.

"I thought you said you had boots!"

"I thought I'd packed them, but I hadn't," lies Imara, sucking breath in through her teeth as Perry pulls off her socks.

"No wonder you have these sore patches! Poor you!" says Perry, briefly cradling Imara's feet in her warm hands. "You must be miserable. But I have some blister patches. They might help."

Perry produces a packet of patches from her knapsack, and carefully applies them to the sore places on Imara's feet. She helps Imara on with her socks and boots, lacing the boots tightly. "Leave

148

the patches on till they come off on their own — probably a week or so. I hope they help," she says, standing.

Imara thanks her profusely, then, lying through her teeth again, says "I'm really enjoying the hike, but I'm thinking about heading back soon."

Perry grimaces sympathetically. "Unfortunately, this is a circular route, and we're at the furthest point right now, so whether we go on or go back, it's the same distance." She helps Imara to her feet and for a moment, as Imara feels the strong arms pulling her up, she is tempted to go in for a hug, but Perry steps back and roots in her pack again, this time pulling out an anorak. "So I think we should go on, don't you? And it's about to start raining, if I'm not mistaken. Did you bring a mac?"

Imara says "No," miserably. She decided it would be too heavy to carry her rain jacket, and has worn a very attractive but very impractical blood-orange woolen jacket instead. Perry laughs, not unkindly. "Well, I think you'll be getting a bit wet." She points at a huge dark-grey cloud that looms over them. "Luckily, I carry a spare poncho for occasions like this." She rummages in her pack and pulls out an ugly, wrinkled green poncho and helps Imara into it. "Best to get going," she adds with a grin, and they set off down the hill. Imara's feet feel only marginally better, and as the cloud releases its burden onto their heads, she resigns herself to a long, wet walk.

Eventually, as dusk is starting to set in, they reach the village again. Imara can see the welcome sign of the Old Gate, which means her car is nearby. She is in quite desperate pain, as well as being utterly exhausted and soaking wet in the areas of her person that the poncho hasn't protected. All she wants in life is a hot bath and a fistful of painkillers.

Perry, on the other hand, looks as chipper and energetic as she had at midday. "All right then?" she asks, and from somewhere Imara summons a smile and says, "Great, thanks for the lovely hike."

Perry laughs. "Hike? Relaxed saunter, more like. Glad you enjoyed it — a bit more conditioning and you could be a decent hiker, I'm sure. Must run — my bus is in five minutes."

Perry gives Imara a quick, efficient hug and walks off at a fast clip.

Later, in her bath at the guest house, Imara fumes. That is not how her day with Perry was supposed to turn out. Her management skills were no match for this oblivious outdoorswoman. She's more intrigued with Perry than ever, though, despite herself, and wonders what tack she might take next time she comes to town.

~

Walking Rugby

"Heads up, Dev!" Daisy passes the ball to Devon. She grasps the unnaturally large, odd-shaped ball and has a moment of glee as she takes two or three long strides toward the end zone *or whatever they call it*, then Evie comes out of nowhere, grabs the ball from Devon's arms, and passes it to another player. Flustered, Devon loses her balance and finds herself face down in a patch of freezing-cold mud. Daisy, laughing loudly, pulls her to her feet.

Devon is furious. "I thought this walking rugby was supposed to be 'less physical' than regular rugby!"

Evie is doubled over. She points at Devon. "You're just *covered* in mud," she wheezes.

Daisy has a bit more sympathy, though she can't hide her hilarity. "Are you hurt, mate?"

Devon does a quick inventory of her physical condition. "No," she says grudgingly.

The practice session halts for a moment while it is determined that Devon is not injured. Evie thumps her on the back. "Sorry to laugh, Dev."

The field of a dozen mostly middle-aged men and women take advantage of the lull to trot to the sidelines and take swigs from their thermoses. They call out encouraging words to Devon, and the practice game starts up again. Despite the slippery grass, Devon is having a blast. The slowness of the game means her ankle is not stressed, and her natural competitiveness spurs her on. The other players are funny and cheerful. She makes a touchdown, which for some reason is called a "try," and everyone makes much of the American.

Two tall women, one of whom has a gigantic dog, are watching from the sidelines and cheering. As they applaud Devon, the huge dog gets away and starts running all over the field, his owner and her friend chasing him. The rugby players join in and in a few minutes, the dog has been taken in hand and most of the players are red-faced and out of breath.

A whistle blows and the organizer, Cherry, declares the practice session over.

Evie and Daisy thump Devon on the back. "Well done, mate!" shouts Evie.

"Will we see you next week?" asks Daisy.

"I don't know," says Devon, looking ruefully at her mud-caked track pants.

"Oh come on, Dev, you did really well," Evie shouts encouragingly.

"Thanks," Devon replies, combing mud from her hair.

"See you in the pub, then?" asks Evie.

"You bet," says Devon. As she limps over the field to collect her gym bag, Devon sees one of the tall women heading toward her, as the other one walks away toward the car park. It's Jess. Her dog strains at his leash and jumps up and down excitedly.

"Ey up, Devon."

"Hey, Jess, how are you? Who's this handsome fellow?"

"This is a very bad boy. His name is Tesla."

"May I pat him?"

"Are you sure you want to? He's a right mess."

"I couldn't be any more filthy."

"All right, then."

As Devon gives Tesla a rub, she grins at Jess.

"Nice to see you again."

Jess nods, smiling. "Same, lass. What a gorgeous job you've done with the B&B."

"Thanks!"

Tesla paws at Devon's hand until she resumes scratching him. "He likes you."

"I really miss having a dog."

"I couldn't manage without one."

"Coming to the pub, Jess?"

"All right, don't mind if I do."

"Is your girlfriend coming?"

"My girl — oh, you mean Nicola?" Jess is amused. "No, she has summat else on. Also, not my girlfriend."

Devon walks with Jess to her van. Devon takes a look inside the sparkling clean van as Tesla is put into his cage with a handful of biscuits. Then Jess and Devon join the rugby players in the pub.

Devon finds it easy to talk with this rough-edged, cheerful woman. They put their heads together and talk about being small-business owners for nearly an hour, as the rugby players leave one by one. Then Jess checks her watch and startles. "Is that the time? I need to go milk me cows."

"You're a farmer, too?"

"In a very small way. Seven chickens. Three cows."

"Might you be interested in supplying my guest house with eggs and milk?"

Jess smiles happily. "I might indeed! And butter! Give us a call, or better yet, pop round." She rummages in a pocket of her tan work coat and comes up with a crumpled business card.

Devon walks outside with her. Tesla is released, and sniffs happily at Devon's hands. Devon runs her hands over his back and scratches his ears. "Say, Jess — do you ever come across dogs that need to be adopted?"

"From time to time," Jess says. "You looking for a dog?"

"I'm not sure yet. I'm a little concerned about the commitment, to be honest. But I do miss my Baxter."

"Well, let's say you were looking, what would you want?"

"Um — not a puppy. A dog that is nice to look at, and calm. Well-trained. Medium-sized. A good walking companion. Oh, and a dog that smells halfway decent."

Jess snorts. "Anything else? Walks on water, does magic tricks, that sort of thing?"

Devon nods. "Card tricks would be great."

"Mind if it's not a purebred?"

"Not at all. I like a good mutt."

"Let me see what I can do. This'll be reyt good!"

They shake hands and part. As she drives home, Devon is warmed by the thought that she has met one more potential friend.

PART SIX: Winter
Yorkshire

Teaching at the W.I.

It's a week before Christmas. Devon is standing in front of a room containing a dozen older ladies. They are all sitting at a long table with sketch pads in front of them, and looking expectantly at her. *Why the hell did I say yes to this?*

Claire is introducing her to the group. "Devon's paintings have been displayed in several galleries in San Francisco. She's just moved here recently and is excited about exploring the moors and the villages. And excited about teaching us some basic drawing skills. Please welcome Devon Rodriguez!"

There is a spattering of enthusiastic applause. Devon looks at the class plan she drew up and hopes these nice ladies will not immediately detect that she has never taught anything before. When Claire invited her to teach this class at the Women's Institute, Devon at first laughed and absolutely refused. But then Claire wheedled her with "What would Anne Lister do?" and Devon finally caved in, knowing that Anne Lister would have accepted the challenge.

Devon hopes her voice won't betray her nervousness. She says, "How many of you have ever…"

"Speak up, love!" someone calls out.

"Sorry." Speaking louder, she says, "How many of you have ever told someone that you can't draw a straight line?" Almost all of the students raise their hands.

"I have good news for you," Devon says. "You don't need to be able to draw a straight line." The whole class enjoys this; various iterations of "phew!" can be heard.

"What you do need is to be able to look. Please come to the table over here by the window and pick up one of the objects on it. A stone, a leaf, a stick, it doesn't matter."

Slowly, they congregate around the table, choose something, and return to their seats. Devon gets over her stiffness and starts enjoying herself as she gets the ladies laughing and being brave as they start drawing their rocks and leaves.

By the time Claire signals that the class ends in ten minutes, everyone moans in protest. Devon gets each student to stand and show her sketch, and leads the class in boisterous applause for each one of them. "Aren't you going to critique us?" one of them inquires querulously.

"No," says Devon. "Did you enjoy looking at your object? And sketching it?" Most of them agree that they did. "Well, then, you're a successful artist already. Give yourselves another round of applause." They do, with enthusiasm, and Devon takes her leave, but not before the ladies have insisted that she have a cup of tea and a fresh-baked scone.

At the front entrance of the Institute building, Claire grabs Devon. "That was amazing, Dev! I'm sure they'll want you to come back!"

"Are you serious?" Devon says.

Claire nods. "You're a natural teacher," she says.

Devon shakes her head. "Let's talk about it in a month or two and see, okay?"

~

Nicola: Winter

The next morning, Devon is working on a second painting of the Shibden trees when she hears a car entering the courtyard. She's glad of a potential interruption — the picture isn't going too well.

She goes to the front door and peers into the rainy courtyard to see a tall, thin woman with a massive mop of curly brown hair getting out of her car and heading toward the Guest House. Devon shouts, "Over here!" and waves as the woman turns towards the Annex.

"Hi!" Devon calls, as the woman hurries toward her. Devon thinks she recognizes her from the rugby practice. "You're Jess' friend, aren't you?"

"Yes, I'm Nic."

"Well, Nic, come on in and get warmed up."

Nicola enters and takes off her raincoat, rubbing her hands together and enjoying the warmth of Devon's living room.

"Tea?" asks Devon.

"Oh, no, thanks, my dog's in the car, I won't stay long."

"The kettle just boiled, come on," says Devon. Nicola accepts, and sits at Devon's table. They chat for a few minutes about the weather and rugby while the tea is steeping. Nicola is awkward, nervous. She pulls at her hair compulsively every minute or two. Devon can't help noticing that Nicola's frizzy, bushy haircut is extremely unflattering to her angular face. Her clothes, too, are dreadful — polyester plaids and clashing stripes. *I'm no fashionista, but this chick needs help.*

Finally, Devon sits down as well. "Well, Nic, what can I do for you?"

The tall woman is embarrassed and looks around, anywhere except at Devon. "Um. I've been getting to know a woman from Leeds. Through the Anne Lister group, you know."

"Mm hmm," says Devon encouragingly, as her visitor seems at a loss for words.

Nicola leans her elbows on the table and plays aggressively with a long curl of her hair. "We've really connected with each other through our interest in dogs. I've invited her to come to Halifax for the weekend of the twentieth. To see the sheepdog trials."

She trails off again. Devon says, "That sounds like fun."

"Yes," says Nicola, savaging her hair and then letting it go and sitting on her hands.

"So has she accepted the invitation?"

"Oh, yes, she has," says Nicola, rocking back and forth a bit in her chair.

"How can I help?" asks Devon gently.

Nicola looks agonized. "Well, is there a room here available that weekend?"

Devon doesn't even have to look at the reservation book. "Yeah, any room you like."

"Fab. Well." There is another long pause, then Nicola's face tightens and she blurts out, "I just don't know what to do with her once she's here. The sheepdog trials won't last all weekend."

"Have you gotten to know her pretty well long-distance?"

"Oh yes, loads of texts and phone calls. We know each other's stories pretty well by now, it's been three months since we started chatting."

"I see," says Devon. "Is it romantic at all?"

Nicola suddenly bursts out laughing, a little hysterically. "Romantic? I've never experienced anything like this. She says she's madly in love with me. She hinted once or twice about wanting to marry me. She sends me presents in the post, cards…"

"What sort of presents? Flowers, chocolates..?"

"And more! Nice hardbound books, a beautiful handmade leather lead for Zorro."

"Zorro…?"

"Dog."

"Wow. What's the woman's name?"

"Megan."

"Are you attracted to her?"

"Oh my God, yes," says Nicola. "Look at her." She pulls out her phone and scrolls to a photo of a glamorous-looking blonde snuggling with a handsome Dalmatian.

"Nice," says Devon. "And how do you feel about her?"

Nicola says in a serious tone, "I fancy her rotten. Feel I can't live another day without seeing her in the flesh."

"You're really good friends with Jess, aren't you?"

"Yeah, we train our dogs together, and we've been mates since we were the odd ducks in our high school," replies Nicola. "Why?"

"I was wondering what she has to say about this…Megan."

"Oh, she doesn't have much to say about it — she's happy for me, I suppose."

"So you're pretty excited about this visit," Devon says, smiling, though alarm bells have been going off inside her.

"Excited isn't even the word, Devon. I'm out of my head, can't sleep, can't eat, all that." Nicola grabs her hair again and starts mauling it. "I've not dated anyone since my ex left me, and that's eight years ago."

"Oh boy. And…?"

"And?"

"Well, what's going on inside you?"

"I'm nervous as owt!" Nicola jumps up and stalks back and forth. "I don't know what to do or what to wear or anything." She looks utterly miserable.

Devon thinks for a moment. "What if you slowed things down a little and asked Megan to meet you halfway for a meal before she comes all the way here for a weekend?"

"Oh," says Nicola. "I don't think she'd be up for that. She's not one for tapping the brakes. She's sort of more full-speed-ahead."

"How can I help, then?" says Devon in her gentlest voice.

Nicola bursts out laughing again. "I have no idea!"

Devon joins in the laughter, then says, "I have one small suggestion, maybe you've already done it."

"What?" says Nicola eagerly.

"Nice new underwear," says Devon. "Matching bra and…what do you Brits call them, not panties —"

"Knickers," grins Nicola.

"Yeah. I find that really good underwear gives me confidence, don't you?"

Nicola perks up. "It's been years and years since I invested in good underwear, so I don't know, but that's an epic idea. I'll go down town tomorrow and see what I can find."

"Good," says Devon, pleased.

"Thanks so much, Devon. Can we make that reservation now, please?"

After the reservation has been made and paid for, Nicola dashes out to her car, waving her gratitude. Devon watches her, despairing. The bad haircut, the terrible clothes…but most of all, the red, red flags.

∿

Devon knocks lightly on the Guest House door. The door swings open instantly and a smiling Nicola stands staring at Devon. Nicola's face falls. Now she looks tragic.

"Hi, how's it going?" Devon asks.

"Oh, come in," Nicola says morosely.

Devon steps inside. Nicola has the fire on in the sitting room and the place is warm and cozy.

"When's Megan supposed to arrive?"

"She was supposed to be here at four," Nicola says glumly.

"What? It's almost eight. I wondered what was going on, because I didn't see another car pull in."

"I can't get her on the phone," Nicola says. "And no answer to my texts. Maybe she's had some accident on the roads, that's all I can think of." She slouches on the couch and pulls at her hair.

Devon sits next to her. "Shit," Devon says sincerely. "That sucks. When did you last hear from her?"

"Two days ago, finalizing her plan to meet me here. But it's odd, because usually we text every couple of hours, and I didn't hear again from her yesterday, or any time today."

"Mmm hmm," says Devon, her heart sinking in sympathy. "Very strange. Have you checked again?"

"Yes, of course," Nicola says impatiently, bending over her phone. "I've been checking about every fifteen sec— oh, wait — she's just posted something on the social group." She reads for a moment.

"What is it?"

Nicola looks up in disbelief. "It's about a movie she says she's going to see in York tomorrow night. But she'll be here, so how can she see a movie in York...?"

"Message her?"

Nicola types furiously, then exclaims, "I think she's blocked me!" Devon asks Nicola to show her. They review the possibilities.

"Why don't you phone her," Devon suggests.

"I don't know her phone number; we always talked through the social site."

They try a few more ideas, but it gradually becomes incontrovertibly clear to both of them that Megan is avoiding Nicola.

Devon gets a bottle of beer for each of them and Nicola drinks half of hers down right away.

"She's ghosted me, hasn't she," says Nicola, smothering a burp.

"It looks like it. I'm so sorry."

"Bloody, bloody hell. God, I feel like an idiot." Nicola upends the bottle and drinks the rest of her beer in three gulps.

"Easy there, sport," says Devon. "Did you two have a fight or anything?"

Nicola looks off into the distance. "No, no — in fact, last time we talked, she seemed very excited about meeting me."

"Jeez. Rough luck."

They sit in silence for a minute. Finally, Nicola looks up at Devon with a grimace that is trying to be a wry smile. "Bloody hell. Well, I guess I'll go home."

"No, don't be silly. You've paid for the room, why don't you enjoy it? Or I'll refund your money if you like. But I think it would be better for you to stay here. Change of scene for you. I'll make us some dinner, and we can watch TV or play Scrabble or something. Better than being home by yourself, I think, don't you?"

Nicola tears up. Devon pretends not to notice. "Come on, help me in the kitchen. We'll have a good evening regardless of the stupidity of stupid women, whaddaya say?"

Nicola wipes her eyes and laughs. "Sounds all right. Thanks," she adds gruffly.

In the morning, Devon texts Nicola to come over to the Annex for breakfast. Nicola trudges over looking as if the weight of the world is on her shoulders. She slumps at the table and mechanically nibbles at the blueberry pancakes and bacon that Devon has served. She does drink three cups of coffee, though. "Bloody hell, that's good coffee," she says.

Devon smiles at her. "California's finest. Costs me a fortune to have it shipped here, but it's worth it." Nicola smiles weakly and looks again at her plate. She eats a few more forkfuls joylessly.

Devon watches her and debates whether to say what's on her

mind. At last, she pours them both another cup of coffee, and clears her throat. "Nic," she says.

Nicola glances over at her. "Yeh?"

"Have you ever been to the Todmorden Women's Disco at the cricket club?"

Nicola nods. "A few times. Not recently, though. It's a good laugh."

"Well, it's coming up in a week, and I'm thinking of going."

"Good, I'm sure you'll like it," Nicola says morosely.

"Well, I was wondering if you'd like to go with me."

Nicola's eyes widen. Clearly, this is the last thing she expects to come out of Devon's mouth. "With you?" Devon nods. "Like a date?"

Devon smiles. "Like a friend."

"I'm not in the mood to go dancing," Nicola says.

Devon laughs. "I know you're not! Neither am I! But I'm planning to get a little group of single women to go together."

Nicola is mildly interested. "Like who?"

"I'm going to invite Jess, and Kim, and Steph. And anyone else you'd like to add. We could call ourselves the Lonely Butch Girls or something."

Nicola smiles. "Sure, count me in. At least if we don't dance, we can talk to each other."

"Oh, we're going to dance. We're going to dance our classy little butts off."

"I love it," says Nicola quietly, combing back her messy curls and tucking them behind her ears.

"That's more like it," Devon says, clapping her on the back. "And you know what? I'm going to get a snazzy haircut for the occasion. And some new dancing clothes." She pauses. "Would you like to come with me? I don't want to be obnoxious, but you could do with a haircut, couldn't you? And a new outfit?"

Nicola scowls and Devon thinks *uh, oh, I've gone too far*. But Nicola starts to laugh. "I was going to resist, but I see that's useless. Yeah, of course, I could do with a makeover. You know what? I'm always sort of nervous to get my hair cut, I don't know what to ask for, and I'm overly eager to have it over with, so I sit there saying

'Yeah, lovely' when they hold up the mirror for me to inspect their work."

Devon laughs. "I'll be with you. Laura's great, but I'll make sure she gives you plenty of time to see what she's doing. If you'll do that for me as well."

"Of course," smiles Nicola. "But new clothes…"

"We'll find something fabulous, even if we need to go into Manchester. Um, is money a problem?"

Nicola shrugs. "Not really."

"We'll be as spiffy as Anne Lister," Devon promises. "But much, much, much more colorful."

"No stupid ear curls," Nicola warns as she gets up.

"Don't worry."

They make arrangements to meet up later in the week. Devon opens the door for Nicola, and walks out to the car with her. Nicola's sadness seems to have returned, but then after she puts her overnight bag in the car, she surprises Devon by throwing her arms around her and giving her a vigorous hug.

"Thanks, Devon," she mutters, her voice cracking.

"See you Wednesday," Devon says, patting her on the back.

Devon goes back into the Annex. She wanders over to her Aunt Amy-Anne Lister shrine and lights a candle.

What's going on, Aunt Amy? Am I becoming the village wise woman or something? Should I tell everyone I'm just a dumb softball player?

Devon is on her way home from a chilly morning walk in the countryside, looking forward to a bowl of the stew she made last night. The breeze carries the scent of cows, the sound of clucking hens. Devon inhales deeply with enjoyment.

On impulse, instead of going straight down the hill towards home, she pulls a crumpled business card out of her pocket, verifies an address, and heads down a side road lined with small fields and low stone farmhouses. She pushes through a squeaky gate and knocks on the front door of a small, neat cottage.

A furious barking ensues from within. Devon can hear the

crash of paws against the other side of the door, and a woman's voice calmly but firmly telling the dog to stop and sit.

The door opens. Jess is holding Tesla by the collar. The huge dog is barking nonstop. "Good God, shut up! Down! Devon, what a lovely surprise! Come in, come in, before this beast tears my arm off."

Devon enters, submits to the dog's greeting, follows Jess and the dog into the kitchen. They sit and catch up on the latest news, and after a few minutes Jess hits herself in the forehead and says "Where are my manners? Cup of tea? Biscuit?"

At the word "biscuit," Tesla barks with excitement and whirls in a circle. Devon accepts a glass of water. Jess gives a dog biscuit to Tesla, who flops down under the table and gnaws quietly. "How's it going, Devon?"

"Quite well," says Devon. "I actually have two items of business to discuss."

Jess adopts a formal posture. "Please, proceed."

"First of all," Devon says, "I'm putting a little group together to go to the Todmorden Women's Disco next week. Would you like to join us?"

Jess holds up a finger. "Great minds!" She reaches over to a file box on the kitchen counter, rummages in it, then holds up a ticket. "I'm already going! They're having a Motown night!"

"Oh, wonderful! Do you have a date?"

Jess laughs. "Who, me? No, I seem to be eternally single. Oh well, that's why we have dogs." She pats Tesla. "Who else are you inviting?"

Devon says, "Steph, you, Kim, and me, and Nicola."

"Nic, eh? I wouldn't think this was her cup of tea."

"What, dancing?"

"Going out and that sort of thing."

"She seems pretty enthusiastic about it. You know, when I first saw the two of you at the rugby practice, I thought she was your girlfriend."

Jess laughs. "She's a good lass. But we've been mates since we were teenagers."

"And?" says Devon.

Jess laughs again. "And…I can't imagine feeling romantic towards her."

"Hmm. And the other thing I wanted to ask about was the dog."

Jess jumps to her feet, excited, and fetches her phone. "I was going to get in touch with you this week. I think I've found one. Want to see her picture?"

Devon sees a photo of a cute black and white dog, its tongue lolling out. It looks like a happy animal.

"Her name's Walker," Jess says.

"Oh, like Ann Walker?"

"Exactly. Her owner, Polly, is moving to Dublin soon and can't take her. Polly's gutted about it."

Devon sighs and hands the phone back. "I still haven't decided whether I can take a dog on. She does look very sweet, though."

"Tell you what," says Jess. "I'll ask Polly if I can take Walker out for a trial run, and if so, I'll bring her over to your place. What do you think?"

"Yeah, wonderful!"

"Right then. Look, I have to feed the bloody chickens. Want to come with me, or…"

Devon gets up. "No, thanks a lot — see you at the disco, then."

Jess throws her hands up and does a creditable imitation of Gloria Gaynor: "Once I was afraid, I was petrified…"

Devon rolls her eyes and joins in for the next few lines. Then they run out of lyrics that they remember, and Devon strides off toward home, enjoying the sunny afternoon and thinking of how nice it would be to have a dog walking beside her.

Nicola's doorbell rings. Tonight is the disco outing. She opens her front door and sees Devon, wearing black blazer and trousers with a white T-shirt. Devon is singing, in a loud falsetto.

"I want to put on my my my my my boogie shoes — and boogie with you…"

Nicola pulls her into the house. "What will the neighbors think?" she scolds. "I have my reputation to consider!"

"Yeah, right," scoffs Devon. She looks Nicola up and down.

Nicola strikes a voguing pose. "Turn around," says Devon, and Nicola turns around slowly. "Nic," says Devon.

"Devon."

"I'm dead serious. I want you to take this in, all right?"

"Eh?"

"What I'm about to say. I want you to absorb it. Okay? Are you ready?"

"Yeah, what?"

"You look absolutely spectacular," Devon says in an awed voice. Nicola waves her arms to dispel the compliment, but she is blushing with pleasure. "I was with you for the haircut, and I was with you for the clothes buying, but to see the whole look!" Devon whistles. Nicola is wearing a dazzling white jacket embroidered with lines of sequins down both arms, over a scarlet boatneck silk shirt and the skinniest of skinny black jeans that make her look even taller than she is. Her haircut is flattering — elegant and short, highlighted with the faintest touch of scarlet to match her shirt.

"Stop," says Nicola weakly.

"No, I'm being dead, dead serious. You look amazing."

"Really?"

"Really. That outfit works so well with your long legs. Love the boots, by the way. And the haircut — absolutely fantastic."

Nicola reaches up in an automatic gesture to play with her hair, but it is too short for that, so she just smooths her hand over the sculpted cut. She allows herself to grin with pleasure. "You look great, too, mate," she says shyly. "But may I ask you something? What was it that Laura said about your hands when she was doing your manicure..?"

Automatically, Devon thrusts her hands into her pockets. "I don't know."

"It was so odd, what she said — 'You're not so angry at your fingers these days.' What did she mean?"

Devon puffs. "I have this horrible habit of chewing on my nails when I'm stressed. I guess she noticed that they're not as bad as they used to be."

"That's good, right?"

Devon shrugs, embarrassed. "I guess so! Clean living! Ready

166

to go?" Nicola nods and heads for a closet. "Wait, let's see the coat," Devon orders.

Nicola dons a knee-length black trench coat. "Okay?"

"Oh yeah. Snap that collar up." Nicola obeys. "You look sensational," Devon says sincerely. They head for the door, then Devon says, "Do something for me."

Nicola replies, "Sure, what, mate?"

"I want you to keep your head up when we go in — no slouching, right? — and look around and see who's looking at you."

"Probably nobody."

"Probably everybody."

"We'll see."

"Yes, we will."

After a short drive, Devon and Nicola arrive at the cricket club just outside the village of Todmorden. They can hear the pounding dance music as they park, and Devon is immediately energized by that old feeling of pre-dancing excitement — a feeling that she hasn't had for a long time.

She and Nicola stand in the car park for a moment, watching women enter the building, then Nicola says, "How would Anne Lister enter the hall?" and they stride in the door with as much attitude as they can muster. Inside, a short, thick-set woman in a trilby stands beside a table that bears a row of shot glasses holding various colors of liquids. She takes their tickets and, bellowing over the music, offers them a free shot to start their evening off.

"Free shots? I've never heard of such a thing — this is awesome," shouts Devon, downing a shot of vodka and shuddering as it hits her throat. Nicola takes a shot of something amber-colored and shakes like a wet dog. They hang up their coats and strut into the dance hall. It's dark, but with a good lighting system casting rotating, flashing lights over the crowd.

No one looks at them — everyone is dancing.

The room is not huge. There are round tables at the edges of the room, a bar at the end, and a dance floor with cushioned seating around two sides.

The dance floor is absolutely heaving with women, flailing merrily to a Supremes medley. Right now they are all acting out "Stop! In the Name of Love" with elaborate gestures. Devon, who can't stop grinning, and Nicola mosey around the edge of the crowd. Then Devon grabs Nicola's hand and they work their way into the middle of the dance floor, bumping up against bodies every step of the way. They start to dance together — now it's "Where Did Our Love Go?" — and the old joyful energy surges through Devon, overcoming her inhibitions, setting her feet and hips and arms and legs and shoulders free. Nicola, to her surprise, is a graceful and dynamic dancer. They relax into the music and riff off each other's moves. *Oh my God this is so much fun. If only Larkin were here.*

Devon feels a tap on her shoulder, and turns to see Stephanie, and beyond her, Kim and Jess. Kim dances over and pulls Devon and Nicola into their circle. The five of them dance together, challenging each other to fancier spins, higher jumps, sillier gestures, laughing inaudibly as the music pounds.

After the medley is over, the DJ puts on a slow dance and the five friends, red-faced and sweating, gratefully go to a table and sit. Kim and Stephanie go to get Coronas for everyone. Devon, smirking, watches Jess, who is trying not to make it obvious that she can't take her eyes off of Nicola.

Jess waves at Nicola, trying to get her attention, but the beers arrive and they all clink their bottles together in a toast. "Great disco!" yells Devon, and they all nod and smile. Conversation is impossible.

The slow dance is over and now a Daft Punk song thunders on.

Jess tries again to get Nicola's attention, but at that moment a curvy young woman in a Manchester United jersey puts her hand on Nicola's shoulder and bellows into her ear. Nicola's eyebrows shoot up in alarm, but she nods, and gets up, and the young woman leads her onto the dance floor. Jess watches their departure, eyes wide. Devon chortles to herself.

Devon drinks two beers very quickly and then finds herself pulled back onto the dance floor by Kim. The old magic takes over and she feels the ecstasy — so vital, so rare — of being completely surrounded by women in motion, dancing in groups, in pairs, alone. She flirts shamelessly with a tall redhead and indulges the attentions of two plump, manic, curly-haired girls who look like sisters. Pleasure and excitement shoot like drugs through her veins and she dances completely uninhibited, wild, free, forgetting everything but the raving delight.

Much, much later, after everybody has danced with everybody else over and over again, after laughter and flirting and many trips back to the bar for refills, the last-call lights start to flash and, moaning, they prepare to leave.

Devon is pulling her jacket on as a cute, athletic girl she's been dancing with thrusts a scrap of paper into her hand. It's a name — Katee — and a phone number. Katee winks and disappears back into the crowd. Devon puts the paper into her jeans pocket but doubts that she'll call the girl. Even in the middle of all this riotous enjoyment, she can't help thinking of Larkin and wondering what she's doing, so very far away.

The friends go to the car park and stand in a knot, shivering as their sweat cools, elated, their ears still ringing.

"Great night!" says Kim. "Thanks for getting us together, Dev."

"We should do this every month," Stephanie says.

"Definitely," says Devon. "And let's — oh, I don't know…" she trails off.

"What? Say it!" says Jess.

"Well, I don't want to be one of those touchy-feely Americans you guys despise."

"Too late!" Kim taunts. "Go on, spit it out."

Cornered, Devon blurts, "What do you think of Nic's haircut?"

Jess says, "I hardly recognized you, mate! You look spectacular!" The others concur.

As Nicola is bashfully dealing with the compliments, Devon says, "Well, what I was actually going to say was — we're all single. Why don't we do a sort of informal group, you know, where we watch out for each other and have permission to call each other when we're feeling lonesome? And go dancing and… stuff," she concludes lamely.

"Yes! We'll need a group name," says Stephanie.

"And T-shirts," adds Nicola.

"And a theme song." says Kim.

"And a website," says Jess.

"All right, all right, it's too cold to brainstorm. I'm glad you like the idea," says Devon. "Group hug?" She holds her arms open and they all step away from her. "Too much?"

"Too bloody American," Kim laughs. "The group is a great idea, let's do it. Good night!"

Except for Nicola and Devon, they all pile into Jess' van. Nicola gets into Devon's car. Feeling a little tipsy, Devon drives very carefully the few miles back to Nicola's house.

Nicola says, "Wow, Devon. I feel like a new person."

"It was a great night, wasn't it!"

"The best night I've had in ages."

Devon parks in front of Nicola's house. They lean across the seats and give each other a quick, firm hug. Nicola says, "The group is just such a lovely idea. I do hope we can pull it off."

Devon squeezes her arm and says, "We'll make it happen." Nicola grins and gets out of the car with a wave.

Devon drives home carefully but quickly. She stands, shivering, in the courtyard for a moment. "Good night," she whispers to the starlit darkness. "I'm starting to feel like a real part of this place."

She goes into her cozy little home and feels the shimmering presence of something that feels like hope.

This is Walker

Devon is shopping in downtown Halifax. She has just gotten into her car when her mobile buzzes with a text. It's from Jess.

- I'm at Polly's. I can borrow Walker if you'd like to meet her.

- *Yes, I'll be home in an hour.*

- Super. I'll bring her to yours.

Devon is ridiculously excited. She looks up pet-supply shops and finds one not too far away. She drives over and goes in. It's a tiny shop, overflowing with all manner of pet supplies. Shuddering, she notices a pile of something that turns out to be frozen rodents. She pokes around a bit, remembering Baxter, and feeling a bit sad.

The cheery man behind the counter comes over to her. "May I help you find anything?"

Devon smiles. "I might be getting a dog soon, and thought I should see what kind of investment I'll need to make in supplies."

"What's the breed?"

"I don't know, exactly. Sort of middle-sized. A friend is getting me the dog."

"Well, whether it's a Great Dane or a chihuahua, you'll need a few basic items."

The man leads Devon up and down the aisles of the shop, and within a few minutes, Devon has made notes of the cost of a heap of dog supplies, including bowls, toys, a bed, and two leashes ("leads"), as well as food and a bag of treats. The total is significant but she can handle it.

"I'll just take this little bag of treats for now," she says.

"No charge for that, m'love."

"Really?"

"Yes. I hope you like your dog, and do come back for anything you need," says the man.

Devon thanks him and hurries back to her car. Her other shopping can wait.

Back at the house, she puts the kettle on and paces up and down in the sitting room. She is more excited than seems logical or sensible. Ever since she saw Walker's photo, she's been envisioning a whole new life with a dog — a companion for her hikes, a living being to care for, a warm animal to curl up with in the evenings.

Jess' van pulls into the courtyard and Devon trots outside and waves to her. Jess waves back cheerily as she gets out. "Ready to meet a real cutie?" Jess asks.

"Yes," says Devon. Jess opens the back door of the van and clips a lead onto the collar of a handsome mid-sized black and white dog. The dog jumps out, looking around and sniffing the cobblestones with a lively curiosity. Jess gives a light tug on the dog's lead and they enter the house. The dog bounces a bit with enthusiasm and goes to jump on Devon — but "Sit," says Jess, and the dog obeys, panting.

Devon goes to pat the dog. Walker sniffs her hand thoroughly and then leans heavily on her leg and looks up at Devon with an expression of total trust. Jess lets her off the lead and the dog wanders around the house, sniffing at everything and then coming back to Devon and leaning on her again. Devon gives her a treat from her pocket and the dog eats it happily.

"I think she's in love," laughs Jess.

"I think I am, too," says Devon, stroking the soft white fur on the dog's head. "Hello, Walker," she says. The dog's pointed ears perk up at the sound of her name.

"Polly absolutely hates having to give her up, but she's moving soon."

"And does Walker like to go for walks?"

Walker hears the word and quivers with excitement.

"Yes, she loves them."

"And runs, too?"

The dog barks and pants. Devon laughs, delighted by this alert personality.

"She loves to go for runs," Jess says. "She's spayed, had all her shots, and she's been very well trained, as you can see."

Devon and Jess settle into chairs at the kitchen table. Walker lies down between them with a deep sigh, closes her eyes, and goes straight to sleep.

"She's beautiful," says Devon.

"Isn't she? I love grooming her," says Jess. "Do you want her?"

"I'm not sure," says Devon, torn. "I have to think about a few things. Does Polly need to know right away?"

"Pretty soon," says Jess. "Why don't you pop over to her house tomorrow and take Walker out for a bit?"

Devon agrees. She pours tea for Jess and herself. Smiling brightly, she says, "I had the best time ever at the disco, did you?"

Jess picks up her cup and clears her throat. "Um." She takes a sip of tea. "Yes. Yes, I did."

Devon waits.

Jess takes a deep breath and says, "Hypothetically, Dev. Have you ever had a friend turn into a girlfriend?"

Devon thinks carefully and replies, honestly, "No, I haven't. I don't know why not, though. Hypothetically, why do you ask?"

Jess laughs. "It's the silliest thing. Nic…" she trails off.

"Didn't she look sensational at the disco?"

"Yes, and I'm so embarrassed."

Devon waits. At last, Jess resumes. "I haven't had many relationships, but they've always been with very feminine girls. So — Nic and I, we've been mates for ever and I've never thought of her as anything but just that, you know, a pal. But somehow, that haircut, and those clothes — even her posture looked different. I found that I really fancied her, and it knocked me for six."

"Confusing?"

"Yes, absolutely, very confusing. I mean, one minute she's my pal, you know, like an old comfy armchair or something, and the next she's this glamorous…creature."

Devon nods sagely. "Of course, that's confusing."

Jess runs her fingers through her hair. "I can't stop thinking about her, and wondering what it would be like to, you know, date her."

"Only one way to find out, I guess," says Devon.

Jess grimaces and rubs her face with both hands. "Ask her out, you mean?"

Devon says, "Sure. You don't have to say it's a date. Just do something normal, something you'd do anyway."

Jess says, "We only ever do dog stuff together."

"You want to break out of that pattern. How about a movie?"

"Hmm, I suppose that's not a bad idea."

"Take her someplace nice for dinner first. Don't let her pay. Treat her like a lady."

"Should I tell her how I feel?"

"Not at this stage. Be subtle."

Jess laughs. "That's not really my style."

"So tell her how great she looks, ask her questions about herself."

"We know each other inside and out, I think, after all these years."

"Well then, ask her about her hopes and dreams. Or see the film first, and talk about it over dinner. Come on, Jess, you can do this."

"Why am I so nervous, then?"

"Because this is a kind of a seismic shift for you. But do you think you'd be well suited as a couple, provided the chemistry's there?"

Jess lights up. "Oh, yes, absolutely. We like all the same things and in all these years we've never had so much as a friendly squabble. I was a wee bit jealous when she was dating a woman from Sheffield a few years ago, and I suppose that should have clued me in that I might have these feelings for her, lying dormant, as it were."

"Don't overthink it," says Devon. "Just be natural."

"I suppose I can do that," smiles Jess.

"It's exciting, isn't it?"

"Excruciating," Jess responds. "Now then, Devon, if you don't mind my asking, do you ever hear from Larkin?"

"Not often," says Devon, a pang streaking through her heart. "She's deeply involved in a project to help women and children who have been affected by the floods."

"Oh, good for her," Jess responds. "What a godawful mess."

At that moment, Walker comes to life. She executes a perfect downward dog pose, stands, and woofs. Jess laughs. "Time to go back home to Polly, eh, Walker?" Jess puts Walker back on her lead. "Thanks for the brew and chat, Dev," she says.

Devon shows them out. "Thanks for bringing her over," she says, patting Walker as the dog jumps up into the back of Jess' van. "She's really lovely. Let me think for a day or two and I'll give you a call."

"Do, mate, and don't leave it too long — I know Polly wants to settle her soon."

"All right," agrees Devon.

"And thanks for the kind advice about Nic," says Jess. "Wish me courage!"

"I do! You'll be fine!" Devon watches the van drive away into the darkening late afternoon, then closes her door with a sigh.

Though she has longed for a dog, she wonders about taking on this extra layer of responsibility — one that will tie her more firmly to this place and this life that she is building here. *How will I be able to leave, even for a brief vacation, if I have a dog as well as the B&B to care for?*

～

A Real Artist?

Christmas and New Year's have come and gone, with a noisy gathering of the Lonely Butches at Devon's on Boxing Day and a group of shivering Australian guests over New Year's.

These days, as winter looks as if it will never end, the guest house is quiet, with only an occasional visitor or two at the weekends, and Devon awakens every day full of an almost frantic energy. The minute she is free from B&B duties, she tears outdoors with her sketching satchel.

As soon as she has hiked to a place with a good view of the moors, sat herself on her portable stool, set out her thermos of coffee, and taken out her sketchpad and pencil, she can feel her blood pressure plummeting and a sense of fully alive contentment wash over her.

On these sketching days, she stays out sketching in ink and watercolor until she is frozen, stiff, starving, and tired, and returns home feeling emptied out, used up in a way that she has never experienced before. It's both exhausting and deeply gratifying.

Then she spends most of the afternoon and evening translating her pencil and watercolor sketches into acrylic paintings on canvas.

She falls into bed at night with no thoughts in her head except where she will go to sketch the next morning. She is forgetting what day it is and whether she has eaten or not.

One bright morning when the weather looks promising, Devon trots upstairs to her studio to corral some supplies for her day's excursion, and to her dismay notices that she has only three blank canvases left, and that all her paint tubes are totally depleted. *Wow, I've been painting a lot,* she realizes with some surprise. She starts making a list of what she needs.

Her phone buzzes. It's Jess. Devon's heart gives a little jump as she thinks of Walker. She is still undecided about taking the dog on.

"Hey, Jess, how are you? How are things going with Nic?" There is a silence and Devon worries that she's overstepped. "Jess? I'm sorry if I'm being too nosy —"

Jess whispers into the phone. "It's going well, she's here now." Devon laughs. "Great to hear!"

Jess returns, with her normal voice. "I'll have to tell you more the next time we talk. But look, why I'm calling — Polly really needs to know what to do about the dog. Do you want Walker or not?"

"I'm deciding right now. I'll call you this evening, all right?"

"Of course. I'm sure if you don't want her, it will be easy enough to get her adopted — she's a lovely dog."

"Of course she is. I'll call you later."

Devon puts the phone away with a pang, as she remembers how much it costs to keep a dog.

She paces around the studio, brooding. Then she decides to look through the work she's been doing. She sets up the easel and puts one canvas at a time on it. During this month of obsessive work, she has produced a stack of about two dozen paintings. Looking at them one at a time, with a critical eye, she feels goosebumps rise on her arms.

She loves them. She loves what she's created. Most of all, she loves this land. For a moment, that love sinks deeply into her and she allows herself to immerse into a totally unfamiliar sense of pride. *Maybe I'm finally becoming a real artist.* And even more than that, she finds a sense of true belonging. She can feel the land beneath and around her reaching her, embracing her; her bones feel connected to the rocks and fields.

But this is swiftly followed by a cascade of worries. Because she has done almost nothing but paint for weeks, she has done little to promote the guest house, and her cash flow has suffered accordingly. She will have to take a break from painting for a while, and hustle for some income. And what will she decide about the dog?

She pulls out her phone and looks again at an email Glo sent yesterday. It's one of a series of frequent messages from Glo begging to see Devon's work, mentioning a gallery she knows in San Francisco. Devon has been putting her off because she doesn't want to take the time away from painting. But now, she sets up some lights and takes a decent photo of each of her favorite dozen paintings and sends them to Glo.

- Just to see what you have to say, Glo. No pressure, I'm having fun.

And that evening, sitting in front of the fire in her lonely, quiet house, Devon makes another decision and pulls out her phone again.

- Jess, yes please, I would like to adopt Walker. Can you tell Polly I'll be over to get her tomorrow? Thanks. And I'd love to get your personal update! Meet me for a pint and tell me about it?

Devon sends the text and puts herself to bed with happy visions of a dog romping around the place and sleeping at the foot of her bed.

~

These Women Are Magnificent

Devon is working in the guest house kitchen on this Thursday afternoon, setting out the ingredients for the weekend's breakfasts and blasting a classic Willie Colón album. Walker has been for a long walk with Devon this morning and is now napping beneath the kitchen table.

The guest house will have all four rooms full this weekend — guests at the wedding of two women who met through the fan group. Devon is a bit envious, though she's not sure she ever wants to be actually married. Still, it must be nice to have someone love you that much.

Thoughts of Larkin rise unbidden. It's been so many months since they spent those three days together. Devon's heart is still sore and angry whenever she remembers that brief, passionate time. *I was an absolute idiot for ever thinking things would work out between us. Obviously, I'm way down low on her priority list. I was such a fool to think I could be at the top of it.*

She wrenches her thoughts away from Larkin and focuses on the task at hand: mixing the dry ingredients for a big batch of cachapas. She sees that she'll need another bag of cornmeal, and scribbles a note on her shopping list. Just as she finishes writing it, the phone buzzes. She rushes to mute the sound system and answers the call.

It's Claire. "Hello, love, it's been too long since we've seen each other. All right?"

"Yeah, I'm okay, how about you?"

"Things are a bit crap, actually. My wife's brother is in hospital in Leeds, very ill, and the family is gathering round him."

"Oh, I'm so sorry, Claire."

"Yes, well, thank you, but the reason I'm calling is to give you a heads-up that Larkin phoned me yesterday, beside herself with stress about the shelter project she's working on."

Devon's heart thuds. "Oh. Well, we haven't communicated in months."

Claire sighs. "I know, love. But she's in this sort of emergency situation now, running out of money from their original grant from the Red Cross. And things have been absolutely hellish over there."

"Sorry, Claire, but I don't see how this involves me."

"Well, it's just that — because of my family situation, I didn't have time to talk with her properly, so I suggested she might call you. I wanted to let you know in advance because I know you've been so upset with her."

"Yes," Devon says simply.

"I did suggest that she get in touch with Imara, but knowing Imara, she might not get far — anyway, please, if she does phone you, give her a bit of a chance, all right? Look, I have to run, I'm catching the 3:10."

"Thanks for letting me know, Claire. And I hope your brother-in-law is okay."

"Bye, love."

The call ends. Devon gets back to her breakfast prep, her heart pounding, her attention distracted by the work of trying to keep her pain under control. Her months-old hurt and rage come roaring back at the very idea of hearing from Larkin. Gradually, she calms down, but her thoughts are as black as night.

As she finishes the last batch of cachapas and puts them in the fridge, her phone dings again, bringing her heart into her throat. But it's just Imara. Devon's heartbeat returns to normal after a couple of deep breaths, and she answers the call.

Imara launches in with no introduction. "Have you heard this about Larkin? This is what she gets for staying in that awful place. That shelter is out of money, and she called me to see if I could make a donation or start a fundraiser or something."

"What did you say?"

"I said of course not, we're all having enough trouble making ends meet as it is. I told her to come home, she has friends and family here."

"You've known her for a long time...?"

Imara snorts. "Of course. We dated for two years in high school. We came out together."

"Do you think she will? Come home?"

Imara sounds exasperated. "Probably not! When has that girl ever done anything sensible? And she sounded awful. Completely knackered."

For an instant, the armor around Devon's heart opens an inch. She clears her throat. "Well, is there anything I can do for you?"

Imara sighs. "No. I just wanted to tell you, she might call you."

"Did she say she was going to?"

"No, I suggested it."

Devon barks a laugh. "Thanks a lot."

"Oh, don't worry, she probably won't. Hey, I've got to run. Bye now."

Devon throws herself into a frenzy of dusting the guest rooms. When she's finished, she goes back to the Annex and lies on her couch, catching her breath and starting to feel almost peaceful.

Her phone dings again. It's Larkin. Devon stares at the phone for a long time before answering.

"Hello, Dev?"

Devon would recognize that voice anywhere. The armor clangs shut around her heart again. She struggles to breathe normally.

Larkin sounds hesitant, shy. "I'm so, so sorry I haven't been in touch, Dev. It's been...I can't describe it."

"It's all right," Devon grinds out.

"How is the guest house doing?"

"It's fine, we have a full house this weekend."

"That's wonderful." The voice is flat.

"What's going on?"

"Oh, everything — I'm calling because — oh, Devon, it's overwhelming. I'm so tired."

She starts weeping as if her heart is breaking. Devon waits patiently, the armor opening just a little again as she hears Larkin's exhausted sobbing and the story she has to tell.

She is in a rural area, living in a quonset hut with five aid workers. Most of the men from the village have long since gone to the cities for work. The floods left many women and children on their own in destroyed or damaged homes. They are in danger from bands of marauding men, and there have been numerous rapes. There is little security, no medical aid, and no reliable source of clean water or decent food. Larkin is working desperately with local women and a handful of foreign aid workers to create a clinic and shelter with a canteen. She's also documenting their stories in photos and videos, trying to get support for the shelter. "These women are magnificent. I'm in absolute awe of their courage, their ingenuity," she says. "But there's nothing to work with — no money, no supplies," Larkin says in a rough, exhausted voice. "I just had to talk to you," she adds, tearfully.

The conversation peters out simply because Larkin has no energy left to talk. Devon glances at her little statue of Anne Lister and takes a deep breath. Her personal pain lowers a little and a spirit of determination shoots through her. She stands up, squares her shoulders.

"Larkin. We're going to try to do something to help."

"You are? What?"

"I don't know. Don't count on it. But if we wanted to make a donation, how would we get it to you?"

"Oh, Dev, really?" Larkin starts crying again, but controls her voice enough to dictate the information to Devon.

Devon takes it down carefully and says, "Go get some sleep."

"All right. Thanks for listening."

"No problem."

Devon ends the call and thinks for a moment, feelings cascading through her. The predominant, reluctant, feeling is one of admiration for Larkin. What she's doing out there. And worry for her. And deep gratitude for the strong walls of her house, the warm dog at her feet, and the ample food in her fridge.

She picks up the phone again and calls Kim. "Are you free this afternoon or this evening for a talk?"

"Sure, mate, want to come for a cuppa right now?"

"Great. Thanks." Devon runs out and jumps in her car.

Devon and Kim have been brainstorming for an hour and a half. Kim's kitchen table is covered with sheets of paper with ideas scrawled on them. Finally, Kim makes a third pot of tea and calls for a break. Devon's neck is sore and stiff, and she has the beginning of a tension headache.

"Why don't we get up and stretch a bit, mate?" says Kim, and they walk around Kim's small, neat flat, whirling their arms, and then giving each other shoulder rubs until they are a bit more relaxed.

With the fresh pot of tea and a plate of Kim's miniature scones in front of them, they look over their notes.

"What do we have in all this mess?" asks Kim.

"Let's each circle the best ideas," says Devon. They work at that for a few minutes. Finally, Devon tosses her pen down. "We have a winner, don't we?"

Kim nods. "Yeah, a raffle, plus a silent auction. It's a great idea, and it won't cost us anything."

Devon says sadly, "I was envisioning a fabulous gala."

Kim pats her on the shoulder. "Don't be daft. Think how much more work that would be."

"All right, we'll have the silent auction at my place."

"We'll need three or four really great items for the raffle, especially if we're going to sell tickets to everyone we know, not just our crowd."

"How much do you think we can actually raise in a month?"

"Depends," says Kim, tugging at her forelock. "I'd think two thousand quid."

"That doesn't sound like very much."

"Just remember, it'll go a lot further over there."

"All right, that's our goal, then."

They look at each other, eyes wide, and in unison scream quietly. Kim claps her hands together. "Well, we'd better get started."

They make lists of people to contact, and divvy up the names. Then they make up an information page ready to post on the social networks. Devon sends a quick text to Larkin asking her to send some photos of the project and the women she wants to serve.

By midnight, Devon and Kim are exhausted and elated. Devon folds up a sheaf of notes and to-do lists and shrugs into her jacket.

"Thanks so much, Kim," she says, throwing her arm around her shoulder.

Kim thumps her back and replies, "Thank you, mate, for getting this started. It couldn't be more important."

Devon heads for the door, then turns. "Um, look. Awkward. Would you be the point person on this?"

Kim looks at her quizzically. "Eh?"

"Things between Larkin and me are…strained. I don't want to be the public face of this, at all. If you'd be willing to be the contact person with Larkin…"

"Of course, mate. No worries at all. I understand."

Devon drives back through the dark roads with a confused jumble of feelings in her mind. When she enters her house, she has one task uppermost in her mind. After letting Walker out and feeding her, Devon trots up to her studio and rummages until she finds the photo that Larkin sent her so many months ago. Nandita, the thin soccer-playing girl.

She props it up where she'll see it first thing in the morning. She'll get it properly framed and hang it in the guest house, to remind her guests as well as herself that they are connected to a wider world of women.

∼

Devon is raking leaves in the courtyard when Kim stops by to show her the design for a flyer to advertise the silent auction.

Devon looks it over quickly. "Love it," she says. "How are you doing soliciting donations?"

Kim grins. "Really well, mate. The women's disco gave us five pairs of tickets, Laura offered a perm or dye job, um, Jesse is offering a dozen eggs every fortnight for a year...and the deluxe weekend at the Guest House is sure to be a big hit."

"That's fantastic!" Devon is delighted. "Well done!"

"Hey, can I come in for a minute? Larkin sent a video."

"Is it any good?"

"I don't know, I've been waiting for you so we could watch it together."

They go into the guest house. Devon fires up her laptop and they stand next to each other watching the two-minute video. Larkin has recorded heartbreaking scenes of shattered houses, small children dressed in rags, teenagers carrying heavy pails of water, painfully thin women begging by the roadside. The wordless sound track consists of soft, sad cello music as one scene follows another.

The last few scenes show glimmers of hope, and feature more upbeat music — women working in teams on the shelter building, smiling children eating from full bowls, nurses giving inoculations to a long line of elders.

Near the end, Larkin's voice comes in over the music. She says a few words about the rebuilding efforts and what kind of support the shelter is looking for, and the screen shows contact information for donations.

At the very end, a familiar face —Nandita, playing soccer with a real ball instead of the bundle of rags. She looks taller and more robust than she did in Larkin's photo of several months ago, but her devilish smile is the same as she kicks the ball past a hapless goalie and lifts her arms in triumph.

The video ends. Kim looks at Devon. They both have tears in their eyes. They laugh, embarrassed.

Kim clears her throat. "I think that might help."

Imara: Winter

Imara has reserved a room, and Devon has decidedly mixed feelings. The last time Imara stayed at the guest house, she texted Devon three times in one evening to ask for more towels, more heat, and a better wi-fi connection. Devon came very close to reminding her that Miss Lister's was not a five-star hotel with a big staff, but she restrained herself.

So it is with a bit of an attitude that Devon greets Imara when she arrives at four p.m. with her usual brusque demand for help with her suitcases.

Devon goes to Imara's car and carries her two bags into the foyer. Then she puts them down and stands with them, holding them hostage. Imara demands, "Would you take them up to my room, please?"

Devon answers in a laconic way, "Sure. Oh, I did hear from Larkin. And it seems she's in need of some funds to get her shelter project off the ground." Imara rolls her eyes. "So we're going to help her with a fundraiser. A silent auction and raffle. We're trying to raise two thousand pounds."

"Yes?"

"And I wondered — since you have such good contacts locally — if you might be willing to contact some of your artist friends to see if they'd contribute some paintings."

Imara nods thoughtfully. "I might be able to do that. Text me all the details, all right? And now, I'd really like to unpack, so…"

Devon reaches for the bags, then, as if a sudden thought has hit her, she stops herself and says, "Oh, and you're friends with Perry, aren't you?"

"Yes, quite good friends."

Devon claps in delight. "Then you'd be just the person to contact her."

"What for?"

"To see if she might offer some personalized poems — you know, the highest bidder can get a poem written about a subject of their choice —"

Imara snaps her fingers. "A better idea would be for her to do a benefit poetry reading."

"Excellent idea! So you'll speak to her while you're here?"

"I think so, yes, why not," says Imara thoughtfully. "I thought I might stop by to see her this evening, actually, surprise her at the White Horse."

"Oh, is that where she's working?"

"Yes, she's there every Wednesday night."

"Super!" Devon picks up Imara's bag.

"Am I in the Chaumière?"

Devon winces. "I'm afraid not — we have a full house, so I thought you might like to try the Argus Room this time, would that be all right?"

"I expect so," says Imara gracelessly, and Devon follows her up the stairs, lugging Imara's remarkably heavy bags.

On Thursday morning, the other three guests have nearly finished their breakfast by the time Imara comes down. They try to make conversation with her, asking Imara to recommend local attractions, but Imara dives into her phone and replies to their friendly overtures with monosyllables. The other three leave the guest house with profuse thanks to Devon for their breakfasts.

Devon puts an insulated carafe on the table in front of Imara.

"What's this?"

"I thought you might like your own carafe of coffee, so it doesn't get cold," Devon explains. Imara looks pleased, and pours herself a cup.

"It really is quite decent coffee," she says, sipping.

"What would you like? You can have a full English. Or porridge and fruit."

"Two eggs, cooked through, a piece of brown toast, and beans, please."

"You got it!" Devon replies cheerily. She makes the order quickly and serves it within a few minutes. Imara eats it quickly and apparently appreciatively. Devon comes back in to collect the plates and see if Imara wants anything else.

"No thanks, I'm just going to read for a while and drink the rest of this carafe, if that's all right," Imara replies, speaking a little more warmly than before.

As Devon puts the dishes on a tray, she snaps her fingers as if just recalling something, and turns back. "Did you get to speak to Perry about the auction?"

"No," says Imara, blushing.

"You didn't see her?"

"Well, I saw her. I mean, I was at the pub. We chatted a little but — well…" She looks down, and Devon realizes it's the first time she's seen Imara look any way other than totally confident. "…I just didn't get around to asking her."

Devon doesn't have to fake her disappointment. "That's too bad. I was hoping to get her commitment by this coming weekend. Will you be seeing her again, by any chance?"

Imara stirs her coffee studiously. "I was thinking of going back this evening. I think they're going to have live music."

"That would be great!" Devon says, then pauses. Gently, she says, "Sometimes people are a bit shy about asking their friends to donate things…you know?"

To Devon's surprise, Imara looks her full on, and looks as if she's about to cry. "I really want to help. But I just can't seem to ask Perry. I don't know what to do — I'm never shy!" She grips her linen napkin as if she wants to strangle it.

Devon sits at the table and thinks for a moment about how to approach this. She looks around the dining room and her eyes fall on a framed quotation from Anne Lister's diaries, a passage in code that means "have some courage." *How ridiculous to be nervous about this woman. I don't want to lose her as a customer, that's all.*

"Why do you think you're shy about this?" she asks, as gently as possible. Imara doesn't respond, and Devon decides to plow on. "Do you think you might have a crush on her?"

Imara snorts. "A crush?" She is looking everywhere but at Devon. "Of course not, I don't get crushes," she says disdainfully. "I admire her, that's all."

"Lots of us admire Perry, but we don't have a hard time talking to her," says Devon.

There is a pause as Imara stirs her coffee. "All right, maybe I do have some feelings for her."

"Nothing to be embarrassed about," says Devon with a smile. "I'm sorry I put you in this position. I'll get someone else to ask her about the fundraiser. I'm sure Kim wouldn't mind. Or Steph. I was just hoping for someone with business experience…"

"No, no, I'll do it," says Imara hurriedly. "I do have the business experience — enough to wheedle a bit of extra value out of her."

"Fantastic," Devon says, relieved. She stands and picks up the dishes. "Tonight?"

"I'll try," Imara replies.

"You can do it!" Devon encourages her. As she is about to leave the room, Imara speaks again, hesitantly.

"This isn't like me, you know. I'm never shy with women. It's quite annoying." She laughs, harshly. "Crazy, eh?"

"No," says Devon, emphatically. "Hold on a moment." She pushes open the swinging door to the kitchen, puts the tray down, returns immediately to the dining room. "No, it's not crazy at all. It shows you have real feelings for her. She's a very attractive woman, after all." Imara looks tragic. "But you are, too," Devon says hastily, and sincerely. Imara is very pretty — at least, when she's not looking petulant.

"Thank you," says Imara.

"You know," says Devon slowly, wondering what she's about to say next, "Being a little uncertain, a little vulnerable, is much more interesting than being on top of things all the time."

Imara looks at her quizzically. "How's that?"

"Being competent all the time leaves no space for someone else to come into your life. I mean, look at Anne Lister. She was very vulnerable when she met Ann Walker. She talked a good game, and came across as very sure of herself, but really she was probably nervous as hell that she'd scare Ann Walker off. A little vulnerability is very appealing."

"Really?" Imara is thinking it over. "Perry doesn't seem to have any vulnerabilities."

Devon laughs. "Oh, sure she does. Every time she gets up to read a new poem in front of an audience — didn't you notice how she was sweating when she did that reading last month? And it was a cold night!"

"I didn't notice," Imara admits.

"Let her see that you're a bit shy with her. She'll know what's up. No need to hide it."

"I don't know…" Imara trails off.

"Well, best of luck, whatever you decide," Devon says. "But let me know in a day or two if you don't feel brave enough, and I'll enlist someone else to approach her."

"No, no, no," Imara protests. "I'll do it."

"That's the spirit!" Devon grins. "I'm rooting for ya." She goes back into the kitchen and Imara stays, sipping the last of her coffee and contemplating the "Have some courage" sign.

Imara sits at the bar, unseen by Perry, who is organizing some receipts. The pub is quiet at eleven-thirty in the morning.

"What'll it be, love?" Perry asks over her shoulder.

"An Irish coffee, please."

"Right you are, love," Perry says without turning around. "It'll be a minute."

"But only if you make it with Tullamore Dew."

"I don't think we have that, love," Perry says, finally turning around. "Oh, it's you, Imara! What a nice surprise!" She leans over the bar and kisses Imara on the cheek. "Did you really want that?"

Imara blushes but smiles seductively. "The kiss?"

Perry puts her hands on her hips and looks sideways at Imara. "The Irish coffee."

"Not really, I really want just a glass of chablis and a word with you when you get a minute."

"A glass of chablis, right you are, no problem. A word…I'll be on my break in ten minutes; we can chat then, if that's all right."

"That sounds lovely."

"Why don't you sit over in the corner there, and I'll join you in a bit," says Perry.

Imara sits where Perry has indicated, and enjoys the quiet of the normally noisy pub on this winter morning. She has butterflies in her belly, which she can scarcely believe. *I'm too sophisticated for this crush business, surely.* She pulls out her phone and scans her emails — but all her awareness is on Perry, who she can see from the corner of her eye, polishing glasses, opening a wine bottle, calling back to her boss that she's taking a break.

Finally, Perry joins Imara, presenting the wine with a flourish and also setting down a bottle of ginger beer for herself. Perry sits with a grateful sigh, folding her long legs under the low table. Her knee touches Imara's and she pulls it away. "Sorry."

Imara reaches over and pulls Perry's knee back. "That's all right," she purrs.

Perry's eyebrows rise and then she smiles. Imara's butterflies flap their wings faster, and she notices that she's incredibly turned on.

"Cheers," Imara says. Perry clinks her bottle against Imara's wineglass, and they drink, looking quickly into each other's eyes and then away.

"How've you been? Done any more hill-walking?" Perry teases.

"No," Imara says, making an effort to smile back. "I'm not insane. Actually, though, I wanted to ask you about this fundraiser for Larkin's project. Have you heard about it?"

"Indeed I have!" Perry says. "I've heard all about it, and I've been trying to think how I might help. Those poor bloody women."

"Yes," says Imara. "Well, that's great, because we think you should organize a poetry evening and donate the proceeds."

"Oh!" says Perry. She thinks for a moment. "I love that idea. Very do-able. We could hold it at the cafe."

"I'll help you with publicity and so on," says Imara. "It needs to happen soon."

Perry thinks for a moment. "I bet we could get a few other poets to help, as well. I'm certain we could raise a couple of hundred quid, at least."

"Wonderful!" exclaims Imara, exceedingly grateful that she doesn't have to do a sales pitch in her state of mingled arousal and embarrassment. "Would you talk to Devon about it? She's organizing the whole thing."

"Of course," says Perry. "I'll phone her tomorrow, first thing."

"Brilliant."

They both sip their drinks, smiling at each other. Imara tries to think of something to say. *I'm never this tongue-tied.* Then a male voice bellows from the back room, "Perry, love, I see customers walking up."

"I'll be right there," shouts Perry, giving Imara an apologetic shrug as she stands up. The street door swings open, admitting a group of raucous men in business suits.

Imara's heart sinks, but then Perry leans down over the table under the pretext of straightening a beer coaster. She says softly, "How long are you in town?"

"Till Sunday."

Perry smiles and Imara's heart starts beating again. "I finally saved enough to fix my bike. Would you be at all interested in going for a little ride and a picnic with me on Saturday? It's supposed to be sunny, if you can believe that. Or if you'd prefer, there's a decent film playing at the Vue."

"Lovely," says Imara, suddenly dry-mouthed.

A customer at the bar whistles loudly for service and Perry shouts, "Just a moment!" then turns back to Imara. "Oh, good. One o'clock suit you?"

"Yes, please," whispers Imara.

Perry smiles at her, taking a backwards step toward the bar. "Which — motorcycle or film?"

"Either, both," Imara says, wondering at herself. "Whatever you like."

"Whoo!" Perry says, pretending to wipe sweat off her forehead. With a wink, she turns back to her customers, leaving Imara with heat burning in her cheeks and a throbbing down below.

The Proceeds

Kim, Devon, and Stephanie are huddled around Devon's kitchen table. Pads of grid paper, pencils, rubber-banded bundles of five- and ten-pound notes, and a laptop are all being deployed to sort and add up the proceeds from the auction.

Because they are also drinking bottles of beer, the results keep coming up differently, so there is some exasperated disputing of the figures.

A motorcycle pulls into the courtyard. "Must be Perry," says Devon.

"Wasn't that poetry reading beyond belief?" asks Stephanie.

"I heard it was epic," says Kim. "I was gutted to miss it, catering that stupid reception. Let's hope Perry remembered to collect the donations."

A knock sounds at the door and Devon yells, "Come in!"

Perry comes in, her helmet under her arm, followed closely by Imara, also with a helmet under her arm and a dented red cash box in her hand. Not only is Imara's face unusually cheerful, but her hair is windswept and her clothes awry. Devon does a double-take.

As the new arrivals are settled at the table with the beverage of their choice, Devon notices that Kim and Stephanie are also staring at Imara. Imara, though, cannot seem to keep her eyes off Perry. *Are they a couple now?*

After a healthy swig of beer, Perry cracks her knuckles and says, "Let's have a look, love."

Imara opens the cash box and gives a handwritten tally to Perry, who clears her throat and says, "Well, shall I read this to you lot?"

Kim shouts "Yes!"

Perry, dead serious, looks at the piece of paper again and says, "Are you sure? Because Imara only added up these figures twice and she might have made an — "

Stephanie snatches the tally from Perry's hand with an impatient growl and silently reads the total, which is circled in red and underlined twice. She gapes. "We're going to go way over our goal," she exclaims.

"Are you serious?" Devon shouts. "How much, how much?"

Kim slaps Perry on the back. "Well done, mate!"

Perry smiles modestly. "I give Imara most of the credit."

They all stare at Imara, who sips her beer with the hint of a smile. Perry nudges her with an elbow and urges, "Tell them!"

Imara smiles more broadly now. *God, she looks like a completely different woman when she smiles*, thinks Devon. "Let's just say that

I have two quite well-off friends in Bradford who asked to make a donation to the cause, once I did a wee bit of well-calculated arm-twisting."

They all cheer and Perry smiles proudly and holds Imara's arm up in a triumphant gesture. Kim and Stephanie add the new funds to the total and exclaim in amazement. Stephanie stands while Kim does a drumroll on the tabletop.

"The grand total is..."

"Wait, wait," cries Devon. "Let's let Larkin be the first to know. Okay?"

Kim says, "What time is it in India, anybody know?"

Devon replies, "I think it's pretty early in the morning, but who cares? We need to call her right now."

They cluster around the laptop while the video call is going through. "Who wants to tell her?" Kim asks hurriedly. "Steph?"

"All right," says Stephanie. "Look downcast, everyone." She stands up straight and adjusts her bolo tie.

Larkin answers the call. Her thin face is positively gaunt, and there are dark circles beneath her eyes, but she lights up with delight when she sees them. Larkin waves warmly and greets each of them by name. Devon's eyes prickle with tears and she feels a conflicting riot of emotions — empathy, resentment, hurt, love.

Stephanie puts on a gloomy expression and says slowly, "We did our best, Larkin. We really did." Larkin's face falls a bit. The others follow Stephanie's lead and adopt sad expressions.

Larkin braces herself. "I'm sure you did. Look, every little bit helps."

Stephanie looks again at the scrap of paper and sighs. "Would you like to hear the total?"

"Yes, please," Larkin says, bracing herself.

"Let's see...." Stephanie draws it out as long as she can, pretending to add some figures in her head as she stares at the paper. Devon and Kim both kick her booted ankles and Stephanie decides to end the torture. She scratches her head and looks into the phone. "Well, Larkin, mate, how's eight thousand, one hundred and fifty quid..."

Larkin gasps.

Kim, pointing at the paper, chimes in, "And seventy-five p? Don't forget the seventy-five p."

Larkin is dumbstruck, but not for long. "Are you lot serious?" Even after they repeat the figure for her several times, she keeps asking the same question. When it finally sinks in, she breaks down in tears. "This will make so much difference, you have no idea," she says, almost incoherent. She sobs and laughs simultaneously for a while.

Stephanie says to her kindly, "Why don't you let that sink in for a bit. We'll wire you the funds tomorrow."

Kim says to the still-teary Larkin, "You know what else would make a big difference?" Larkin, wiping her face with her sleeve, shakes her head. "If you came home to see us," Kim says. "And get a rest, which it looks like you really need." Larkin starts crying again. "Cheers for now," Kim adds gently, and ends the call as they all wave and blow air-kisses.

Then they all sit looking at each other. Finally, Kim says, "She looks like shit."

"Absolute shit," Perry agrees. "Glad we were able to help brighten her day a bit."

Stephanie says, as they are all hugging each other and collecting the money into the cash box, "Fingers crossed she takes your advice, Kim."

After they leave, Devon remains alone with Walker. She takes her out into the chilly night to do her business, and can't get Larkin's face, gaunt and frail-looking, out of her mind.

Kim and Celia

The voice on the phone is warm and deep.

And famous.

"Hello, Devon? This is Celia Denton."

Devon's heart stops, then races. She consciously controls her breathing so as not to sound too much like a fangirl.

"Yes, hello, Ms. Denton — are you settling in all right?"

"What a lovely space this is! Do you live in the little barn across the courtyard?"

"Yes. I'm right here. Is there anything at all that you need?"

The famous voice laughs and Devon can imagine the angular face, the generous smile.

"I'm afraid I haven't planned very well. After a long day of shooting, I'm absolutely ravenous. I've eaten up the biscuits and things that you so very kindly left but I'm starving for a proper meal — and I just can't go out. I can't deal with one more autograph request…"

"I'll take care of you! What would you like?"

"Anything — something hot, I don't care what's in it. Meat, vegetables, anything edible, as long as there's lots of it, and it comes as quick as possible."

"I'll see to it, Ms. Denton, you can count on me. I'll have something delivered straight away."

"Oh, thank you, thank you. You're brilliant. Tell you what, I'll leave the courtyard door unlocked and they can just come in, all right? I desperately need a bath, as well."

"Absolutely. Enjoy your bath."

With some effort, Devon banishes from her mind the image of Celia Denton in her bath, and gets to work on the phone.

"No way!" shouts Daisy in disbelief. She throws the lump of dough she has been kneading down onto the counter.

"I swear!" replies Kim, dashing through the industrial kitchen and simultaneously tearing her jacket off and throwing her "Kim's Catering" apron on.

"What? What is it?" yells Evie from over near the oven, her face even redder than usual with the heat.

"Kim says she's been hired to bring supper to Celia Denton!"

"No!" says Evie in disbelief. "Not really!"

"Yes! Really!" shouts Kim, running to the coolers and throwing refrigerator doors open.

"When?" asks Daisy.

"Tonight! Now! Sooner than now!" shouts Kim, pulling out

plates of food from the fridge, sliding them onto the steel counter, and assessing them critically.

The twins drop their tasks and crowd around Kim, firing questions at her.

"Where is she staying? At Devon's?"

"Yes!"

"Do you need help delivering, boss? I could smarten up a bit," says Daisy, wiping her brow with a floury hand.

"No!"

"Really? Celia Fuckin' Denton?" asks Evie, punching Kim's arm in disbelief.

"Ow! Yes! Get off!"

"Sure you don't need any help?" asks Daisy, putting a beefy arm around Kim's neck.

"Just get out of my way, you great pillocks!" shouts Kim, shaking them off as she pulls a meal together from the day's leftovers.

Daisy and Evie return to their tasks, every few minutes staring at each other, wide-eyed, and stage-whispering "Celia Fuckin' Denton!"

As Kim puts the food into boxes for delivery, the twins survey her.

"Comb yer hair, at least," says Evie.

"And wear that tie," says Daisy. "The blue one."

"Where is it?" cries Kim in a panic.

Evie finds the tie in the back room and knots it for Kim while Daisy helps Kim into her white chef's jacket.

Kim runs her fingers through her hair, grins at them, and lugs the boxes to the street door. "Wish me luck!"

Evie gives her a thumbs-up.

Daisy opens the door for her and yells after her, "Details, we'll want details tomorrow!"

Kim loads the boxes into her van and roars away.

Celia is toweling off after the luscious bath when she hears small sounds coming from the kitchen below. As she walks out to the landing, she can smell delicious food odors wafting up the narrow staircase.

She puts on her navy fleece tracksuit and slippers and limps painfully down the two flights of stairs. Her knee is acting up and no one, not even this catering person, can know.

"Hello, hello," she cries, not wanting to startle the person in the kitchen.

"Oh! Hello!" comes the reply. A young woman's voice. She sounds a bit panicky, Celia thinks.

Celia winces down the last few stairs and then, calling on her acting training, walks normally into the kitchen. Standing at the counter, putting the finishing touches on several covered dishes, is a wiry, tanned young woman with a flop of dark hair over her forehead. She looks up and Celia recognizes her as a member of the catering team who have been feeding the cast and crew. Celia feels a huge grin creeping over her face. *I like this girl.*

"Oh, I know you! Um… Kim, isn't it?"

Kim flushes. "I can't believe you remember my name! Yes, so, um, here is just a collection of things I thought you might like, and if you want to tuck in right away, here's a snack." She gestures with her elbow at a plate stacked with cheese and crackers.

Celia thrusts a cracker into her mouth and peeks under the cover of the largest dish. "Roast beef and Yorkshire pud! Yes, please!"

"I'll just warm it up for a moment and then where shall I serve it, ma'am?"

"Out here — I'll set the table." Celia goes into the small dining room and roots around, discovering silverware and place mats.

Kim brings in the meal and places it on the table. Celia plops gratefully into a chair as Kim uncovers three steaming plates.

"White wine all right, ma'am? I mean, that's all I've got."

Celia smiles. "Lovely, yes. No more 'ma'am,' please. Just Celia. I'm a local lass, you know."

"Yes, from Barnsley — I know."

Kim goes to the kitchen, miraculously finds wine glasses in the first cabinet she tries, uncorks the wine bottle, and returns to the dining room. Pouring the wine, she notices that Celia has set two places.

Kim says, "Oh, are you expecting someone else?"

Celia suddenly seems hesitant. "Well, you, I thought, if you'd like to join me — "

Kim looks straight at Celia for the first time and is unnerved by this close-up view of the face that has filled her fantasies for so many months. The strong lines of the jaw, the sensual, rather sad lips, the sleek silver hair that is so different from the brown wig she wears to play Anne Lister. And *oh my God* the piercing sapphire eyes focused intently — incredibly — on Kim. Celia Denton is close enough to touch. Kim finds that she has lost the ability to breathe, then remembers how. "Oh, no, thanks so much, I've eaten."

Celia, looking quite disappointed, says "Have a glass of wine with me, then? Come on."

Kim says, wondering where her words are coming from, "Thanks, but I have to go, really — is everything all right?"

Celia, after taking a hearty gulp of her wine, is piling roast beef onto her plate. "Oh my God, this looks so good, thank you so very much, Kim! Sorry you can't stay — maybe next time, eh?"

Kim stutters. "Next time, sure." She heads back to the kitchen but then remembers her business cards. She pulls one out of her wallet and goes back to the dining room. "Here's how to get hold of me. Um, any time, day or, you know, night. I'll be very happy indeed to serve you."

Celia reaches out to take the card. Her eyes widen. "Oh! Kim's Catering — that's you! You're the boss, then!" Kim nods, bashfully. Celia says, "Please forgive me for thinking you were just an employee — you're so young. Your food is absolutely amazing, Kim. I've been enjoying it so much this whole week. It has a kind of…soul…that's truly unique, certainly on location shoots." Looking Kim directly in the eyes again, Celia carefully puts the card in her pocket. "See you on set then, Kim, and thank you so very much. I won't forget this. Good night."

"Just leave all the dishes in the kitchen and I'll pick them up tomorrow morning. You can lock up, I have a key. Um, good night, then." Dizzy and sweating, Kim stumbles out of the kitchen and throws on her jacket.

Outside in the chilly dark, Kim mentally kicks herself as she tramps over the cobbles to her van. "Why on earth did I turn down a chance to spend time with Celia Fucking Denton? What's wrong with me?"

~

"I never should have told you two!" Kim exclaims over the noise in the pub the next afternoon. Daisy and Evie are jumping up and down in their seats.

Daisy screams, "Celia Fucking Denton invited you to eat dinner with her and you said no?!"

Evie grabs Kim by the neck and swings her back and forth. "You daft chuff! Celia Fucking Denton?"

Kim throws Evie off. "I felt too shy. I mean, there she was, looking at me..."

Daisy says dreamily — "...With those amazing eyes..."

Evie interjects, "You're always whingeing about how boring it is here and you want to move to London....if you had, you'd have missed this!"

Daisy says, "It's because of the tie. I told you you were irresistible in that tie."

"Yes, I was irresistible. But I couldn't stay — I just knew there was no way I could carry on a conversation with her." Kim's friends hoot. "Come on, you two. What would you have done? What would you have talked about?"

Evie says, "Are you joking? So many things!"

Daisy and Evie trip over each other's words.

"'Are the rumors true?'"

"'We know you date women, but anyone serious?'"

"'Did you enjoy your love scenes with Serena?'"

"'In the scene in the stagecoach, did you really use your tongue?'"

Kim rolls her eyes as the twins keep firing increasingly obscene suggestions at her. Then her phone vibrates, making her jump. She pulls her phone from her pocket. There is a text from an unfamiliar number.

- Hello, Kim, Celia D here. Any chance of another delicious

meal tonight? Pasta with veg, or anything you've got?

Wordlessly, Kim holds up her phone. Evie and Daisy lean to see the text, their heads touching. They squeal in harmony.

Kim takes the phone back and types,

- Absolutely, Celia. Wine, as well?

The reply comes almost immediately.

- By all means. And I insist you stay and eat with me, so no arguing allowed. See you here at 7-ish? Xo

Standing, Kim says, "Sorry, girls, I better go — I have a new menu to organize." As she attempts to put the phone back in her pocket, Evie grabs it from her hand. "'I insist you stay and eat with me' — oh my God — xo. XO!?"

Kim reclaims the phone as Evie and Daisy sit with their mouths hanging open. She shrugs into her anorak. Her phone buzzes again and she checks it. Another text from Celia. "PS Please wear that tie again." Kim stares, then shoves the phone back in her pocket and addresses her friends again with a broad drawl.

"Oh my dears, don't you know — all the film stars end their texts to me with 'xo.' Well, good night then," says Kim, heading for the door.

"You better text us every minute," yells Daisy. And then Kim is out on the rainy street, hurrying towards her kitchen and wondering if Celia Denton likes home-made ravioli. *I hope my blue tie doesn't have any gravy stains on it.*

Celia Denton slowly swallows her last ravioli.

"Mmmmmmm," she moans, closing her eyes. Kim drinks her in. Celia opens her eyes and sees Kim staring. She smiles. "So good, Kim."

"Glad you liked it."

"Serious question, Kim, your food tastes different from anything I've ever eaten. Has anyone else ever said that?"

Kim hesitates and says, "Yes, actually."

Their dinner conversation has been quite extraordinary, Kim marvels. Celia's ease and genuineness has completely disarmed her. Kim has gone from being intimidated by Celia's star status to seeing her as a sensitive, caring woman with a restlessness that Kim can't quite identify.

During the hour and a half that they have lingered over the meal and quite a lot of wine, they have shared anecdotes about their families, a bit of relationship history, and hysterical laughter about mishaps at work. Celia tells a somber story about how wrenching it was to have to quit elite fencing when she tore up her knee — "Just before the bloody Olympics." She sighs deeply, then brightens. "But if it hadn't been for that, I'd never have started in the acting game, and it's really been a lot of fun."

Kim would think that they are like two old friends, except for the fact that she has never felt this vibrating desire for any other old friend. Nor, she reflects, does she have any old friends who just happen to be world-famous. Kim has become increasingly aroused as the evening progresses, and is fairly sure she is not imagining Celia's attraction to her.

"Well, why is it?" pursues Celia. Her voice is so rich and warm, Kim could wrap herself up in it. "Why do people say that about your food?"

"This will sound absolutely bonkers."

Celia smiles, encouraging. "Try me."

"I try to sort of…listen to each main ingredient. I try to see if I can detect what it wants to be. Or what it wants to do. And then as closely as possible, I do that. It's a matter of, like, feeling it, or listening to it and what it wants to be. I often start all over on a recipe if I feel that one of the vegetables isn't ready to be in a stew. I sort of fall in love with each ingredient and — try to help it do what it most wants in the world. I told you it was bonkers." Kim fidgets, embarrassed to have said so much.

Celia stares, a soft smile on her face. "Not bonkers at all. You know, when I have to do a love scene — sometimes with an actor I barely know or maybe even someone I dislike, or maybe someone with atrocious breath — I do what a director taught me and try to fall in love with a part of the other actor — lips, or eyes, or whatever it is."

Kim smiles. "Yes! It's a bit like that."

"Hmm. Does your listening talent extend to people?"

200

Kim thinks. "If I listen really carefully and don't get distracted, yes. It's as if I can...see inside them. It's quite odd sometimes, especially if there's something they don't want anyone to see. Or something they don't even know about themselves."

Celia nods thoughtfully and mops up the remaining sauce with a bit of bread. Kim remembers a question she wanted to ask. "I noticed this week that you were directing as well as acting. Is that difficult?"

Celia rolls her eyes. "You have no idea. It was stupid of me to accept both roles. I get so absolutely fed up with making all the decisions and calling all the shots. It's truly exhausting. Sometimes I wish someone else would just take over, honestly."

Kim clears her throat. "But then you might not get the results you want. I'm sure you're a genius director."

Celia's eyes crinkle with a beatific smile as she chews the bread. Even her jaw muscle is gorgeous. "Thank you so much! You, my girl, are a genius in the kitchen." She wiggles one eyebrow suggestively. "And I bet you're pretty great in the other rooms as well. Good Lord, I'm drunk. Such a lightweight." She picks up the wine bottle and swishes it around playfully. "One more glass, want to share it?"

Kim is quite tipsy herself. She loosens the knot in her tie and holds out her glass. "Why not?" she says, and Celia pours half the wine into Kim's glass and the other half into her own.

"Shall we have a toast?" asks Celia.

"All right. What shall we toast?"

Celia thinks. "Success and love?"

Kim raises her glass. "To success and love!" They clink their glasses together. Celia is staring intensely at her and does not break the gaze as they both drink. Kim has journeyed past her incredulity and now absolutely knows that Celia is flirting with...no, seducing her. She just doesn't know what to do about it.

Celia leans back in her chair, playing suggestively with the stem of her wineglass. Celia says, "I think we've talked about success quite a bit this evening — you know about my ambition to write a film script, and I know about yours to move your catering business to London. So I think we've got success covered. But what about — "

201

"Love?" Kim hears herself blurt.

"Yes," Celia says. "What about love?"

"You first," says Kim.

"No, no, no, you first."

Kim takes a big sip of the wine. "As I told you, I've been single for over a year now. It was a horrid breakup, took me months and months to feel like myself again. And I've just been working really hard on the catering business, so I haven't had the time to think about dating."

"What if you did?"

"Think about dating?"

"Yes, what would you be looking for?"

Kim smiles. "I couldn't say."

"Of course you could! Come on." Celia raps her knuckles on the tabletop.

"I'd be looking for….." Kim fades out.

"Come on!" Celia snaps her fingers, grinning.

Kim takes a deep breath. She knows it's a once in a lifetime opportunity and decides to go for it.

With a heroic effort, Kim maintains eye contact. "Well, someone feminine but strong. Athletic. Sensitive. Intelligent. Funny. Confident. Um, beautiful." She smiles. "Maybe — I don't know — a former fencing champion. About five foot…seven. Someone like…" She shrugs helplessly.

Celia looks up at the ceiling and Kim has no idea what is going through her head.

Celia smiles suggestively. "Someone like…?"

"Well, I suppose, someone like — well, like you."

"Someone like me, eh?" Celia sits quietly for a moment. "Then it would have to be someone impatient, fidgety, disorganized, impulsive, and quite selfish."

"Okay," says Kim. "All part of the package. And what about you?"

"Love?"

"Yes."

Celia looks sad. "There hasn't been anyone really special for a long time, not since my marriage ended fourteen years ago. I go out with men sometimes, but that's just for the photographers."

Kim can barely breathe. "Really?"

Celia nods. "Yes, really. I see women, rather quietly."

Kim absorbs this. "But no one special?"

Celia shakes her head. "No, my work takes up so much of my energy lately, it would be unfair." She pauses, looks down at her glass. "But I do have my eye on someone. The only trouble is, it's so difficult to know if someone's trustworthy. Obviously, it requires a person who would be incredibly discreet."

"Of course," Kim whispers.

"Incredibly discreet," Celia says slowly, emphasizing each syllable with a ping of her fingernail on her glass.

"Like the tomb, basically, right?"

Celia nods again. "Like the tomb."

"Discreet, check. I know what that's like — some of my catering clients are MP's and people like that…"

"Oh really, who?" Celia asks innocently. Kim wags a scolding finger at her.

"…and my business would go bust immediately if I wasn't discreet."

Celia smiles, approving. Kim continues. "What else would you be looking for? If you were, you know, looking?" Kim buries her nose in her wineglass and half wishes she was on another planet and half knows that she wouldn't trade places with anyone on earth.

Celia leans back in her chair, breathes deeply, and looks again at the ceiling. Kim can't help taking a look at her slender, strong body as Celia's chest expands, stretching the fabric of her tailored white linen shirt.

"I'd be looking for someone sincere…energetic. Someone a bit younger and a bit…taller than me. Someone who's good with her hands. Someone with experience of being a boss. Someone who wouldn't be intimidated by me, but quite the opposite — someone who'd see me as a challenge. Someone who would take charge and tell me what to do so I could relax and just let it happen. That would be heaven."

She pauses for a long moment and lowers her gaze from the ceiling to Kim's face. "And someone who doesn't want anything from me. I'm surrounded all the time by people who never really see me. They want to be close to me for my fame or my money or what I can do for them. Nobody ever sees me, really — Celia from Barnsley, who has some bloomin' arthritis she can't tell anyone about because it might affect her earning potential and the fate of the next movie…"

She drifts off into a reverie, her face long and sad, then smiles ruefully at Kim. "So — someone who would really see me. What do you think are my odds of finding someone like that?"

Kim is finding it hard to talk, but she stammers, "Pretty good, actually."

Celia says "Hmmmmm."

The room is crackling with tension. They both sit still for a moment, just staring at each other, slight smiles on their faces.

Without breaking her gaze, Celia finishes her wine, puts down her glass, and rises. She walks around the table and takes Kim's hand. Kim looks up at her, half afraid. Celia pulls her to her feet. Kim licks her lips. Celia looks her frankly in the eyes as she folds her fingers slowly around the knot in Kim's tie.

"And she would have to be…someone who can really rock a tie." Celia pulls gently, and Kim leans forward. She puts her hand on the back of Celia's head, and looks into the famous sapphire eyes. Kim, not believing what is happening, lowers her lips to Celia's and they share a light kiss. Then Kim pulls Celia closer and kisses her harder. Celia responds instantly, following Kim's lead and relaxing her body into Kim's.

Suddenly, all fear and shyness vanish from Kim's soul. She forgets that this is a famous actress, a movie star. All she knows is that Celia is kissing her deeply, with passion, making small inarticulate sounds of delight. Kim dares to lower her hands to Celia's bottom — her famous, firm bottom, she thinks drunkenly — and pulls her closer.

The kiss continues for a long time and eventually Celia pulls back to breathe. She grins ruefully and puts her hands on Kim's shoulders as she steps back. Celia says, "Oh God, I shouldn't have done this tonight." Kim's heart sinks through the floor.

Celia puts her hand under Kim's chin and raises her head up.

"Don't look so tragic. It's just that tomorrow is the last full day of shooting on location here. It's not going to be a terribly long day, but I'll need all my faculties, so I really need to go to bed early. Alone, I'm afraid."

Kim nods understandingly, though her body is on fire and she can't take her eyes off Celia's lips.

Celia caresses Kim's cheek. "But what are you doing tomorrow night?"

Kim's heart starts beating again. "Let me check my packed social calendar…nothing I can't cancel, I'm pretty sure."

"Come back here for dinner. Please. My treat, I'll get a carry out. I don't want you to have to cook. We'll celebrate the end of the shoot."

Kim brightens. "Really?"

"Yes, and bring a toothbrush, if you like. Stay the night. If you like. I'm off back to London the next morning and it would be lovely to spend my last night here. With you."

Kim somehow summons up a cocky smile and says "All right then. When shall I come?"

"Come early — about six?" Kim nods. Celia reaches out to take hold of Kim's tie again and kisses her lightly. "Wear this."

"All right," Kim replies. Celia releases her. Kim starts to collect the dishes but Celia stops her. "I'll do those. Are you OK to drive?"

"Yes, I'm fine."

Kim opens the door to the street in a daze. Celia pulls her back into the kitchen and kisses her again, then says, "Good night, Kim. See you at six, then."

Kim steps out into the courtyard and turns to wave. Celia leans out the door and whispers something.

Kim whispers back, "What did you say?"

Celia whispers a bit louder. "Come hungry." She closes the door slowly and Kim stands for a moment in the dark courtyard, swaying on her heels, until she remembers how to walk.

All day, Kim can barely concentrate. She is working alone. She's not needed on set, but has a restaurant order for five hundred hand-made gyoza, a laborious process. Luckily, she can do it more or less automatically — slapping the round wrapper into her left hand, stuffing it with pork and onion mixture, carefully crimping the wrapper around it to create a tiny dumpling and put it on the baking sheet — a fairly enjoyable task, and one that allows her imaginings about her upcoming evening with Celia to run wild. Really wild.

The time goes quickly and when she has finished the job, she's surprised to realize that she's been working for four hours and that her shoulders are cramped. She lays the last dumpling down on the last baking sheet and pushes it into the freezer.

She stretches luxuriously, folds her apron, closes up shop, and drives to the park for a jog. The cool, drizzly weather suits her mood and clears her head as she runs. She revisits her memory of last night. Did Celia Denton really kiss her? It is unbelievable. She wonders what Evie and Daisy would say and realizes that the hardest part of this will be to keep absolutely quiet about it.

Kim runs her usual three and a half miles, stops at the florist's to pick up an order of a dozen pink roses, drives home to her flat, showers, and irons her nicest button-down shirt.

She looks at herself in the mirror while she knots her blue woven tie, practicing her facial expressions. She settles on a cocky one-sided grin that she hopes doesn't look too much like a smirk, checks her watch, realizes she will be right on time if she leaves immediately, and goes to the hall closet to get her brown bomber jacket that one ex-girlfriend had said made her look like Amelia Earhart.

Then she pops into the kitchen to pick up the bouquet. She sniffs the roses and notices a small blank card that the florist had tucked into it. She wonders what she should say. She writes a brief message off the top of her head, slips the card back into the flowers, looks at herself one last time in the mirror, growls "Go get 'em, Boss Lady!" to her reflection, and clatters down the stairs.

∾

"Come in!" shouts Celia as Kim knocks. Kim steps into the guest house and sees that it is aglow with a couple of dozen electric candles, scattered throughout the dining room, lounge, and kitchen. A jazz trio plays through the sound system.

Celia is wearing a striped apron over black jeans and a pale blue oxford shirt with the sleeves rolled up. She is taking food from styrofoam containers and arranging it on plates. She looks up at Kim and gives her that famous gleaming smile. "Done!" she says. She picks out a mushroom canapé from a tray and carries it over to Kim. "Open up," she orders, and when Kim obeys, Celia pops the morsel into her mouth, following it with a light kiss on the cheek.

Chewing the hors-d'oeuvre, Kim bows and hands the roses to Celia, who takes them with wide-eyed delight, smells them, says "Gorgeous!" and pulls out the little card. "To C from K with admiration and affection," she reads aloud. "Oh, how sweet, Kim. Tell me about your day." Kim makes an attempt to find something humorous to relate, but fails. "Made five hundred gyoza. Went for a jog. Came here. Can I help?" Kim shrugs out of her jacket and Celia takes it from her and hangs it on a hook on the wall.

"Oooh, great bomber jacket. Yes, please, light the fire, would you? It's all laid." By the time Kim has lit the wood fire in the lounge and prodded it a bit with a poker, Celia has put the roses into a vase and brought wine and hors-d'oeuvres in.

Celia hands Kim a glass of wine and lifts her own. "A toast?" she asks.

Kim says, "Yes, what shall we toast to?"

"You decide," says Celia.

Kim thinks hard and blurts, "To delicious adventures."

Celia smiles broadly. They drink, and Celia takes both glasses. She puts them on the coffee table and stands gazing at Kim. There is no sound except for the crackling of the fire. Kim suddenly feels ridiculously brave. She steps to Celia, puts her arms around her, and sweeps her into a close embrace. Celia hugs her back and they stand like this for a moment, swaying back and forth a little, breathing together.

Kim, remembering last night's conversation, feels deeply into Celia and tries to determine what she really wants. She holds Celia tighter and Celia responds, like a dancer following her partner's lead.

Celia whispers into Kim's ear, "Are you hungry?"

Kim whispers back, "Only for you."

Delighted, Celia steps back and says, "Oh, really?" Kim nods.

Celia says, "Do you think we should go upstairs and inspect the bedroom?"

Kim rolls her eyes and pretends to mull this over. "Yes, I suppose we could do that." Her heart is thumping. Celia smiles a small secret smile and gestures for Kim to go first.

They take their wine glasses and the bottle up the narrow staircase to the Chaumière, which is also lit by electric candles. It is cool now but Kim knows it will warm up when the heat rises from the fire below.

Kim quickly looks around the spacious room and notes the king-size four-poster, with its cast-iron headboard and puffy white duvet; a chest of drawers strewn with items of clothing; and a bedside table holding a lamp, a couple of paperbacks and a black eyeshade. Two narrow windows show the lights of the village, just flickering on as night falls, stretching below.

Kim takes a breath. She is about to take charge. She points at the heavy purple curtains and says in her most authoritative voice, "Would you draw the curtains, please."

Celia steps eagerly to the windows, pulls the curtains closed and turns to Kim. Kim points at the wine bottle. "And pour us another glass."

Celia pours the two glasses. Kim notices that Celia's hands are trembling just a little.

They drink slowly, looking at each other. Kim's heart pounds. She evaluates the risks of her plan and makes a decision. She takes their wine glasses and sets them down on the bedside table.

Turning to Celia, she kisses her and embraces her firmly, pinning Celia's arms to her sides and immobilizing her. Celia gasps with delight. Kim moves her lips to Celia's ear and bites the earlobe. Another sharp intake of breath affirms that she is on the right track.

Kim whispers into the famous ear, "What do you want?"

Celia whispers back, "I want you to take charge of me. Ravish me. Do whatever you want."

Kim growls, "You like my tie, do you?"

Celia breathes, "Very much."

Nodding towards the bed, Kim asks, "And do you like that headboard?" Celia looks, and nods quizzically. Kim kisses Celia's neck and releases her. Stepping back, heart pounding, she says roughly, "What would you say if I told you I'm going to tie your wrists to that headboard?"

Celia's eyes roll back in her head and her lips part. "I'd say no, no, that would be terrible, I'd hate that," she says — so convincingly that Kim is worried for a moment, then remembers that Celia is an award-winning actress.

"Go to the loo," Kim says authoritatively, "And take off everything except your shirt. And come back here. Hurry up."

Without comment, Celia leaves the room. She is gone only a couple of minutes, just long enough for Kim to throw the duvet back to reveal beautiful pearl-grey sheets.

Celia comes in, wearing only her shirt. Kim looks at the actress' legs and almost forgets how to speak. "Finish your glass of wine if you like," says Kim. "And stay right here."

Kim goes to the loo, freshens up, and looks for a moment at herself in the mirror. She is smirking in disbelief, and gradually changes her expression to a stern scowl. Taking a deep breath, she says to her reflection, "Go get 'em, Tiger."

When she returns to the bedroom, Celia is standing, looking a bit cold, and finishing her glass of wine.

"Come over here." Celia goes to her. "Take my tie off me." Celia fumbles with the knot and pulls the tie off. Kim says, "Give me the tie." Celia does so. Kim says "Turn around." When Celia has turned her back to Kim, Kim reaches around her and caresses Celia's breasts, feeling the nipples stand at attention through the shirt. Kim kisses Celia's neck at the same time, causing the actress to moan quietly. Kim takes her time, pinching the prominent nipples lightly, and running her hands all over Celia's taut torso. She has been fantasizing about this moment for days and is not going to rush through it. She can smell Celia's arousal and notices her own wetness growing. And she can feel Celia's desire — need — to be dominated, relieved of all responsibility.

"Get on the bed. On your back." Celia climbs onto the bed and

Kim goes to stand over her. "Hands up." Quickly, Kim ties Celia's wrists to the headboard and then covers her with the duvet. She reaches to the bedside table and gets the eyeshade. She puts it on Celia, testing that it fits firmly.

Slowly, Kim removes her own clothes. "All right?" she asks. Celia murmurs, "Mmmm."

"You don't make any decisions after this. I'll tell you what to do and all you have to do is obey me — or tell me to stop, and I will. No other decisions. Sound all right?"

Celia sighs deeply and says "Oh my God, yessssss."

Kim gets in bed next to Celia and pulls the covers up over both of them. She gazes at the beautiful body, starts thinking about what to do to please her, and then stops thinking and starts feeling. She reaches out her hand and touches Celia's heart. Kim closes her eyes and listens to what she feels. Celia growls.

"I want you. I want you in me," she whispers harshly.

"Ssssh," says Kim. Very slowly, she unbuttons Celia's shirt. Pressing her body to Celia's, Kim kisses her mouth gently, firmly. Celia responds hungrily. After a long time, Kim lowers her mouth to Celia's neck, then to her breasts, kissing them with infinite care. Celia is moaning, tossing back and forth impatiently, but Kim continues at her own pace. Time disappears as Kim moves down Celia's body, listening to Celia's inner world as she strokes, bites, and kisses her. Celia stops struggling, breathing deeply and revealing herself in detail to Kim's inner vision — Kim can feel Celia's fears, her history, her hurts and dreams and joys. Kim could live here for days, just savoring Celia's rich inner landscape. She keeps kissing Celia, lower and lower down the slim, toned slopes of her body. Celia rocks and moans again, aroused and desperate for release.

When Kim reaches Celia's knees, she stops, listening. There is pain and fear here.

Kim runs her hands gently over both knees and then lowers her lips to the left knee. She kisses it with utmost tenderness, sending all her love into the bones and flesh and cartilage. She takes her time, loving the knee as warmly as if it is the most precious thing in the universe. After a while, she notices that Celia is shaking.

Kim moves back up to lie by Celia's side. "Are you all right?"

Celia shakes her head. Instantly, Kim unties the necktie, releasing Celia, and pulls the eyeshade off her. Celia is weeping.

Celia throws her arms around Kim and sobs uncontrollably. For quite some time, Kim just holds her, rocking her gently, patting her back in wonder.

Celia pulls away at last, wiping her face. "I needed that — your gentleness — so much and I didn't even know."

Kim smiles quizzically. "I wasn't sure — I thought you wanted to be ravished."

Celia looks at her, stroking Kim's cheek. "I thought so, too. But it turns out that this was what I wanted. Your…tenderness. Especially to my poor old knee."

"Well, good."

"How did you know?"

Kim shrugs. "No idea. Was it all right?"

Celia pulls Kim close and whispers, "It was way beyond all right." She pauses. "I realized while you were kissing it — I can't just go on pretending my knee is healthy. I need to get it looked at properly. Fixed. I need to be kind to it instead of being cross with it all the time."

Kim runs her fingers through Celia's silky hair. "That sounds right."

Celia says, "I don't know what you did. But thank you."

"You are so very, very welcome," Kim says softly, reaching one hand down to cup Celia's left knee.

Celia rests in Kim's arms for a long moment and then whispers, "May I tell you a secret?"

"Of course."

"I'm starving."

Kim kisses her again and gets up. "So am I. Come on."

They pull on their clothes and slowly, hand in hand, descend the stairs.

Kim is already at work the next morning, rolling out a batch of pastry dough, when Daisy and Evie come in. They instantly pepper her with questions.

"How did it go the other night?"

"Did she like your food?"

"Did she ask you to stay?"

"Why weren't you at the pub last night?"

"Did you get a big tip?"

Kim shakes her head in mock exasperation. "Shut up, you two! It went well, she liked the food, she's quite nice but she was very tired and I only stayed long enough to set the meal out for her. I was at home last night because I needed some bloody peace and quiet. And yes, I got a very nice tip, and here's your share." She hands them each a 50-pound note. Daisy and Evie exclaim and make a show of holding the notes up to the light to see if they are genuine. Kim returns to rolling the dough.

"If you're quite finished with the hilarity, we need to make a dozen quiches for a reception at the hotel — the ingredients are in the fridge and the recipe is on the board."

The doorbell rings, and Daisy goes to answer it. She brings in a box the size of a large dictionary covered in gold paper and tied with a red ribbon. "Oooh, it's for you, Kim," she says, and stands waiting expectantly.

"Thank you. Don't you have something to do?" Kim takes the box into the back room and closes the door. There is a small envelope on top of the box. She opens the box and sees that it is a triple-layer assortment of the very best kind of chocolates, the kind she can never afford. She pops a dark-chocolate-covered raspberry into her mouth and lets it dissolve on her tongue while she opens the envelope. There is an extremely generous cheque inside, along with a note.

Dearest, most brilliant Kim, Thank you beyond words for taking me away from everything last night, in such an unexpected and lovely way. I'm off back to London today, and I'll make an appointment to have my knee looked at as soon as possible. Please, please come down and see me next week, if you can. I have a serious job offer for you. How would you like to be my personal chef, to cook for me while I'm shooting the rest of the film at the London studio? And to stay for as long as you like each time. I have a guest flat over the garage that I think you'd like. It comes with the job. Don't say yes or no now — come and see for yourself. Please come. I need you. Text me when you can visit. Thanks again for the most delicious evening. Xo.

Kim is catching her breath when she notices that there are also a few words on the back of the card. She turns it over.

P.S. I do hope that ravishing will be on the menu. Bring that tie.

••• ⟨ ● ⟩ •••

PART SEVEN: Spring
Yorkshire

A Call from Miremba

Devon's phone pings. It's Miremba, calling to say she is thinking of coming to Calderdale in a week.

Devon's heart does a cartwheel.

"Yes, please, come and stay with me! How soon can you get here?"

Miremba's throaty chuckle warms Devon through and through. "You must have a big job to do if you're so excited to see me."

"No, I don't," said Devon. "Well, I have a medium-sized job, but I don't care if you help me with it or not. I just want to see you! I only need to finish painting my spare bedroom. I have a feeling the B&B will fill up this summer, and I could use an overflow room."

"I want to see you, too, before I leave."

"Leave?"

Miremba sighs. "I'll tell you when I see you."

Dawn, Lindsay, Perry: Spring

It's a beautiful week for the Anne Lister birthday gathering. At the historians' workshop, Dawn is sitting on the stage, next to Dr. Finley, waiting for the session to start. Shyly, she closes her eyes and pretends to go over her notes. She takes the opportunity to reflect on the happenings of the past months.

Lindsay wrote to Dawn a lot for several months after their meeting last year. They engaged in a lively correspondence discussing the ongoing research into Anne Lister's life. Lindsay applied to be accepted as a codebreaker, but the work was too intense for her and after a while she confessed to Dawn, "I'd really rather be out on my bike, I'm afraid."

Dawn took that as a hint and backed off, though Lindsay kept writing to her for quite some time — Lindsay got a cool new job that she loves; Lindsay is dating a woman she met in her birdwatching group; Lindsay got a new bike; Lindsay broke it off with the birdwatching woman because she wasn't the slightest bit interested in Anne Lister ("Can you imagine, Dawn?! There was no future").

But for most of these past months, a great deal of Dawn's spare time has been taken up with deciphering Anne Lister's journals and also continuing to write her own fanfic, which for her is like entering another world. When she's writing it, as "Louise Alexander," she is brave and sexy. The love scenes are vivid, juicy, shameless — things that she really wishes she could be in real life. Her usual modesty dissipates as she enters the world of her alternate reality and marvels at the explicit adventures her characters engage in. "Louise" is all the things Dawn is not, but aspires to be: bold, forthright, daring, sensual, passionate.

After she had posted the first few chapters, nothing much had happened beside a few likes.

But more recently, her tantalizing experience with Lindsay and Perry inspiring her, she posted the next chapter, which included a provocative scene of her characters nearly making love. Dawn knew it was a good chapter for two reasons. First, she was incredibly turned on each time she edited the scene, so she knew it was hot. And secondly, the word started to spread about the story. A fan posted fervent praise of it on the group page, and immediately, "Louise Alexander" was overwhelmed by fan messages, urging her to hurry up and get to the dirty part.

She then posted three more chapters, spacing them a couple of weeks apart, building slowly and, according to her fans, agonizingly, toward the promised climax. The fans expressed their pain and impatience in dramatic terms that made Dawn laugh with delight. *If they could only see what a plain wee mouse I am.*

Dawn decided just for fun to wait to post the last two chapters until she is visiting Halifax, feeling quite sure that some of her fans will be at the gathering and reveling in the fact that, as adept as many of these women are at deciphering the coded journals of Anne Lister, none of them suspects who "Louise" really is.

Dawn has made some changes in her life, emboldened and inspired by her experiences with the Anne Lister researchers. The biggest change in Dawn is the new, Anne Lister-inspired self-confidence that has unexpectedly grown in her. She finds herself saying "yes" to all kinds of things that she usually would have avoided completely. She has had her curly hair cut radically short and streaked with a few red highlights, which has attracted new kinds of attention from women at the parties she occasionally attends. To her great surprise, she has been asked out by two of these women in the past few months, dating one for three weeks and the other on and off for a longer period. At last, she lost her virginity. It is an enormous relief.

But neither of these women understood her passion for all things Anne Lister, and Dawn found it hard going without that crucial shared interest. She challenged herself to take riding lessons — not for her, as it turned out, since she had a heretofore unknown allergy to horses and ended up sneezing for hours each time — but an adventure nonetheless. She has continued her research into the Wilkinson family, and made some more discoveries that have resulted in her being invited to give a talk at the current workshop, and to her own astonishment, she agreed to it. And she has taken a class in public speaking, which terrified her so much when it was her turn to give a practice speech that she thought she would keel right over, but eventually it got easier and even, almost, enjoyable.

All the same, as the time for this gathering approaches, Dawn is quite nervous about it — not just about her talk, but also about seeing Lindsay again. She is apprehensive about the memories that staying at Miss Lister's Guest House would be sure to bring up. So Dawn is staying at a hotel in downtown Halifax, which is not terribly comfortable but has the advantage of anonymity and privacy.

This morning, she finally indulged her fanfic readers and posted the final two chapters.

And now the lecture is about to start. As Dr. Finley introduces her, Dawn takes a moment to look down at her notes, on which she has written "SMILE! PROJECT! BREATHE!"

There is a spattering of applause as Dr. Finley concludes her introduction, and Dawn rises and steps to the microphone. She surveys the small, intent audience and spots both Perry and Lindsay, sitting near each other and giving her encouraging thumbs-ups as she begins.

Dawn gets through her talk — "Unveiling the Mysteries of Local Cemeteries," — without stumbling on her words too much, and her slide show works flawlessly. She actually relaxes and enjoys giving the talk, sprinkling in a few spontaneous jokes. When she finishes and steps down off the podium, the applause is enthusiastic and sincere. Lindsay stands and waves eagerly at her, beckoning Dawn to come and sit with her. As Dawn gets to the chair, Lindsay steps forward and hugs her hard. "That was amazing!" she whispers into Dawn's ear. Perry leans over and slaps Dawn's back.

When the session is over, the attendees, talking loudly, crowd into the entry hall, where refreshments are on offer. Lindsay runs to get an orange squash for Dawn, who is surrounded by women peppering her with questions.

After about 20 minutes of this, Dawn is exhilarated and exhausted. Luckily, at this point a volunteer comes out and makes a loud announcement that the next session is about to start. The crowd recedes like a tide, leaving only Perry, Lindsay, and Dawn.

"Going to the next talk?" Perry asks.

"No, exhausted," says Dawn, feeling shy again. "Going to my hotel for a bit."

Perry helps her gather up her notebook and rucksack. "Not staying at Miss Lister's, then?"

"No, a hotel just seemed…simpler," Dawn replies. She thanks Perry for her help and starts toward the exit. Lindsay and Perry look at each other with raised eyebrows, then chase after her.

Lindsay exclaims, "Well, but you can't just go off like that…I mean, you can, of course, if you want to…"

Perry jumps in. "I'd love to spend some time together, wouldn't you two? To catch up? It's been ages."

"It has been ages," Dawn agrees.

They plan to meet at the pub in two hours, and Dawn, feeling relieved to be away from people, walks the short distance to her hotel, where she lies down for a while and then changes into jeans and sweater. She looks herself over in the en-suite's mirror. "I am relaxed, spontaneous, and open-minded," she reminds herself, trying to believe it. As she walks through the streets to the pub, Dawn reflects on her confusing, colliding feelings about the two women she is about to see. Her attraction to Perry returned the moment she saw her, but it is much less powerful than it was a year ago. *Interesting.*

And Lindsay — their correspondence was eager for a few months, but has faded out to a trickle recently. Dawn is not even sure how she feels about Lindsay, though the main issue has been the seven hours' driving distance between them.

But her memory of that moment with Lindsay, that intense look on the landing, makes Dawn pause and catch her breath for a moment before she steps through the door into the pub.

She sees Perry at a corner booth and waves. Dawn orders a half bitter at the bar and carries it over, and sits across from Perry. The woman's perfectly weathered leather jacket, her confident, welcoming smile — infuriatingly, Dawn can't help blushing, and is glad of the low lights as she and Perry clink their glasses together.

"Congratulations to the star!" Perry says. As they raise their glasses, Lindsay appears and slides into the booth next to Perry.

"Wait, wait," Lindsay says. "What are we toasting? Can I be in on it? Are we toasting Dawn for her incredible presentation, and if not, why not?"

"Yes, of course that's what we're toasting," says Perry.

"Hail, Dawn!" Lindsay says, and they clink their glasses together. After taking a sip, Lindsay adds, "Oooh, is that an actual bitter you're drinking, Dawn?"

"Yes," Dawn says. "I decided to try this alcohol stuff that everyone seems to like so much."

As the three women start to catch each other up on the events of their lives — Perry has had several poems published and has finally saved enough money to buy her dream motorcycle; Lindsay has ditched her annoying flatmates and moved to a tiny studio by herself — Dawn can't help noticing that they have a new attitude towards her. Where they were once a little bit condescending, now they stop talking as soon as she says anything, and look at her as if she is dispensing pearls of wisdom instead of just talking about her new job title and the kittens she is thinking of adopting.

Perry says, with an uncharacteristic hesitation in her voice, "I've been seeing Imara, do you know her?" The other two shake their heads. "It's been fun, but I don't really know what's in her mind. And now that I've got enough money to buy this bike, I'm intending to go to Germany to pick it up, and then travel on the Continent for a while."

Lindsay says, "That's good, isn't it?"

Perry stares into her pint glass. "The trouble is, I'm afraid to tell Imara I'm leaving. Silly, eh?"

Dawn is about to say something but at that moment, a pair of women who Dawn recognizes from the workshop approach their booth, waving shyly at them. Perry notices them and says, "Hello!" The newcomers merely glance at Perry, focusing their attention on Dawn. One of the women says "So very sorry to interrupt you —"

The other says, "But we absolutely loved your talk this morning and we just had to tell you!"

The first one chimes in, "Would you sign our programs?"

Dawn looks down at the two programs that have been placed in front of her. She doesn't know what to say. One of the newcomers gives her a pen.

"I've never, um, been asked for an autograph before," Dawn stutters.

"It's all right, just sign your name," Perry advises, and Dawn does so, her heart swelling. She hands the programs back to the two women, saying sincerely, "I'm very glad you liked my presentation."

"Thank you!" The two women giggle like schoolgirls and scurry away.

Lindsay rolls her eyes. "She's a star, now she'll be too good to hang out with the likes of us."

"I'll say," drawls Perry, shading her eyes with her hand. "She's so high on that pedestal I can hardly see her."

Dawn finds it impossible to wipe the grin off her face.

Perry slaps her hands down on the table. "So! Any gossip?"

"Not really; what about you, Perry?" asks Dawn, noticing that she is no longer feeling shy.

Perry says, wearily, "Just working like mad."

"Same for me," says Lindsay sadly. Then she brightens. "Oh! That fanfic writer we liked so much — Louise — remember?"

"How could I forget?" says Perry, pretending to wipe sweat off her forehead.

Lindsay: "She's almost finished her story! Did you see all those comments by women *demanding* that she post the last two chapters? They were in an absolute frenzy."

Perry: "I'm so glad she's near the end — everyone is dying of suspense and lust."

Lindsay: "Have you read it, Dawn?"

Dawn looks down. "I've looked at it. Quite well done, isn't it?"

Perry: "Understatement of the year. It's far and away the best one I've read. I've been checking every day…"

Lindsay pulls out her phone. "I wonder if she's posted the next chapter yet." She scrolls and suddenly shouts, "Oh my God! She's posted the last two chapters!"

Perry pulls out her phone and searches it.

Dawn says, authoritatively, "Wait!" and they both stop looking at their phones and look at her in surprise.

Dawn stammers, "Well, I mean, maybe we could go somewhere a bit more private —"

Lindsay, excited, says — "Come to the guest house! Right now! We can start a fire and read it aloud!"

Perry checks the time. "We really would have to get a wiggle on — I'm due at work in two hours."

Dawn, disappointed, asks, "How many jobs do you have, anyway, Perry?"

"Four at the moment," Perry grins. "But not for much longer! Come on, let's go. I'll meet you there."

Lindsay drives Dawn to the guest house, and when they arrive,

Perry is just dismounting from her cycle.

Once inside, Dawn is momentarily overcome to be back in the place where so many emotions had come forth a year ago. But then she pulls herself together and makes a pot of tea while Lindsay and Perry build a fire. The tea is ready just as the fire starts crackling.

Lindsay and Perry settle on the green leather sofa and pull out their phones. Dawn sits on the big, comforting brown armchair and experiences a storm of feelings as they start to read her words aloud, taking turns. Dawn gazes at Perry, who is reading dramatically and making Lindsay laugh hysterically with her vivid voices. Perry gets to her feet and strides about during an especially arousing part of the story. And just as the characters in the fanfic are starting to make love, Perry sits down and says to Lindsay, "Your turn." Lindsay begins to read, and Dawn — in the oddest position, since she had been visualizing Lindsay in the role of her heroine when she was writing it — hears Lindsay saying the words she wrote. She can't help noticing once again how adorable Lindsay looks, especially here and now in the firelight. She doesn't have the dramatic flair that Perry displayed, but reads with feeling and intelligence, not hesitating during the truly sexy parts. Perry whimpers and rolls around a bit on the sofa. Lindsay snorts. "Are you all right, Perry? Shall I stop?"

Perry hides her face in the sofa cushion. "No, keep going, but I have to go to work in a few minutes, so this is agony."

"Your turn to read, Dawn," says Lindsay.

Dawn shakes her head vigorously. "No, no. You go on. You're doing a fantastic job."

Lindsay takes a deep breath and launches into the last chapter. Dawn looks surreptitiously at both of them. Perry has her eyes closed and her legs wrapped around the cushion. She moans periodically and rocks her hips a little as Lindsay continues. And Lindsay is actually gasping as she reads.

Dawn is thrilled by the impact of her erotic prose. She covers her mouth with her hand to conceal her delight at the power she is evincing. She can't take her eyes off Lindsay, who is perspiring a little now as she reads the very explicit climactic scene.

At last, Lindsay reads "The End." She collapses back into her chair, letting her phone fall to the floor. Perry and Dawn applaud loudly.

"Oh my GOD," says Lindsay.

"That was hotter than hot," says Perry.

Realizing she must say something if she is to disguise her authorship, Dawn adds, "Aye. Wow, that was really something."

"Any idea who the author is?" asks Perry.

"No," says Dawn.

Lindsay says, "I wish I could meet her. I'd…"

"We know, we know," laughs Perry, disengaging from the sofa cushion and standing. "Wow, I have to leave right this minute."

The other two moan with disappointment, and also stand. The three of them embrace, and Lindsay and Dawn promise to keep in touch with Perry. "You'd better, you cuties," says Perry, kissing them in turn, then throwing on her jacket and helmet. "Talk soon, all right?" she calls as she lets herself out into the alley. Dawn and Lindsay go to the door and wave as Perry guns her motorbike and roars away.

They close the door against the evening chill and look at each other.

"Peckish?" asks Lindsay.

"A bit, yes," says Dawn.

Lindsay gathers things from the fridge and larder while Dawn makes another pot of tea. They make sandwiches and go back into the lounge. Lindsay stirs up the fire and they relax onto the couch. For a few minutes they are busy eating their snack. Then they put their plates and cups aside and sit looking at the fire.

Lindsay, after a silence, says, "There was something I noticed in that last chapter, and I rather think I might know who the author is, after all."

"Oh really?" says Dawn casually, though her heart has stopped for a moment.

"Yes. There's that word, 'trauchled,' the main character uses a few times."

"So?" says Dawn, blushing uneasily. "That's a pretty common expression, isn't it?"

"In Scotland it is," says Lindsay. "My dad's a Scot, and he used to say it all the time. But I never hear it used down here."

"Hmmm," says Dawn.

"There's just one person I know who says that."

"Oh yes?"

Lindsay looks her in the eyes.

"Yes."

Dawn suddenly doesn't know where to look. She stands and starts to put the plates on the tray. Lindsay rises as well, smiles gently. "Did you write it?"

"Yes," Dawn says, somehow finding the courage to look back at Lindsay. They are standing so close, Dawn can feel her body heat.

"Well, you are absolutely bloody amazing," says Lindsay, putting her hand on Dawn's shoulder and shaking it slightly. "I've read loads of these things and this one is the best. The hottest. But also the ... deepest."

She looks at Dawn with a sort of awe in her eyes.

Dawn is torn between two impulses — to escape or to embrace this moment. She asks herself what Anne Lister would do.

Dawn reaches up, putting her hand on Lindsay's. "What did you say you'd do to the author?"

Lindsay breathes, "I don't know, what did I say?"

Dawn says, "You said you'd 'bang her so hard,' I believe."

Lindsay looks mortified. "I didn't mean that, really —"

"Oh no?" says Dawn. "What a shame," and pulls back with a disappointed expression.

Lindsay says, "Wait, wait..."

Dawn turns away, and Lindsay pulls her back. Lindsay says, "I only meant that I'd like to — you know — well, kiss you, if that's all right."

Dawn turns back to Lindsay, puts her arms around her and kisses her. Lindsay returns the kiss with passion and heat. They stand there for a long time, kissing as if they had just invented it. Though it is hard to focus, Dawn vows to herself that no matter how far apart they live, she will find a way to pursue this.

And as Lindsay kisses her neck and her knees start to buckle, Dawn realizes with her last coherent thought that for the first time in her adult life, she feels thoroughly at home in her own skin.

❦

Imara: Spring

"Come over to Germany in a week or two," Perry suggests. "I'll have my bike, and I'll be ready to start the adventure." She and Imara are walking slowly down the pavement near Imara's Halifax office on this foggy afternoon.

Imara laughs dismissively. "I can't. I have employees. A business."

"Surely they can get along without you for a few days, a few weeks."

"Very difficult," says Imara, unyielding.

Perry reaches out and grabs Imara's arm, spinning her around. Smiling at Imara beseechingly, she says, "We've been having a nice time together, haven't we?"

Imara spins away from her and continues walking down the street. "Yes," Imara replies. "So why don't you stay here?"

Perry follows her closely. "Let's stop and sit somewhere so we can talk properly."

Imara turns to face her. "We can talk here."

Perry sighs. "I've been dreaming about this motorcycle for years, saving up for years to be able to find one. You know this."

"You're obsessed."

"Yes, exactly. It's my Moby Dick. My dream. And I've also been dreaming of riding it around Europe, free to see all the places I've not been able to visit because of my financial situation. This is a once in a lifetime thing."

"Good."

"I really want you to come with me."

"For how long?" Imara asks, looking anywhere but at Perry.

"For as long as you like."

"To do what?"

"Tour around with me. All the great places — not looking out at them from the window of a car, but being out in them, immersed. The Stelvio Pass, the Gorge du Cians, the Black Forest...with no plan, just stopping to sleep in a hostel or a campground, experiencing..."

"Stop right there," says Imara. "Hostels? Campgrounds? You don't know me very well."

"No," Perry says, deflated. "I suppose I don't."

"Have a nice time," Imara says. "I mean it. Perhaps we'll see each other when you return."

"Yes."

"Goodbye, Perry." Imara reaches up to hug the taller woman and kisses her on the cheek. She starts to walk away.

"That's it?" calls Perry.

"That's it for now," Imara calls back. She turns a corner and is gone.

Perry punches her right fist into her left hand and stands breathing heavily for a moment.

She checks her watch. Over an hour till she needs to be at her job. And she's near her favorite cafe for writing in. She turns and walks quickly towards the cafe, an idea for a new poem starting to form already.

~

A Rumour of Larkin

Kim texts Devon with disturbing news.

- Hey, Dev, heard a rumour that Larkin is heading back to the UK. Have you heard anything?

- *No. Why's she coming back?*

- I gather that she caught some parasitic disease.

- *Oh, ick.*

- And something about coming home to see someone named Belle... do you know a Belle?

- *No. As rumors go, this is annoyingly vague.*

- Yeah, sorry. I'll let you know when I hear more.

Belle? Despite her most strenuous efforts, Devon is plunged once again into a morass of helpless anger.

~

Honour and Stephanie: Spring

As she drives to Halifax for the Anne Lister birthday gathering, Honour is reminded over and over of the last time she drove in this direction, just over a year ago. Now, in early April, the fields are beginning to turn greener and the sun comes through the clouds occasionally, hinting that spring really is coming to this valley.

So many changes have come about in her life. The complete absence of communication with Stephanie was the first big change. Honour had not realized how many hours a week had been spent writing to Stephanie. After their wonderful weekend together, she wrote hundreds of texts to Stephanie in her mind, but never sent any.

She started going to a pastoral counselor through her church to work out why she desired an affair, and in hopes that the counselor could help Honour get over her desire and settle into domestic contentment with Nora. Luckily, the counselor was insightful and gentle. He asked sensitive questions that affirmed Honour's feeling that her life with Nora was stifling.

She tried to persuade Nora to come to a session with her, but Nora refused, saying bluntly to Honour, "If you're so bored with me, you can move out. I don't care, really. I'm ready for a new start."

Honour started job-hunting, and sooner than she'd expected, found a good new job with a higher salary on the other side of town. Then she found and moved into a nice flat, and after an awkward month or two, she and Nora started living separate lives. The whole process was remarkably quick and amicable, which confirmed Honour's perception that Nora, too, had been bored with their static life together. And indeed, by that autumn, Nora was dating a new woman and appeared to be happier than she had been in years. It was all very surprising, and more than a little annoying.

Honour was still reeling from the dizzying rapidity of these changes, and adjusting to her newfound freedom, when she signed up to attend the Anne Lister birthday events in April. She wanted to see Stephanie again — she had not stopped thinking of her in all these months — but now found that she lacked the courage to tell Steph she was coming.

There will be several hundred people at the celebration, Honour knows, and she imagines that if she and Steph do bump into each other, she will know right away if Steph is happy to see her. And if not, well, there will be plenty of other women to talk to.

～

Honour arrives in Halifax after her long drive, checks into her hotel, and goes out to walk around the town. It's a cool but sunny afternoon and Honour is delighted to see Anne Lister devotees everywhere. *This is heaven*, Honour thinks, as she sees friends falling into each other's arms with squeals of delight, couples walking hand in hand, and clutches of women laughing loudly and clapping each other on the back. Honour breathes in the ambiance as she makes her way to a lecture at the Piece Hall by one of the foremost Anne Lister historians.

The lecture hall is crammed and hot, and the lecture not all that riveting, so at a break, Honour slips out to the entryway and browses the books displayed on a table. She has just picked up a volume about Anne Lister's famous diaries when she catches a whiff of a familiar perfume and hears a soft voice just behind her. "I was wondering if you'd be here."

Honour spins. "Stephanie," she says, and to her dismay finds tears springing into her eyes. Stephanie smiles happily at her, then sees the tears and reaches out to hug her.

"I'm so happy to see you, Honour," Stephanie says quietly.

"Oh, Steph. I'm so happy to see you. How are you?"

Stephanie just stares at her, drinking her in, then says, "Let's do one and go somewhere we can talk, shall we?" Honour nods, and they leave the building and walk downstairs to a quiet tearoom.

As soon as they are seated, with tea on order, Honour blurts out, "I'm so sorry for how I left you. So very sorry. But I've broken it off completely with Nora now, I'm living on my own, and — well, you're probably seeing someone now but I thought at least we could be friends or—"

Stephanie puts her hand on Honour's forearm and squeezes. "No, I'm not seeing anyone."

Honour again feels tears in her eyes. The tea arrives. "What a pretty pot," Honour says inanely. Stephanie laughs and pours her a cup.

"Milk and two sugars, if I remember correctly."

"Yes," says Honour. "You remember correctly."

Stephanie says quietly, "Good."

"I'm so, so glad to see you, Steph. Are you all right?"

"I wasn't, at all. I was really, really gutted for a long time. Until something happened."

"Oh," says Honour, staring into her tea. "What was it that happened?"

"I saw you at the book table."

"Oh," says Honour. She finally gains the courage to look into Stephanie's eyes. They are blue as ever, and filled with kindness and affection.

They talk for an hour, and the heaviness flees from their hearts until they are wiping their eyes — this time from laughing so hard.

At last, Stephanie asks, "What are your plans for this evening?"

"I was going to go to a panel discussion."

"Can I tempt you to skive off and come and have tea at mine? It's in a right state, but it's where I live."

"If you'll have me."

"I will," says Stephanie sincerely. "I will have you." Honour smiles with deep joy and reaches out to take Stephanie's hand. Stephanie leans closer to her and whispers, "Whether you're wearing a corset or not."

∾

Lambing Season

The morning after Miremba's call, there is intermittent rain, but the sky shows a brightness that speaks of spring. Devon heads into the village with Walker by her side. Walker heels obediently, except when there are cats. Over the past weeks, the dog and the woman have become buddies, and a massive empty space in Devon's heart has been filled. At an intersection, she gives the "stop, sit" command as Polly taught her. Walker obediently stops and sits. Devon pats and praises her, and is just reaching into her coat pocket for a doggie treat when her phone rings.

It's Glo. Devon's heart knocks against her ribs — Glo never phones her without texting first. Hoping nothing is wrong, she answers the phone while simultaneously handing the treat to Walker, who gobbles it down. Glo is shouting so loudly that Devon can't understand what she's saying.

"Slow down! What? Are you okay?"

"The Turner Gallery — you know, that one in Noe Valley?"

"Yes? Walker, sit! Nice gallery — what about it?"

"Oh, nothing — just that they want to feature your work in a big headliner show! This June!" Glo's joy is palpable across the many miles that separate them. "They're focusing on this theme, 'The Female Gaze in the Landscape,' and you'll be the featured artist. You're sure to sell most of your pictures. It's an unbelievable opportunity, but you have to jump on it right away. Oh, and there's a five thousand dollar honorarium that comes with it, and you'll be in residence at the gallery for a month. You can stay with me and Tanisha!"

Devon is speechless. *I never thought in a million years...*

Glo chatters on, giving details about shipping, catalogues, and commission rates that Devon is too overwhelmed to take in. Finally, Glo runs out of breath.

Devon finds her voice again. "When do I have to let them know?" she asks.

"Two weeks from tomorrow. Can you do it?"

"I'm gobsmacked. And I'm out in the middle of the street in the rain. But yes, yes, yes!" Devon speaks so loudly that Walker whines, disturbed. Devon pats her reassuringly.

Glo sounds almost as emotional as Devon. "Congratulations!" she cries.

"How can I thank you?" asks Devon.

"I don't know yet, but we'll come up with something."

Devon goes about her errands in a daze. *I'm a real artist*, she keeps saying to herself as she walks in and out of the shops, filling her backpack with purchases. She intends to take her load straight home, but the rain has stopped and Walker is so full of energy that

Devon relents and takes her to the park near the train station. Two older ladies are having a chat on a bench. As Devon approaches, she sees that they were in her class at the Women's Institute.

"Excuse me, may I leave my backpack here for a few minutes while I take my dog for a little run around the park?"

"Of course!" says one of the women. "You're Devon, aren't you? We loved your class!"

"Yes," says another, "When are you coming back to teach us some more?"

"I don't know!"

"Well, we'd love to have you. We'll watch your backpack, don't worry."

Devon puts Walker on the long lead and runs her around the park until they are both panting and happy.

On the long walk back up the hill, Devon starts thinking again about the proposed show in San Francisco. *It will be an unbelievable shot in the arm for my finances, not to mention the prestige — and I'll be able to command much higher prices for my paintings in the future.* She is lost in a joyful delirium.

They near the guest house. The low sun shines through a gap in the clouds. Turning into her courtyard, she sees the old stone buildings momentarily illuminated; shiny with rain, they radiate light.

As Devon turns the key in her front door, she turns to survey the golden buildings and looks over to the emerald-green fields in the distance, and down at Walker, who is panting and wagging her tail with excitement to be home.

Scratching Walker behind her ears, she says, "Walk, how can I bear to leave this? And you? Even for just a month?"

The dog leaps indoors and Devon goes inside with this question echoing through her.

Larkin is walking slowly, supported by her cane, down the street in Halifax. It is spitting rain. Pedestrians are sloshing along, hunched inside their anoraks and under umbrellas. Larkin wonders, not for the first time since she returned a week ago, why on earth she came back to England, instead of recovering somewhere warmer.

Then she remembers, and smiles to herself. *Belle. Lovely Belle.*

She walks as quickly as she can past the pub where, a year and a half ago, she and Devon had dinner the night before Larkin left for India. A deep, sad longing passes through her in a sickly wave, followed by the sour taste of guilt. She wonders if she hurt Devon. No, she knows that she did.

Larkin looks up and sees the hotel where Devon had stayed, where they had slept together for the first time. A pang of grief clutches her heart. She hopes fervently that she won't bump into Devon during the next few weeks. She sighs deeply and walks on, remembering their three days together. *The closest I've ever been to heaven*, she thinks sadly, as she stands at a pedestrian crossing waiting for the light to change.

At that moment, a sunshine-yellow Toyota Supra roars past, then skids to a stop and reverses in the middle of the traffic. The driver's window rolls down and a woman yells, "Larkin! Is that you?"

A line of cars, horns sounding furiously, are backed up behind the Supra. Larkin bends down and sees that the cause of this disturbance is Imara, who is now leaning out of the window.

"Larkin! Come here!" she shouts, waving vigorously.

Larkin limps over to Imara's car and grins at her former girlfriend.

"Nice car."

"What are you doing in England? You're all wet! Come and get in — I'll take you wherever you're going."

Larkin recognizes an old habit as she unquestioningly obeys Imara's order — it has always been far easier to do what Imara wants than to argue with her. She pops into the car to a chorus of horns and Imara leans over to embrace her, then starts to drive slowly down the street.

"Ugh, you're soaking! What are you doing here?"

"I got a bit ill in India. Parasite thing. I have pretty bad anemia, so I feel weak. I've come home to get healthy again. Doctors say I should be all right within a month or two."

"You will insist on going to these unhealthy places, Larkin! How long have you been here? Where are you going?"

"About five days. Right now? Just to do a bit of shopping and see the town again," says Larkin.

"Let me buy you a coffee," orders Imara, and Larkin, shrugging with a smile, agrees.

Soon they are sitting in an elegant cafe on Market Street, with steaming lattes in front of them.

"Tell me everything," says Imara.

"Well, I told you about being ill. Boring!"

Imara is happy to see Larkin smiling with that familiar grin.

"What about that money we raised, eh?"

Larkin's smile widens. "It was a miracle. I can't tell you how much difference it made. Morale on the project had been quite low, and the money made everyone feel hopeful again. Thank you for your part in doing that, Imara. Deeply, deeply appreciated."

Imara nods.

"And then I got really ill," Larkin continues. "My co-workers told me to go away to recover. I didn't want to leave the project, but then I heard from my brother Derek. You remember him. He and his wife just had a baby. She's a sweetie." Larkin shows off some photos on her phone. Imara glances at them and makes appropriate baby-admiring sounds.

"Congratulations."

"Thank you," Larkin smiles. "Mum got on the phone with me and bullied me mercilessly until I agreed to come home. And I'm so glad I did." She gazes at the photos on her phone again, even though she has them memorized. "I'm absolutely besotted with her," says Larkin, remembering the comfortable density of the baby's warm little body in her arms, the little quiff of fluffy brown hair on her head. "I'm going to be the best aunt in the world."

"Lovely. So you're back for good, then?"

"No, no — just until I recover. A month or maybe two. I'll need to go back to take the rest of the photos for my story and help get the shelter to the next stage."

"Where are you staying?"

"At my sister's flat in Tod."

"How is dear Coral?" asks Imara with the hint of a sneer.

Larkin laughs. "Oh, she's all right. She's not nearly as homophobic as she was when you and I were in school. All the same, it's a bit cramped and chaotic in her place — I'm staying out of her way as much as possible, but really all I'm doing most of the time is sleeping." Larkin looks terribly tired, but suddenly her eyes widen and she reaches over to touch Imara's hand. "I haven't asked about you! You were seeing that poet…"

"Yes, Perry," Imara says, gritting her teeth.

"How's that coming along?"

"Oh, it's not," says Imara airily. "She's gone off to Germany to buy some special motorbike, and then she's going to ride it around France and Italy for some time, I don't know how long. I suppose till her money runs out."

"Oh, what a shame!"

"I suppose so," says Imara. There is a bitter note to her voice. "She offered to take me with her, but can you just imagine me on a motorcycle for more than half an hour?"

"No, I can't," Larkin admits, keeping her face straight. "You must have been disappointed."

"Yes, I suppose I was, a bit."

"Is it all over, then?"

"I don't know," says Imara.

"Well, I'm really sorry that happened," says Larkin. "And I know how much you hate uncertainty."

Imara takes Larkin's hand and squeezes it. "Why on earth did we ever break up?"

Larkin takes a breath to answer but Imara breaks in again. "Never mind — old news. I'm just so glad to see you! Come and stay with me! I have a new flat that I just rented for when I'm in Halifax for business, it's very simple but comfy enough, and I'm not even here very much. Really, it makes sense. You can have the second bedroom to yourself. Make it into an office or — I don't know — whatever you like." Imara looks seriously at Larkin.

Larkin melts a bit, gazing at Imara's delicate, heart-shaped face, her dark brown eyes and her pretty, pillowy lips. A small alarm bell goes off in her mind, and a condensed memory of Imara's bossiness flashes into her awareness, but then is supplanted by a feeling of relief at the prospect of a more peaceful, less cluttered place to sleep.

"All right, thanks, I'd like that," says Larkin.

Imara claps delightedly. "Let's go and get your things right now and move you in," she says, standing and putting her jacket on.

"I'm too knackered to do that today," Larkin says.

"You do look awful," Imara says, surveying her. "Never mind, I'll come and get you tomorrow morning."

"All right," says Larkin, with the last bit of her strength. The prospect of a peaceful place to stay is really very comforting.

"Let's go, then," says Imara, handing Larkin's anorak to her and tossing some money onto the table. "I'll take you straight to Coral's." Larkin shrugs into her jacket. Imara takes her by the elbow and steers her efficiently out the door.

Miremba and Devon stand side by side, admiring the paint job they have done on Devon's spare bedroom. It is a pale primrose yellow. The room feels sunny and airy in the late-morning light.

"Awesome work, Miremba. I love it!" Devon throws her arm over Miremba's shoulders. "But I feel bad about putting you to work the minute you appear."

"It's all right, boss," Miremba smiles. "It's wonderful to see what you've done with the house. And of course to see you." She winks at Devon. "Let's have tea."

"Yes, and catch up on everything."

They collect the paint pans and brushes and go into the kitchen. Miremba makes tea while Devon washes the paintbrushes. Then they sit down to eat.

Miremba points at the little shelf in the corner of the kitchen — a shelf with a photo, a candle, and a small vase, full of tiny fresh wildflowers. "What's this?"

Devon looks over. "Oh. That's a little sort of shrine to help me remember my Aunt Amy…"

"She took you in when your parents chucked you out."

"Yes. She saved my life. And that little statuette…"

Miremba smiles. "Anne Lister, of course." She leans over, takes a closer look at the photo. "How lucky you were to have your Aunt Amy," she says, with an unfamiliar note of melancholy in her voice.

Devon touches Miremba's hand on the tabletop. "I've missed you so much."

"Oh, boss, I've missed you more," Miremba smiles, picking up Devon's hand and squeezing it affectionately.

Devon notices a strain in Miremba's face. "I haven't heard from you in weeks. Please tell me what you've been doing."

Miremba lets go of Devon's hand and leans back in her chair, eyes closed. "My father lost his job, and my mother's ill. My family needs me rather desperately at the moment. So I'm going back to Uganda."

"Going back? But will you be able to return to the U.K.?"

Miremba opens her eyes and looks bleakly at Devon. "I probably won't, boss."

Devon feels as if someone has kicked her in the stomach. "Well, are things any better for gay people than they were when you left?"

Miremba shakes her head and takes a gulp of tea. "It doesn't matter," she says. "I have to go. That's all there is to it."

Devon sits, stunned, for a moment, her heart full of rage at the world. "When will you take off?"

"On Sunday."

"This Sunday? Four days from now?"

"That's right. I'll need to sell my car right away. And my tools, if I can. Then I'm taking the train to the airport on Sunday afternoon."

"Oh, Miremba, I'm so sorry."

"Yes, so am I."

"And of course I'll drive you to the airport."

"All right." Miremba smiles radiantly.

They spend the afternoon walking by the canal, and the night cuddled in Devon's bed, sharing hugs and tears.

Devon awakens very early, as the first rays of sun are lighting up her walls. Miremba's arm is flung over Devon's waist, and tears come to Devon's eyes. She feels a depth of affection for Miremba that she knows will never dissipate. They will be lifelong friends. She makes a firm inner commitment to visit her in Uganda as soon as she can. She slithers out of bed quietly.

Over breakfast, Miremba says, "I'm going to drive around a bit today to see a few friends and see if anyone wants to buy my car and tools."

Devon says, "Let me buy them."

Miremba argues. "But you already have a car, and plenty of tools."

"Yes," Devon says. "But I'll buy yours so you can have the cash right away, and then I can sell them at my leisure."

"Are you sure, Dev?"

"Yes," says Devon resolutely. "I want you to be able to relax and enjoy these last three days. Go visit your friends without this worry on your mind."

Miremba looks at her thoughtfully. "That's very kind of you, Devon. I accept. Thank you. Well, I think I will go and see my friends." She laughs. "It will be a bit easier to say goodbye if I'm not trying to sell them anything."

Miremba returns in the early evening, laughing with stories about her encounters with old friends. "Let me make dinner for you tonight, Devon. I'll make luwombo. So you can have a taste of my native comfort food. Most of the ingredients should be fairly easy to find in the village, but I fear that we will have a difficult time finding goat meat, plantains, and banana leaves. We will have to improvise."

"Let's go!" says Devon, pleased at the prospect of cooking with Miremba.

They walk to the shops and just as Miremba has predicted, are unable to find the more exotic components. But they load up their shopping bags with enough ingredients to make four servings of the dish. Miremba gets to the cashier first and pays, over Devon's loud objections. Once out on the pavement, Devon wrestles with Miremba, trying to push a twenty-pound note into her pocket. They are laughing helplessly as they tussle with each other.

Two women walk by on the other side of the street, observing their struggle. One of them calls out, "Oh, a free show, how fun!" Devon, focused on escaping from Miremba's half-nelson, does not look up. Miremba calls back, "This part is free, but we charge for the mud wrestling." The other women laugh and walk on.

When Devon finally surrenders, Miremba tucks the twenty back into Devon's pocket and releases her. Devon looks around, but the two women have turned the corner.

"Who was that?" asks Devon, panting from the tussle.

"The woman who yelled? That was Imara. You know her."

"Oh yes," says Devon, wrinkling her nose.

Miremba laughs. "She is a very bossy person. But she's not really so bad."

"Yeah, I know."

As they reach the door of Devon's place, Miremba says thoughtfully, "I didn't know Larkin was back in town — she looks awfully thin."

Devon stumbles, then regains her equilibrium. "Larkin?"

"Yes, didn't you see her? She was with Imara." Noticing Devon's shocked expression, she adds, "Oh, did you not know she was here?"

"I heard she was planning to come back, but that's all," replies Devon.

She resolutely swims through the wave of pain that has washed over her, and focuses on the interesting challenge of making a Ugandan dish with only two-thirds of the necessary ingredients.

As soon as they have turned the corner, Larkin, in some shock, turns to Imara and asks her a question to which she knows the answer. "Who were those women?"

"That was Devon. And Miremba, she's from Uganda, I think."

"Are they…a couple?"

"I didn't think Devon was seeing anyone, but it certainly looked like it."

Larkin's heart hurts as if someone had punched her. Then she reminds herself that she is over Devon, has given up on the possibility of their relationship.

They reach Imara's car and get in. "You're taking me to my sister's, right?" asks Larkin.

"Oh, no, Lark, we're going to mine."

"Not today. I need some alone time, and my sister's going to be out tonight, so I can have her place to myself."

"You shouldn't be alone while you're recovering," says Imara.

"Imara! You just drove past Coral's street!"

"Yes, relax, let me plop you in front of the telly and make you a nice tea."

"You're not listening to me."

"Of course I am listening to you. I'm very good at listening to people. It's one of the three cornerstones of my success."

Larkin feels a storm starting in her head. "Then listen to me now. I need some alone time."

Imara pulls up to her building and turns the car off. "Come on, Lark, let's have a nice cuppa." She pats Larkin on the knee and gets out of the car.

Larkin gets out slowly. Imara is holding the front door open, with an ingratiating smile. "Come on, love, it's nice and warm inside."

"I don't care," says Larkin. She grabs her bag and her walking-stick from the back seat of the car. "Good night." She walks down the street, fuming.

"Where are you going? Are you going to walk to Coral's house? Are you mad?" Larkin keeps walking.

It is a beautiful night, with a cold breeze but no rain. The sky is clear and the stars look like a river of tiny diamonds. Larkin is hot with anger, and she is grateful for the cold air. It's only five miles to Coral's. She can make it.

After a minute, she hears a car pull up next to her, and Imara telling her to stop being such an idiot. She gets into the car and they drive in silence. When Imara drops her off, Larkin feels her mood shift. She thanks Imara, agrees to call her the next day, and waves goodbye.

She stands for a moment looking at the amazing stars. She is focused on the fact that she saw Devon. That Devon is nearby. Very close, in fact.

If she had the energy, Larkin could walk over there right now and — well, she doesn't know what. Larkin imagines the humiliating scene that would ensue if she were to go over to Devon's and see her in the embrace of that beautiful African woman. In any case, Larkin feels a shivering weakness throughout her body and knows she's not strong enough to undertake either the walk or the confrontation.

By the time she enters Coral's flat, Larkin is faint with the relief of being alone at last. She goes in and turns on the heat and pours herself a small whiskey while the flat warms up. Still in her coat, she paces up and down, muttering to herself. Her heart is tattered, her body distressingly weak. She feels directionless, unsure of when she will be strong enough to go back to work.

At that, Larkin thinks of Belle. The real reason she came back here. Her heart cracks open. She gulps down the last dram of her whiskey and pours another.

And then she thinks of Devon — those sad hazel eyes, that dear crooked nose — and she sits on Coral's messy sofa and rocks back and forth, holding herself, holding her aching heart, for a long time, before summoning her last ounce of strength and lurching to bed.

The next day dawns blustery and dark, but after a near-sleepless night, and a morning spent moping uselessly from one room to another in Coral's messy flat, Larkin gets on a bus and takes her hangover out to the canal-side path for a shivery afternoon walk, hoping for clarity, hoping for relief from her feelings of grief, yearning, and regret.

She is trudging along the path, head bent, hoping that the light rain won't turn to a downpour and that her energy level will stay up for a couple more hours.

The project in India is pulling at her. Every day, she gets two or three texts from her team at the shelter, saying how eager they are for her to return, to document their progress and to help with the challenges they are still facing.

But pulling just as strongly at her heart is her tiny niece. *How can I leave, when the baby is just getting started on being a person?*

Her family is being so considerate, so concerned about her recovery, so not-smothering. She has no idea what's come over them, but she'd quite like to stay and enjoy it.

And there is Devon. The brief glimpse she had of Devon the other day practically destroyed Larkin. She groans inwardly — *I can't go on living in fear that I'll see her.*

The rain is falling in earnest now, as Larkin approaches a low stone bridge that arches over the canal. She is glad she brought her cane. She watches her feet carefully on the muddy path as she ducks under the bridge's shadow — it's slippery and she doesn't feel terribly steady on her feet.

Just as she comes out from under the bridge, a black and white dog appears from nowhere and tears past her, trailing its lead, then doubles back and stops next to Larkin, sniffing her feet.

A woman calls out from the other side of the bridge, "Walker! Come! Come, girl!" The dog perks her ears up, tears away, then rushes back again to crouch playfully near Larkin, panting and evidently having the time of her life.

The woman jogs toward Larkin, emerging from under the bridge. It's Devon. Larkin's heart lurches. She doesn't want to deal with her. But here she is — it was bound to happen at some point.

Devon stops, out of breath. She stares. "Shit — Larkin, is that you?"

"Devon! I — are you looking for that dog?"

"Yeah, have you — oh there she is."

The two women stand looking at Walker, who is now lying on the wet grass beside the path, flopping around voluptuously.

"Let me help you, Devon."

"I don't need any help."

Devon lunges for Walker's lead but Walker dodges.

The two execute a pincer movement. Larkin distracts the dog and Devon tiptoes up behind, grabbing the lead. "Good girl," she says, giving Walker a treat from her pocket.

Larkin pats Walker's head. "Gorgeous dog," she says. "How long have you had her?"

Devon is breathing normally now, focusing on the dog. "Not too long. We're still getting used to each other."

The rain is falling harder.

Larkin keeps patting the dog so she doesn't have to meet Devon's eyes. "How's the B&B going?"

"Pretty well," says Devon. "Are you all right? I heard you were sick."

"Getting better every day, thanks. Oh, Devon, I can't thank you enough for helping with that fund-raiser. You have no idea how much it accomplished."

"I'm glad," Devon says. "Well, I have to go. Have a nice day." *Have a nice life, thanks for nothing.* Torn between anger and longing, Devon trots off down the path, the dog at her side.

Larkin looks at Devon's retreating back with despair in her heart. Her world, her life, swings around her, dizzying.

"Wait, Devon, please!" she yells, walking after Devon as quickly as she can.

Devon slows down but does not turn around. "What?" she snarls.

"Oh please, can we talk? Just for a minute?" Larkin says to Devon's back.

Devon keeps walking. "What about? In the pouring rain?"

"About...about how you are."

Still Devon doesn't turn. She stops, though, and Larkin catches up to her. The dog sniffs at Larkin's feet and leans on her leg, further dampening Larkin's jeans. Larkin pats her on her head. "What's your dog's name?" she asks, her voice quavering.

Finally, Devon turns and faces Larkin. Larkin's heart stops. Even the dark expression on Devon's face doesn't mar her beauty. Those eyes. That lovely mouth, twisted now in anger. That broken nose that Larkin so longs to touch again.

Devon scowls at Larkin, then mutters, "Walker."

"Walker?" answers Larkin, confused.

"Dog's name. You asked." Devon takes a few more steps down the path, then stops and turns. "Fuck. It's pouring. What's with the stick?"

"I'm not very strong yet. Anemia."

Devon processes this for a moment. "You have a car?"

"No, I walked here from the bus stop."

"My car's right down here. Come to my place and dry out, if you want. Or I'll drive you home."

Larkin's heart soars. "I'd love to see your place."

They walk silently the rest of the way to Devon's car, getting soaked. Larkin couldn't care less.

Devon drives them to her house. They stand in the Annex's entry for a minute, shedding their shoes and socks, and hanging up raincoats. Devon points to a pair of slippers and Larkin puts them on.

Devon lights the gas fire. Walker finds a rawhide toy and lies in front of the hearth, chewing happily. Devon says, "Would you towel her off a bit while I get tea. Please." She tosses a ragged towel to Larkin and steps out of the room. Larkin rubs the dog until her fur is fluffy and dry.

Then she looks around the lounge, appreciating the simple, richly colored furniture, the dark wood bookcase, the whitewashed walls, the old red Persian rug. And her breath catches when she sees, leaning on a wall in the corner, the photo of Nandita that Larkin sent all those months ago. Devon has had it matted and framed beautifully. Behind her, Devon enters the room and sets a tray on the coffee table.

Devon says quietly, as if the words are being pulled out of her, "I love that picture. Just got it back from the framers. I'm going to hang it in the guest house."

Larkin turns and looks at Devon. "I'm so glad. And you seem to be doing all right — you and that, what's her name — that woman you were wrestling with?"

"Miremba," Devon rasps. "She's gone back to Uganda. Family stuff. Political stuff. It all sucks. I might never see her again."

"Oh, Dev, I'm sorry."

"Are you?"

"Yes. Very sorry."

They fall silent, and Larkin tries to think of something to say to break through Devon's icy wall. Then her phone buzzes in her pocket. She pulls it out, glances at it. "Scuse me," she says to Devon, who sighs and walks out to the kitchen. Larkin answers the phone impatiently. "What's up, Imara ?"

Imara sounds petulant. "Where are you? I'm worried about you."

"Well, don't worry about me. I'm out for a walk. I have some thinking to do."

Imara sighs. "Are you still mad about that silly thing yesterday?"

"Yeah, I'm still mad. I'm moving back to my sister's."

"That's crazy, Larkin."

"We'll talk about it when I see you."

"When will that —"

"Sorry, gotta ring off, bye."

Larkin turns off the phone and jams it back in her pocket. She looks up to see Devon leaning in the doorway, smirking at her.

"Trouble in paradise?"

Larkin laughs. "Paradise? With Imara? No worries."

Devon softens for a moment, lets a grin through. "I've had some dealings with Imara. Can't imagine you two together."

"Oh, God, not in a million years."

"But you were her girlfriend — "

"In school. Another lifetime. Oh, fuck it, I don't want to talk about her."

"What do you want to talk about?" Devon's tone is hard, unyielding.

"I'd like to know about the guest house. It's going well, I take it?"

"Well enough. It would be better if I spent more time promoting it, instead of spending all my time out on the moors with my sketch pad."

"I was going to ask you about your art. So you're painting?"

Devon smirks. "A bit."

"I'd love to see your work. If you'd let me."

Devon stares at her for a moment, considering. Then, with a sigh, she leads Larkin upstairs to her studio. She indicates the leaning pile of canvases and Larkin starts slowly looking through them, making inarticulate sounds. Devon leaves her to it and goes back downstairs.

When Larkin comes back down to the kitchen after half an hour, she is alight. "Devon. Your paintings are all of the moors."

Devon raises an eyebrow. "Yeah, and?"

Larkin closes her eyes, trying to find the right words. "This is a ... great love story." She opens her eyes to see Devon looking at her quizzically.

"Love story?" Devon snorts.

"Laugh if you like," Larkin says, irritated.

"No, tell me what you meant."

"You and the moors. I've seen a thousand paintings of these views but yours are extraordinary — you've found the soul of this place — you've found the essence — in such a short time, too. You've painted everything I've loved about this place my whole life. I especially like the three views from Stoodley Pike."

Devon can't resist a smile of pleasure, which sneaks onto her face before she remembers she is still angry and hurt. "A gallery in San Francisco is going to give them a special show in June."

"That's wonderful, Dev!"

"Yeah. They're flying me over there; I'll be away for a month."

Larkin is crestfallen. "Oh, no."

"Oh, yes. I have to start packing them up tomorrow, so they can be shipped in time."

"Tomorrow."

"Yeah."

"Well, I'm so glad I was able to see them. I suppose you'll sell a lot of them at that gallery."

"I hope so," says Devon. "My cash flow's not so great."

"That's only because not enough women know about the guest house! You probably just need to do better publicity. It should be full all the time."

"Yeah, well, anyway, I need to find somebody to be a caretaker for it while I'm away, so if you know anybody who might be good at that, please let me know."

"All right," says Larkin.

"And what about you?" asks Devon, grudgingly. "How's your work going?"

Larkin sighs. "I haven't done much paying work for the past few months, since I've been helping with the shelter project. But now the A.P. is pushing me to go to the Philippines for a feature on the typhoon rebuilding efforts. As soon as I'm healthy enough."

"That's good, right? That you get to go back to that part of the world."

"Yeah, it's good. I suppose."

"You don't sound very excited about it."

"Yeah, I'm a bit tired of taking photos of people whose lives have been torn apart, actually."

Devon winces. "Of course. Well, if I don't see you again, I hope it goes well."

"Thanks," says Larkin, on the edge of tears.

"Let me give you a ride to Coral's."

"No, no, I'll catch the bus, it's not raining any more."

"All right. The stop's just fifty yards away."

"I know."

Larkin pulls on her shoes and jacket, which are only slightly less damp than when she arrived. She finds her cane. Walker trots over to her, nudges Larkin's hand. Larkin pats the dog. She feels tears coming and doesn't dare say goodbye. Devon grabs the dog's collar and holds her as Larkin steps out into the courtyard.

"Thanks for letting me see your paintings. They're beautiful."

"Yeah. Take care of yourself. Feel better. 'Night." Devon waves and closes the door.

Larkin stands in the cold street trying to breathe normally, then sets out for the bus stop, her heart a leaden lump in her chest.

Late the next morning, Devon, having just arrived home with two huge rolls of bubble wrap, is lugging them upstairs to her studio when her phone vibrates in her pocket. She swears, runs up the last few stairs, and drops the bubble wrap on the floor. The phone says that Larkin is calling, and for a moment Devon is tempted to let it go to voice mail, but her curiosity gets the better of her and she answers.

Larkin sounds very nervous. "Devon, hey, look, I'd like to talk to you about the house sitting job."

"Okay, go ahead."

"Well, would you mind if I came over for a bit? I'm not far away."

"I suppose. Give me half an hour."

Devon hangs up and turns her attention to the bubble wrap. Her hands are shaking from the adrenaline rush of hearing Larkin's voice. She shoves her feelings aside.

She finds the process of wrapping up her paintings for the gallery incredibly difficult — not the physical act of packing them, but the prospect of potentially never seeing some of them again. *Never mind, most of them won't sell and you'll have them back here by the end of the year.* All the same, she feels unable to pack a few of her favorites — the three paintings she did at Stoodley Pike — and sets them aside to keep out of the sale.

She debates with herself about one painting — one of her first pictures of the moors, done when she was just, as Larkin put it, falling in love with this landscape. No, she can't bear to part with it. She promises herself to stop this sentimentality right now. Resolutely, she wraps the next canvas on the pile.

As she is taping the bubble wrap, Walker barks and the doorbell rings. Devon trots downstairs to open the door to Larkin. Larkin greets the dog, ruffling her fur, and smiles tentatively at Devon, but Devon is not anywhere near ready to relent. She notices it has turned out to be a beautiful day and reaches past Larkin to take Walker's lead off the hook.

"I need to take her for a little walk," she says, clipping the lead to Walker's collar as the dog jumps up and down in excitement. "Sit!" The dog sits, panting. "Want to come?" she asks Larkin, not looking directly at her.

"All right," agrees Larkin. Devon locks the door and they start walking slowly along the road. The unaccustomed sunshine makes them both squint. Walker trots along happily, sniffing at every clump of grass, doing her business here and there.

Devon turns to Larkin. "So what's going on? You have a house sitter for me?"

"Well, I might."

"Who, then?"

"Me."

"Seriously?"

"Seriously."

"I thought you were leaving the country."

Larkin takes a deep breath. "I thought I was, too, but I've decided not to go after all. I decided last night."

Devon stares. "But you said the A.P. was pressuring you —"

"Yeah, they are," Larkin says, stretching her arms over her head, releasing tension. "It's basically career suicide if I don't go. But I did some soul-searching and I just can't bear to leave my little niece. And my family. They're being incredibly nice to me. I still need some time to get healthy. And I'll miss…" She glances at Devon, licks her lips, turns away. "And, well, I'm just not going. I'll be all right staying at my sister's. And I expect I'll be able to get some local photography jobs with estate agents or something." She looks at Devon and proceeds, a bit timidly. "And meanwhile, I thought I might house sit for you while you're in the States. Help us both out."

Devon laughs, bitterly. "You don't have any idea, do you?"

Larkin's face falls. "Idea of what?"

"How much you hurt me."

"I guess I don't…"

Devon feels rage rising in her, a red flood. She struggles to restrain her voice as a mother and toddler walk slowly past them. "A whole fucking year, Larkin. Longer. Months and months of wondering what the hell I did wrong to make you stay away and not even write to me. For over a year."

Larkin is stricken. "I felt we needed to break it off."

"But you didn't even give me the consideration of talking it over with me! Do you know how that felt? Like I was too unimportant for you to even communicate with. Like I was just a nothing to you."

Larkin is shocked. "A nothing to me? Are you joking?"

"Then why did you dump me?"

"I didn't want to string you along. I wanted you to be free. I didn't know how long I'd be away."

Devon stands, paces, unsure of how much to believe. "I thought you really liked me."

"I did. I — liked you — a lot. Too much."

"What does that mean?"

"I was afraid that if we — you know, lived together or whatever — you'd keep me from being able to travel and do my job."

"Why the hell would you think that?"

"That's how it's always been for me. If it's not my family, then it's girlfriends — jealous of my work, wanting me to stay home. Girlfriends who get annoyed that I'm always traveling someplace."

Devon is exasperated. "I'm not like that! I'm glad you have your work. I'd have supported you to travel wherever your work called you. You never gave me a chance to — you never asked me about it."

Larkin's face shows both remorse and skepticism. "Really?"

"Yes, really!" Devon shouts. "Jesus!"

Larkin still struggles to look her in the eye. "Well, you were living in the States then, anyway, and you knew I'd never move there."

Devon turns away, fists clenched in frustration. "You never gave us a chance, Larkin. Look, I can't do this any more. Not today."

Devon and Walker trot back toward the guest house, leaving Larkin behind.

Devon awakens late the next morning to the sound of her phone ringing. As she gets up and fumbles around for it, she groans a little — her back is very sore from the hours spent crouched on the floor of her studio last night, working with her paintings. Walker is up, too, barking with excitement to see her awake at last.

She finally finds her phone, buried deep in her bedclothes. It's Larkin.

"Oh, Devon — I nearly rang off. Look, I'm actually five minutes from your house, can I come and talk? I have something to say to you."

Devon sighs, though her foolish heart is beating faster now. "Yeah, all right. Come on over."

Devon fends Walker off as she throws on a sweatshirt and jeans, and starts down the stairs. She rakes her fingers through her hair and splashes some water from the kitchen sink on her face, then takes the dog out for a minute to do her business. Squinting at the sky, she sees pale sunshine behind the high clouds. Looking down at her flower border, she sees that a few brave daffodils have emerged, bright yellow, into the light. And now around the corner comes Larkin, on foot, holding what looks like a bouquet, wrapped in brown paper.

Larkin hasn't seen Devon yet. Devon's heart surges again, seeing Larkin's face, seeing her rather shaky gait as she walks along. She's not using her stick today, which Devon figures is a good sign. Then Larkin looks up, and smiles a tentative smile. Walker whimpers and tugs at her lead until Devon relents and lets the dog pull her over to Larkin.

"'Ey up, Walker," says Larkin. "Are you allowed to have a dog biscuit?" she asks, pulling one from her pocket.

"Yes, she is," says Devon. Larkin smiles. The two women stand watching Walker crunch the biscuit.

"Let's go in," says Devon gruffly, and leads Larkin into the house.

Kicking her shoes off, Larkin holds the flowers out to Devon. "These are for you."

Devon looks at the bouquet suspiciously, then takes it. She opens the paper wrapping and sees chrysanthemums, purple ones and white ones. "Oh, my favorites," she says, taking a deep whiff of the spicy scent. "You remembered that."

Larkin says, so quietly that Devon can barely hear her, "I remember everything."

Unable to look Larkin in the eyes, Devon takes the flowers into the kitchen and busies herself finding a vase and a pair of scissors.

"So, uh, thanks," she says roughly, indicating the flowers, as she starts to trim their stems.

Larkin clears her throat. "I wanted to talk to you again about about house sitting —"

Devon holds up her hand. "Wait. Before you say anything."

"But I want to do it."

Devon looks at her. "Wait. Maybe sit down."

Larkin looks apprehensive, but sits. Devon remains standing.

"Look. I'm not going to need a house sitter after all, because —"
Larkin looks tragic. "Oh," she says. "You've found someone."
"No," Devon says. "It's just —"
Larkin is on her feet. "You don't have to explain."
Devon slaps the flowers onto the counter. "Please!"
Larkin's eyes widen and she sits back down.

Devon paces up and down the kitchen floor. Walker, excited, starts to whirl around. Devon banishes her to the bedroom and closes the door.

She turns back to Larkin. "I was up till one wrapping the paintings. But then I was taping up the three you liked so much. The views from Stoodley Pike. And I just suddenly realized — I can't leave this place right now, not for a month. Not in springtime. And I can't send these pictures all the way to California. I don't even know if I can bear to sell any of them, but if I can..." She stops, tears welling up in her eyes, her voice breaking. "If I can bear to sell them, it will have to be to people who already know this place, people who love this land. You know?"

Larkin nods, and Devon sees that tears are in her eyes as well.

"So," says Devon, roughly wiping her eyes with the back of her hand, "I'm not going. For better or worse, I belong here now. I belong in this countryside, but even more, in the community of women that I've found here. It's more important than I'd ever dreamed."

"You're turning down that opportunity in San Francisco?"

"Yes."

"But you said it was such a great chance."

"I know."

Silence follows. Larkin says, tentatively, "Oh, well, I'm sad. I was looking forward to taking care of your place, and Walker. But I understand." She stands and takes a step toward the door. Devon grabs her arm to stop her. They stand there, not moving, for a moment. Devon says, "What are the flowers for?"

Larkin looks down. "For you."

"Why? Why did you bring them?"

"As a peace offering. And because I...care for you."

"I care for you, too." Devon looks at Larkin. "Goddammit."

Larkin says in a rush, "I don't know why I stopped communicating with you. I was so overwhelmed with all the pain and distress around me — and I just didn't know what to say. The world I was in was so...so far from Yorkshire."

Devon nods, then grits her teeth and blurts, "I heard you're seeing someone."

Larkin looks blank. "Seeing someone? Me? No. What did you hear?"

It's killing Devon but she grinds out the name. "Someone called Belle."

Larkin inhales, then doubles over with laughter. "Belle!"

Annoyed, Devon says, "Is there someone called Belle? Or not?"

Larkin can barely speak. "Yes!" she manages to choke out. Finally getting her breath back, she wipes tears of laughter from her eyes. "And I'm absolutely mad about her. Want to see her picture?"

Devon says, "Fuck," and tries to turn away from the phone as Larkin holds it up, but Larkin grabs her arm and makes her look.

"It's a baby," Devon says stupidly.

"My niece! You wally!"

"I don't get it," Devon growls.

"Her name is...?" Larkin prompts.

Devon stands dumbly as her world reconfigures itself and clicks into place. "Belle?"

Larkin rolls her eyes and nods. "Yes! Isn't she gorgeous?"

A wave of hysterical laughter now sweeps over Devon. "I was so jealous!" she manages to squeak out, inciting another gale of laughter from Larkin.

They both laugh until they are completely out of breath and collapse onto the couch, side by side.

As the wave of laughter ebbs, Larkin shows Devon all her photos of Belle. "I'm going to be the best auntie ever."

After a while, they are sitting in silence. Larkin starts to say something but Devon holds her hand up, looks over at the little shrine in the corner. Then she closes her eyes and focuses on what her soul is saying to her. She summons Aunt Amy's face, hears her saying *Be true to your heart, Dev.* She wonders if this, right now, is an invitation from the world to step into a larger life. And then she thinks of Anne Lister's fearlessness, and reaches deep inside herself, and finds some courage.

Devon opens her eyes but can't quite look at Larkin. Haltingly, she says, "When I didn't hear from you, I got depressed. I finally realized that rejection always sends me into depression…"

"I'm so sorry…I was so confused and … wrong about everything … wrong not to give you…and us a chance."

Devon squeezes her arm and Larkin stops. Devon continues, "But the good thing is that I didn't stay in that darkness. Being here, starting this new life, the magic of this place, the community of women we're creating, the art I've been able to do — it helped me, even while I was so angry and hurt. I did a lot of thinking out on the moors. A lot of thinking, and I realized that so many of my mistakes go back to when I was sixteen. Sometimes I think I even see rejection where it doesn't exist." She stops for a moment, very near to tears again.

Larkin says, her voice breaking, "I've never stopped loving you, you know. Not for a minute. I tried and tried to stop but…"

Devon lets go of her arm. "I tried and tried, too, but —"

Larkin whispers, "In my heart, I never left you. I just couldn't turn my back on all the suffering that was around me, and I couldn't see how you could understand and be with me in that. Every single night, I dreamed of coming back to you. But I couldn't abandon those women. I should have told you what was going on, but I had no words. Devon, I'm so, so sorry."

Devon reaches out to Larkin, tucks a wisp of hair behind her ear. "I'm so sorry, too. For all the time we've lost, and —"

Larkin puts her hand over Devon's, kisses her palm. "Don't worry about that, Dev," she whispers. She turns Devon's hand over. "Your nails!" she exclaims.

"What?"

"You're not chewing them anymore."

"Oh. I guess I'm not."

Larkin kisses Devon's fingertips. Devon's words pour out in a torrent. "Live here with me, Lark. At least give it a try. I'll take care of you till you're completely better. You can do whatever you want, go wherever — help me promote the guest house, set up a studio for yourself, work with me if you like. We can still send money to your people in India. You can have your own room, your own life — bring Belle over whenever you —"

Larkin stops her with a warm, lingering kiss on her cheek. Devon almost faints from the joy of feeling those lips again after all this time.

And at that moment, she feels the armor that she has built around her heart fall completely away, leaving her open, vulnerable, free to say yes to this invitation.

She wraps her arms fiercely around Larkin, embracing the slim, strong shoulders she thought she'd never feel again. Alarmingly, heart-breakingly thin, now. And then Larkin pulls back, gazes into Devon's eyes, and whispers, "Let's not lose any more time, then."

Devon stands, pulls Larkin to her feet, and sweeps her into a deep, gentle kiss.

This kiss goes on and on, as if their eager lips and hands, their bodies pressed together so fiercely, have the power to repair the months of longing, the regret, the hurt; can convey the forgiveness, the hope, the joy that fills their hearts like the sunlight that is now pouring down, illuminating the street, the village, the moors, the bright green fields with their newborn lambs, shining on and on over the whole valley, over their whole lives, as their future together begins.

From the Author

The generosity and helpfulness of so many women have enabled this novel to come to life.

I am grateful beyond measure for the insights of my readers — Jill Hutchinson-Walker, Una Walsh, Janet Lea, Jenny Crakes, Carissa Meisner Smit. Thanks for encouraging me — and for urging me to go back to the drawing board to find the novel's heart.

'Ey up! to my two Yorkshire experts — Rosie Hayes and Tessa Hankinson. Thanks for giving me great guidance on dialogue, vocabulary, and locales, and for weeding out my Americanisms.

Jane Wingfield, your lovely line drawings are incredibly helpful for a book with so many characters. You were a dream to work with.

Geraldine Aikman, your cover art and book design skills are stunning. Thank you so much.

And Jane Crisi Tufts — I always knew you were a great editor, but only now do I know how very excellent you are. I hope this was even more interesting than your usual economics textbooks.

Thanks to my partner, Nancy Flowers, for your patience and understanding.

And thanks to all women, worldwide, who are creating safe spaces for women, especially lesbians, to find support, joy, and camaraderie.

To learn about Anne Lister and her fascinating diaries, a good place to start is www.annelister.co.uk/

Thank you for reading! I'd love to hear from you.
www.miss-listers.com

Amanda L. Aikman
Everett, Washington
February, 2023